CLOSE TO FAMILY

SUZANNE FERRELL

Copyright © 2022 by Suzanne Welsh

All rights reserved.

No part of this book may be reproduced in any form or by any electronic or mechanical means, including information storage and retrieval systems, without written permission from the author, except for the use of brief quotations in a book review.

❦ Created with Vellum

Dedication

*For my Mother and Father.
I miss you both more every day*

ACKNOWLEDGMENTS

The Ferrell team always deserves a big thank you!

I'd like to thank my cover artist, Lyndsey Lewellen of LLewellen Designs. Your covers are making the fictional town of Westen come alive!

Thank you to LIBRIS en CAPS for the editing. You know I have comma issues.

A special thank you to Stacy Taylor who walked me through the inner workings of hair salons! And David LeVay for chatting with me about field medic assessments for trauma injuries. Any mistakes I made in any of these areas are purely my own.

Author's note

Dear Reader,

Thank you so much for trying my Indie published book. I understand that there are many options for you to spend your money on and am honored that you chose one of my books. For that reason my team and I strive to put out the best product we can from the awesome cover design through the entire editing and formatting process. For my part, I hope to deliver an entertaining story that keeps you wondering what's going to happen next.

If at the end of this book you find you simply loved the story and characters, please consider giving it a positive rating or review. In this brave new book world, the only way for a good story to find its way into the hands of other readers is if the people who loved it let others know about it. We authors appreciate any little bit of help you can give us.

If, when you reach the end of this story, you think, "Wow, I'd love to know what's next in Suzanne's world of characters," then consider joining my newsletter mailing list. I only send out newsletters a few times a year, plus extra ones in anticipation of any new releases, so it won't be flooding your inbox on a weekly basis, but will keep you abreast on any changes I may have coming.

Also, I love to hear from readers. If you have any questions or comments, or just want to say "hi", please feel free to visit my webpage for some extra tidbits or check out my Pinterest boards. You can connect with me via Facebook, Twitter or through my email: suzanne@suzanneferrell.com

Now the important part: Here's Dylan and Sean's story. I hope you will love them as much as I did while writing **Close To Family**

Suzanne

CHAPTER 1

The early autumn sun filtered through the canopy of leaves shading the drive up to the cabin, followed by the rustle of the leaves on the gentle breeze.

Peaceful.

It was one of the things Dr. Dylan Roberts loved about visiting her sisters in the town of Westen. Since her sister Chloe's wedding to one of the town's deputies four years ago, and her sister Bobby's marriage to the sheriff the year before, she'd come to think of the town as her vacation home. A place to relax, enjoy family and friends.

Compared to the chaos of her life in the big city hospitals where she'd trained in trauma, coming to Westen felt like taking a deep, soul cleansing breath. It was why she visited now. She needed the peace and quiet to think. She'd finally achieved her life goal of becoming a trauma surgeon, yet living in the urban setting where almost all her time seemed focused on patching people up from their bad decisions, felt...empty.

Coming to stay in Westen, at least long enough for her sisters to deliver their babies, she hoped to find the next step for her career. Of course, the past week she'd been here, both her siblings had pitched the idea of her bringing her medical practice to Westen. She knew their efforts were out of love for her, but she wasn't sure that at this stage of her life, Westen was where she belonged.

Three SUVs pulled into the drive leading up to the cabin, breaking her train of self evaluation.

"Here comes the baby brigade," she said, thankful for the distraction.

"Don't make fun. They're here for the baby shower and I'm very flattered they're thinking of Wes and me," Chloe said, lowering herself onto one of the porch chairs and patting her stomach. "And this little person."

Eight months into her first pregnancy, she'd started doing a pregnancy waddle. Dylan had to admit it was only a slight waddle, given Chloe's height of nearly six feet, but it was definitely there.

A moment later the front door opened, and their older sister, Bobby, stepped out onto the porch, resting her hand over the top of her own rounded abdomen. Being nearly six inches shorter than Dylan and Chloe, she looked like she was carrying twins instead of an eight-month gestation single baby—her second child, a girl this time. Her three-year-old son Luke, a whirlwind of activity and a bundle of questions, was spending the day with his father Gage at the sheriff's office, well out of the way of the party goers.

"Is Dylan complaining about the baby boom we're experiencing here in Westen?" Bobby asked, waving at the women climbing out of the SUVs like clowns from a clown car. "I think it's lovely. So many new families moving to town, so many children the same age to become friends and grow along with."

"You *would* think it's great," Chloe said with a laugh. "You started the whole thing."

"No, she didn't," a brusque voice said seconds before Harriet stepped onto the porch. "Emma and Doc Clint did."

The septuagenarian nurse that ran Doctor Clint Preston's medical clinic like a drill sergeant always amazed Dylan with both her cognitive alertness and her physical spryness. No bigger than five feet with her shoes on, Dylan had seen her quell any number of the husbands of the women coming to the party today, including her brothers-in-law Gage and Wes, with nothing more than a raised eyebrow. When Dylan arrived here this morning to help Chloe get the cabin cleaned for the baby shower, she'd found her sister parked on the sofa with her feet up and strict orders not to move except to visit the bathroom from Harriet. Then her own orders were issued.

"Doc, you're in charge of putting out dishes and silverware," Harriet said, swishing past her with the floor dust mop. "Only put out the smaller plates. Don't want these ladies filling up a huge plate and then we run out of food for them."

"I have plenty of food," Lorna Doone, the owner of the Peaches 'N Cream Café, said from the corner of the kitchen, where she and her daughter Rachel were unloading coolers of food they'd prepared at the café. "You just worry about getting everything clean and tidy."

Harriet stopped mid-swipe of the broom to eye her oldest friend. "Half of them are pregnant and don't have a clue when to put aside the sweets. I doubt the all-you-can-eat buffet over at Tilly's could be enough food."

Dylan quickly got the suggested plates from the cabinet and exchanged an amused look with Rachel, who tried hard not to laugh at the two feuding honorary grandmothers of all the town's little ones. They'd quibbled about things for years.

Bobby had arrived with decorations, and the younger women were quickly hanging things while the two older ladies gave directions, often countermanding each other. Then Harriet dismissed Chloe's pet wolf-dog Wöden to the forest behind the cabin. The big animal that had saved Chloe's life years ago was attached to her like a shadow. Only three people in the world could get him to do what they said, Chloe, her husband Wes, and Harriet. From what Dylan witnessed over the years, no one, man or beast, balked at orders given by the taciturn nurse.

"Doc, help Sylvie get that baby in here out of the sun," Harriet said, and Dylan jumped to her feet.

One of the first things she learned as an intern was when an experienced nurse told you to do something, it was best to listen. She hurried down the steps and took the baby carrier from the red-headed pixie-like Sylvie, surprised how heavy it was with the newborn inside.

"Oh, thank you Dr. Roberts. I'm still adjusting to getting out and about after giving birth to Sunshine six weeks ago," Sylvie said. "My doctor said my incision was healing up just fine and I can start back to work whenever I want, but not to lift anything heavier than ten pounds for another month. But Sunshine is almost ten pounds already."

"You had a cesarean section?" Dylan asked as she helped Sylvie to the steps and carried the baby up onto the shaded porch. She understood why Harriet was insistent little Sunshine stayed out of the sun. She had the same bright red hair as her mother and the pale skin to go with it. Thankfully, Sylvie had one of those carriers with the shade visor built in.

Sylvie sank into the other porch chair by Chloe. "My doctor was going to give me a chance to have a natural birth, but then she met Cleetus," Sylvie giggled. "One look at him and she decided no way would I be able to birth a baby he fathered."

Everyone laughed. Cleetus, one of the town's deputy sheriffs, was a mountain of a man. The kindest, most courteous of men, but huge, nonetheless. A gentle giant who loved Sylvie with his whole heart.

Dylan set the baby carrier on the table between Sylvie and

Chloe and peeked inside at the sleeping baby. "She's so cute." She reached in to snap open the safety harness—

"No!" eight voices hissed quietly at her.

Dylan froze, looking around at all the mothers. "What?"

"Never wake a sleeping baby," Emma Preston said.

"No matter how cute they look sleeping," Libby Reynolds added, walking past with her own baby carrier with her newest little boy inside.

"You can hold her when she wakes up," Twyla Howard, the owner of the Dye Right hair salon and Sylvie's boss said, carrying several giant gift bags with pastel tissue papers inside.

Maggie Landon, the town's new mayor, draped one arm around Dylan's shoulders and leaned in. "Just be glad you're not a man or we'd insist you change her diaper when she wakes up before we let you hold her."

Harriet scooped up the baby carrier with Sunshine inside, and assisted Sylvie out of the chair. "Let's get this bunch fed before we're all as cranky as hungry babies."

Dylan watched the gaggle of women disappear inside, leaving her standing in their wake with only Chloe and the town's female paramedic, Maggie's cousin, Aisha. Both shrugged her way.

"I feel your pain," Aisha said. "Sometimes I wonder if I just don't have any maternal urges or if it comes with getting married."

Chloe motioned to Dylan to come give her a hand. "I don't think it comes with being married," she said as Dylan hauled her out of her chair. "It's more like—and here's where I'm going to sound like some old-fashioned romantic—but when you find that one person who completes you, having a baby becomes one more link that holds you together."

Another car pulled up and five more women climbed out, one an older lady who carried a large white box. Willie Mae was the owner of the Yeast & West Bakery and Dylan's mouth already watered imagining what creation was inside that box.

"I hope it's lemon," she said.

"Or red velvet," Aisha said, with a twinkle of lust in her eyes.

"Chocolate," Chloe said. "I begged for chocolate and it's my party."

"Might be a little of everything," Rachel said, joining them on the porch. "But mom said come on the food is ready and Harriet says the pregnant guest of honor has to go first."

As the others were swept inside by the second wave of women and gifts, Dylan brought up the rear and stood by the screen door as the others milled about chatting, filling plates with finger foods and salads. Bobby and Chloe seemed so relaxed here among this bee-hive of femininity.

Sadness washed over her.

For years it had been just the three of them. She'd been all of six years old when their parents died in that tragic car accident. Bobby had become not only her care giver and second mother, but her lifeline in a sea of fear and despair. Chloe became her biggest champion, confidant, and defender against bullies. They'd both pushed and encouraged her through med school and been there on those nights of her residency when she needed to either vent her frustration with the medical world or cry over the death of patients. She was happy her sisters had both found a community where they not only belonged but seemed to be loved.

Suddenly, she felt like that tall, skinny girl with braces and big thick glasses all the kids made fun of in school again. Odd man out. The geek. The outsider.

CHAPTER 2

"This might make a good human-interest story," Sean Callahan, editor of the Westen Chronicle, said as he stepped into the sheriff's office that suddenly resembled a daycare center.

Currently Deputy Cleetus Junkins was seated in the center of the common space floor with three male munchkins climbing on him like he was a giant mountain. The boys belonged to Sheriff Justice, Doc Preston and Nick Fisher. The doctor's five-year-old daughter was sitting at a desk with reams of paper and crayons in front of her, while Nick and Gage sat in chairs blocking off the exit to the rear and the main entrance, drinking coffee.

"You print this in the paper, and I'll see you have traffic tickets for the next six months," Gage said with a laugh and grin.

Sean swallowed a retort and the irritation that flared deep inside him. The sheriff didn't know his joke was eerily similar to the comment made by the editor who'd fired him for reporting an unfavorable story about a businessman and politician the newspaper owner supported. Gage had never pressed him on the reason he'd left New York and come to Westen, and Sean had never volunteered the information.

"So, why are all of your kids and a few extras here?" he asked, trying to keep his voice easy going. "The county starting a daddy daycare here?"

"Hardly. All the mothers are out at Wes' place throwing a baby shower for Chloe," Cleetus said, pulling one of the toddlers off his shoulders.

"We've been put in charge of the kids for a few hours," Nick said, catching his son before he climbed on a swivel chair. "So, we decided to join forces and keep them all in one place."

"And how did Doc Clint get out of this?"

"He had medical training classes at the new hospital and baseball practice for the twins," Gage said, referring to his twelve-year-old nephews and the doctor's stepsons.

"Lucky him," Sean said, looking around at the chaos of kids, toys and grown men. He maneuvered a desk chair into the aisle between two desks to do his part in corralling the kids in the center. "Is Wes over at the baby shower?"

"Why would a guy go to a baby shower?" Cleetus asked, dodging a toddler's foot to his gut as the doctor's son tried to climb up his front.

Sean gave a shrug just as the front door opened and in walked the father-to-be bearing food boxes from the Peaches 'N Cream Café. "Back in the city a few years back it seemed to be the big thing that the husbands were all invited, too."

"Welcome to small town life, newsman. Our women know we'd be useless at a party with little finger-sandwiches and talk about babies," Wes said, handing boxes to the others, finally handing one to Sean and taking a seat. "We do a little childcare, eat big man sandwiches that Lorna packed up for us and stay away from all the little baby things."

Sean opened his box and burst out laughing.

Inside were small tea-style sandwiches, little tarts with fruit on top and other types of finger appetizers.

"Looks like Lorna wanted to give you guys the babyshower experience even if you weren't attending."

Gage took out a sandwich and ate it in one big bite. "Not bad. But it's going to take more than one of these to fill me up. Good thing there's about six of everything in here."

"Samich, Papa?" Gage's son, Luke, held out his hand.

Gage scooped him up to sit on his thigh and handed him one of the sandwiches that fit the little boy's hand perfectly. He grinned up at his father then took a bite.

Sean looked around to see all the other men doing the same. Nick's son was seated on his lap, munching away. Cleetus had the doctor's son in his lap on the floor eating while his sister sat at the desk, alternating between coloring and munching on one of the tarts. Usually when small humans were involved there was a woman in the vicinity—mothers, grandmothers, aunts. Not one to be nostalgic, Sean had to admit it was reassuring to see how these men cared for their children and the young children of others.

"So, your place is overrun with women today?" he asked Wes.

"Started yesterday, when the doc came to town," he said, then plopped another small sandwich into his mouth, chewed and swallowed. "Brought two suitcases with her."

"Two?" Gage asked. "Usually she travels with just the one overnight bag."

Wes shrugged. "She's finished her residency and decided to come and stay for a while. I for one am glad she's taking a little time to relax."

"And having a doctor in the house when your wife is almost ready to give birth isn't a bad thing," Nick said, and all the men chuckled.

Wes joined in, then he got a little serious. "It's not just that. She's had a difficult time of it this past year."

That piqued Sean's attention. "Doing the trauma surgery fellowship was that hard on her?"

"Not for Dylan. She had that in the bag with her skills," Wes said, a little sadness crossing his face. "Bulldog dying on that hostage rescue mission in Africa shook her pretty hard."

"Whose bulldog? One of those rescue K-9s?" Cleetus asked.

Wes shook his head. "No. Bulldog wasn't a dog, but a man. One of my former black ops team members, Steven Janowski, nickname Bulldog."

"How did the doc know him?" Sean asked, trying not to act too curious or too put out that some strange man's death had affected the youngest Roberts sister so deeply.

"When Bulldog wasn't on a mission, he worked as a surgical assistant. Damn good one, too," Wes said.

"Remember when Chloe had that stalker down in Cincinnati a few years back?" Gage asked.

"You mean the stalker Wes here brought her back from Cincy to stay isolated in his cabin during the biggest blizzard to hit the area in decades, and didn't realize he had his own stalker that almost killed him and Wöden trying to protect Chloe? Don't have a clue what you're talking about," Sean said, stuffing another miniature chicken salad sandwich into his mouth with a half-assed grin. He knew that story well, had written about it for a few weeks, and didn't remember anyone named Bulldog being part of it.

"For a newsman, you have a lousy memory then," Gage said with a laugh. "Anyways our resident black ops expert had his man Bulldog insinuate himself into Dylan's surgical team at the hospital where she was training. Turns out, not only did he help keep her safe and calm throughout that mess, they became friends."

Friends? The let's-go-catch-a-game-and-a-beer kind of friends? Or the-whole-gang-is-going-bowling kind of friends? Or the I-like-you-and-you-like-me-and-maybe-it-could-lead-to-more kind of friends?

Since the night he met her at Gage and her sister Bobby's wedding, she'd intrigued him. Who wouldn't be attracted to a tall, sexy, smart woman who loved to do the chicken dance and laugh at his bad jokes? For the next four years she'd come and go on visits to her sisters, somehow finding time to hang out with him. Each time she left he missed her a little more. But knowing she had obligations in her career, he hadn't pushed things.

If she'd been in a deep friendship-relationship with this Bulldog guy, that might explain why she'd kept him at arm's length all these years.

"I don't remember anything coming across my desk about Americans dying in some hostage rescue in a foreign country. How long ago did this happen?" he asked Wes.

"Less than a year ago, and no, you wouldn't have heard about it because officially they weren't there." Wes fixed him with an if-you-publish-this-I'll-hurt-you stare. "It's why it was a black ops mission."

Sean nodded that he got the message that this conversation was off the record, but he couldn't help his own curiosity. "Did they get the hostages out?"

Wes nodded, his lips pressed tight, as he swallowed hard, his eyes misting over. "Every last one of them," he finally said. "Even the little girl Bulldog was carrying when he was shot in the back."

Well, that settled it. He might be able to fight the memory of a ghost. But the memory of a *hero* ghost? Yeah, he was on the losing end of that battle. It didn't change how he felt about

Dylan, and it wouldn't stop him from being there as a shoulder to lean or cry on while she was in town.

"How long is this hen party going to go on at your place?" he asked Wes. Maybe he could get some photos and quotes, make it a local human-interest post for the online newsletter.

Wes glanced at his watch. "Chloe told me to be gone until two, so about another thirty minutes?"

"You'd best stay gone for an hour," Nick said. "That way you'll miss most of the clean-up."

All the men laughed.

∼

"Did you see how much Twylla was holding Sunshine today?" Bobby settled onto the couch beside Chloe. "It's like she's her grandmother."

"More like her older aunt. Twylla's only a few years older than you Mrs. Sheriff. And it looks to me like you're not in the grandma business," Lorna said, stretching out her legs as she sank into the overstuffed chair near the fireplace and gave Bobby's baby bump a pointed nod.

Bobby laughed and rubbed her tummy. "I hate to tell you this, Lorna, but there are women my age who are grandmothers. I just got a late start on the mothering end of the business."

"Well, I've got ten years on you—"

"More like fifteen," Harriett said, taking a seat on the fireplace hearth beside Rachel and Wöden.

Dylan bit back a laugh but met Chloe's grin across the room. In the years since both her sisters had moved to Westen, she'd gotten to know the nurse and café owner well. Best of friends, they liked to pick at each other, usually with Harriett's one-liners from her dry wit causing at least one of the Roberts sisters to choke on whatever was in their mouth at the time. Lorna took the comments in good humor, often continuing on as if she'd never heard her friend's quips—although the occasional lifted brow and slight hesitation implied she had.

"And I'm not planning on being a grandmother any time soon," Lorna finished, with a pointed-look directly at her daughter.

Rachel held up her hands in a defensive manner. "Don't look at me! I have this last year of nursing school to get through, and as cute as I find all these little people everyone keeps having, I want to travel a little before I even think of settling down."

"Don't travel too much or too far from home," Lorna said, a little sadness in her voice.

"Yep," Emma said. "That's what happened to Twylla."

Everyone's attention turned to Bobby's cousin-in-law, who was finishing up packing take-home food packets for everyone with leftovers from the party. She paused and looked at them all. "What?"

"Okay, Miss I've-lived-here-all-my-life-and-know-the-hairdresser's-secrets," Bobby said. "Spill."

"Yes, I've lived here *most* of my life, if we don't count the years of college and living with my ex-husband, may he rot in hell," Emma said, squeezing into the spot on the sofa between Bobby and Chloe. "But that doesn't mean I know all of Twylla's secrets."

"You know more than the rest of us," Chloe said, munching on celery covered in peanut butter. "I'm with Bobby. Spill."

"Well, Twylla was about six years ahead of me in school," Emma said, propping her feet up on the coffee table like the sisters. "She sang solos in church on Sunday and was the lead in the high school musicals every year."

"Wait," Bobby said. "Twylla sings?"

Emma nodded. "Her voice could do everything from gospel to Broadway to hard rock. Someone once told Mama that Twylla had a four-octave range."

"Wow! That's impressive," Rachel said. "Why haven't I ever heard her sing in church? What happened?"

"She left town. Right after graduating high school, she took the savings she'd earned working at the diner and headed for New York. She wanted to be a singer."

"This was before Mom and Dad bought the diner, right?" Rachel asked.

"Your daddy and I came to Westen a couple of years later," Lorna said. "The previous owners wanted to retire to Florida and your daddy wanted to try owning our own business. Twylla had already left town by then."

"So, you didn't know her until she came back?" Chloe asked.

"I knew of her." Lorna's lips pressed into a thin disapproving line.

"What did she do?" Dylan asked. From what she'd seen over the past five years, Lorna and Twylla were on very friendly terms.

"She broke her mother's heart." Lorna shook her head. "Twylla changed her name and got some roles in Broadway musicals, mostly chorus lines. Helen never really told me much of what happened to her daughter in New York. I'm not sure she even knew. First, Twylla stopped coming home to visit. I think I met her once when we first moved here. Then she stopped calling every week. Then she stopped writing. Then Helen never heard from her again."

"Never?" Bobby asked.

Lorna shook her head. "Nope. Poor Helen died. Twylla didn't even come back for the funeral."

"Wow," Rachel said and everyone else grew very quiet.

"Tell them the rest," Lorna said.

All the younger women looked to Emma who simply shrugged. "I was away at college when Twylla came back home."

Rachel held up her hands. "Don't look at me. I think I was two."

"The girl came home two years after her mother died," Harriett said. "Classic case of abuse."

"Physical?" Bobby asked.

"Emotional?" Chloe asked at the same time.

Dylan finished the trifecta, "Sexual?"

"Yes."

"All of them?" Emma said.

"And a good case of anorexia. She weighed all of about ninety pounds. Covered in bruises and scars." One who usually wasn't given to emotions, Harriett blinked a few times and stared out the large window into the woods as if deciding how much information she could divulge of her former patient's history. "I know you love Twylla, so it's time you knew some of her story," she finally said. "Doc Ray admitted her to the clinic for months when she got to town. We started off with small amounts of food. IVs with vitamins and it took us a while to get her electrolytes in order."

"Why didn't he put her in the hospital?" Dylan knew how hard it was to treat someone with severe anorexia. The constant weight loss, dieting and self-starvation from psychological problems stressed their bodies, in particular electrolyte imbalances, and could cause heart issues for them. One of her rotations in med school had her caring for a girl in the Medical Intensive Care Unit who ended up dying from heart failure because of her condition.

"Doc Ray delivered Twylla, same as he had most of the kids her age in town. He wanted to be sure she got not just the physical care she needed, but the emotional care."

"But he wasn't a psychiatrist," Dylan said. She'd never met the town's former doctor. He'd retired along with his wife to Florida a couple of years before Bobby first came to town, leaving his practice to his nephew Clint, Emma's husband. As far as she knew he was a general practitioner, no specialized training.

"True, but he had something the hospitals didn't," Lorna said.

Everyone waited for her to continue. Finally, Chloe asked. "What?"

"Caroline," Harriett said, and Lorna nodded.

"Doc Ray's wife?" Emma asked, looking surprised in the other nurse's direction. "She wasn't a nurse or a doctor."

"No, she wasn't. She was something special." Lorna took over the conversation. "She was a listener. That woman could coax anyone in any circumstance to talk to her. She'd make them tea or a sandwich, sit across from them, and they'd just share all their darkest secrets."

"So, what happened to Twylla in New York?" Chloe asked.

Lorna shook her head. "I don't know details."

There was a long pause in the room.

"*You* don't know details?" Bobby asked with a surprised look. Dylan didn't blame her. All the others had the same expression, and she was pretty sure she did too. There wasn't much that went on in Westen that the owner of the Peaches 'N Cream hadn't heard.

"I know it's hard to believe, but I could never persuade Caroline to tell me."

"It wasn't for lack of trying," Harriett muttered.

Lorna narrowed one eye at her friend. "You complained the chart wasn't complete without the facts, as I recall. And Caroline still wouldn't reveal Twylla's secrets." She turned to look at all the younger women. "Caroline wasn't just a good listener. She never, ever, *ever* gossiped. Never told someone's private thoughts. That's why she was integral in helping Twylla."

"While the doc and I healed her body, Caroline healed her

heart and her mind," Harriett said. "Took us nearly three months, but she walked out of the clinic healthier and ready to live her life. She bought the salon space and opened the Dye Right."

"The months she was in the clinic didn't go unnoticed by everyone in town, despite Caroline's resolute muteness," Lorna said. "We'd all seen or heard about the shape Twylla was in when she got here. It took the sting out of her ill treatment of her mother. And all the ladies in town started going to her shop. We wanted to support her recovery."

"Doesn't surprise me," Emma said with a nod. "Even as a teen, Twylla always had a way with hairstyles and always was in step with the newest fashions."

"I love how walking into the Dye Right is like walking into a Parisian fashion house," Bobby said.

Chloe nodded, waving her celery around like a wand. "I know! Especially since she expanded into the empty store next door two years ago."

"She had to," Emma said. "With all the new people moving into town, she had to put in more chairs and hire more stylists. It was getting near to impossible to get an appointment without planning ahead a month or two."

Dylan listened as the other women talked about the changes that had gone on in Westen over the past five years. When Bobby came to town as a private investigator, she and Gage had stumbled into a Meth lab that was supplying the drug to the entire state. A scandal between a DEA officer and a corrupt DA in the county housing the state capitol—who also happened to be Gage's ex-wife—that covered up the knowledge of the lab nearly blew up the town and almost killed Gage. The state, to make amends, poured quite a bit of money into the town to rebuild and develop the area, as well as improving the highway and roads in this rural community. With all the construction had come an influx of urbanites fleeing Columbus to a quaint town within driving distance of the big city. Westen was having growing pains of its own.

"So have you had a tour of the new hospital?" Emma asked, and Dylan realized she'd lost track of the conversation.

"Uhm, no. Not yet."

"She just got into town yesterday. She's taking a sabbatical and hanging out with me until this little one comes," Chloe said, patting her tummy.

Dylan didn't miss the exchange of worried looks between her sisters. She knew they were concerned about her. She'd finished her surgical residency and then an extra year fellowship in trauma surgery this past year. Because of her training and resume, she'd been offered positions at some of the most impressive hospitals in big cities around the country. One of the few physicians who didn't come out of medical school owing huge student loans to the government—she'd worked all through college and part-time as a surgical tech during medical school. Also, their parents had left money for all the girls in trust when they'd died, and Bobby had raised them on her teacher's salary to save the money for her and Chloe's education—she didn't feel the pressure to make a decision right now. Unfortunately, it left her feeling adrift, especially after Bulldog's death.

"Well, when you're ready, I know Clint would love to hear your opinion on the functionality of the place," Emma said. "Let me know when you have time and I'll go with you." Then she paused. "Well, except for tomorrow."

"What's happening tomorrow?" Dylan asked.

"Baseball," Harriett said.

Dylan looked at the others, all of whom were nodding as if they understood the one-word explanation. "Okay, who's playing baseball tomorrow?"

"Lexie Löwe and Sadie Landon," Chloe said with a grin.

"Lexie? The little girl you were the court appointed advocate for a few years back?"

"Yep. She and Sadie, Mayor Maggie's daughter, are on the town's co-ed little league team. They're playing for the Great Lakes championship to enter into the Little League World Series playoffs tomorrow up in Mt. Vernon."

"You're not going," Dylan said, but it was almost an order.

"The hell I'm not." Chloe stared at her like she was daring a witness on the stand to lie under oath.

Dylan gaped at her, then switched her attention to their older sister. "The last thing she needs to be doing is sitting in the hot sun watching a baseball game in her condition. The same with you."

Bobby simply shrugged, obviously also planning to go to the game.

"Half the town is going," Rachel said. "The first time our team's gotten this far and with Coach Löwe and Coach Hillis, they could make it to the finals. And with a girl starting pitcher and a girl short-stop. It's going to be so cool!"

"And I'm part of Lexie's life. I facilitated her adoption and I'm going to watch her pitch."

The finality of that sentence told Dylan there was no talking Chloe out of going.

"Well, looks like I'm going to a little league baseball game."

CHAPTER 3

"So, how did you get dragged to this game?" Sean asked, coming to stand behind Dylan in the concession stand line.

"Hey Callahan," she said with a happy surprised glow in her eyes. Then she looked over his shoulder and nodded. He followed her gaze to the visitors' bleachers completely filled with Westen citizens. "Both of my very pregnant sisters insisted on coming for the game, so I figured it wouldn't hurt to have another doctor hanging around. Why are you here?"

"Rooting on the local team, of course." He motioned for her to move up in line.

She stepped up. "Oh, I thought maybe you were here as a journalist."

"A journalist can't support his own town's team?"

"Sure they can. But given that two of the players on the Westen team are girls, it might make this game newsworthy."

"I could highlight that, but they're not the only stars on that team. Dan has the whole team playing at a really high level. If they win today, they go to the Little League World Series, and that would be news for the whole town, not just the girls."

She moved forward, ordered three bottles of water and a bag of cotton candy. "Gage and Wes already got everyone food, but in this heat I'm going to make sure my sisters stay hydrated."

"And the cotton candy?"

She grinned. "Figure I need to make my nephew a sticky mess."

"Gage is going to love that," he said, stepping to the side and ordering two hot dogs and a large soda.

"I know," she laughed, and the sound sent tingles down his spine. He loved to hear her laugh, had since the minute they'd met. "I take my job as aunt and pain-in-the-ass-sister-in-law very seriously."

They paid for their food and headed back to the stands.

Calls of "Hey, Callahan!" from the group greeted him as he settled onto the bleacher seat beside Dylan, who handed water bottles to her two sisters. He nodded at everyone, listening to them chat as he ate his hot dogs and watched Dylan feed bits of sugary sweetness to all the toddlers in the group.

He grinned to himself. She was going to have more than her brother-in-law unhappy with the sugar rush and mess her treat was going to leave behind.

While he ate, he studied the crowd. The visitors' section was full of parents of the team, including Coach Löwe's wife Melissa. The couple had adopted Lexie, the star pitcher, four years ago, and they'd become a very happy family. Lexie's four foster brothers were all there, too. Two still lived in town and two were home from college. Mayor Maggie Landon and her husband, along with their son Tre, a star running back for the Buckeyes, were here too, to support their daughter, the team's hot-shot short stop Sadie. Lorna had closed the Peaches 'N Cream Café, and all her staff, including Pete the cook, were in the stands. It was one of the things he'd come to love about Westen. They might have differing opinions about politics or the state of the world, but they loved their town and supported each other.

When their team lined up on the third base line for the national anthem, everyone stood and cheered like it was the Super Bowl. All the men took off their hats and everyone sang along with the young trumpeter who managed the song without hitting any sour notes. One voice seemed to stand out from the others. A strong alto that hit every note with pure accuracy and a bit of a jazzy sound to their vibrato.

He looked around, finally landing on the source of the wonderful sound.

Twylla Howard stood next to Lorna two rows back and to his left, singing along with the crowd. For some reason, she seemed to be holding back, trying to blend in. If he didn't have perfect pitch himself, he might not have noticed.

"She used to be a professional singer." Dylan leaned closer to almost whisper in his ear as the song ended.

"Twylla?" he asked as they sat, and the team came in to bat while their opponents, who looked to be really tall for little leaguers, took the field.

Dylan nodded, still leaning close. "That's what Lorna said at the baby shower yesterday. She went to New York to try to get a singing career going."

"Really? I've never heard of her as a professional singer." He reached in her bag of cotton candy and snagged a pinch.

"Apparently, she had a few chorus-line gigs, but then no one knows what happened to her. And she keeps that part of her life there a big dark secret."

"Really?"

Sadie Landon came up to bat and the mystery of Twylla's past faded to the background.

∾

The game progressed until the bottom of the sixth inning. The score was tied, and as the designated home team, the Westen Red Hawks had a chance to win it with a walk-off run. Gavin Schmidt was on third base and Sadie was at bat once more with no outs. One base hit would win the game.

"Come on, Sadie!" yelled her mother.

"You got this, Sadie!" her father shouted.

"Go Red Hawks!" Sean yelled through cupped hands beside Dylan, and she let out a huge "Woot! Woot!"

The pitcher threw the ball. It went high and outside.

Sadie didn't swing.

Ball one.

More cheers for Sadie came from both the Westen fans and the players in the dugout.

She stepped out of the batter's box and took a deep breath as she rubbed her hands, one at a time, on her thighs and took one practice swing before stepping back in the box.

The pitcher held the ball and glove close to the chest while reading the signs from the catcher, gave a nod and hurled the ball at the plate.

Sadie swung.

A crack sounded as the bat hit the ball towards second base. She dropped the bat and ran for first.

Gavin tagged and ran for home.

The second baseman threw to home. The catcher moved to block the base.

The ball hit the catcher's glove.

Gavin, running full speed, dropped to slide in feet first. The crowd was on their feet.

Then he crashed into the catcher, who dropped the ball. Safe!

The Westen fans erupted in cheers and high-fives.

Dylan—her eyes on the boy holding his ankle and rolling on the ground, wailing in pain—flew down the bleachers to get to the field.

The boy's coach and a couple, who were probably his parents, reached him first.

"Hold still, Jeremy," the coach said, squatting down.

"It...really...hurts, Coach," Jeremy cried.

The mother knelt at his side, holding one hand over her mouth and using the other to smooth his hair from his forehead—something Dylan had seen mothers do in a sign of comfort for their kids—tears welling in her eyes and shock on her face.

"Is there a doctor here?" the man, who looked like Jeremy's father, yelled.

Dylan maneuvered through all the teammates, parents and umpires crowded around the injured boy. "I'm a doctor," she said, coming to squat by the coach at Jeremy's feet.

The father and coach stared at her.

She'd experienced this skepticism before. Because she was a young woman, people at first didn't believe her. Usually, it occurred in the hospital and once they saw her lab coat and read her name tag stating Dr. Roberts, Trauma Surgeon—she'd specifically requested the wording that way to save explanation—most patients and their families accepted her qualifications. But today she was in jeans and a t-shirt with her hair up in a ponytail.

"Do I need to call the paramedics, Dr. Roberts?" Callahan asked, coming to her side.

At that moment she could've kissed him. Immediately, the coach and father inched away to give her room. Jeremy's mother moved to lift her son's head into her lap.

"It hurts, Mommy," he whispered, still holding his leg, but he'd stopped rolling from side to side.

"Can I take a look at your leg, Jeremy?" Dylan asked, staring into the boy's frightened brown eyes, purposely keeping her voice calm and soothing.

He gulped in air and looked up at his mom, who nodded it would be okay. Then he let go of his leg to clench his mother's hand.

Dylan studied the crowd that now also contained the concerned parents and kids from the Westen team. Gavin, who'd crashed into Jeremy, was crying, and his mother Glenna and older brother flanked him. Grasping Jeremy's leg beneath the calf with one hand and his foot with the other, Dylan held it steady and motioned for Sean to come closer.

"What's up, Doc?" he asked, bending down.

"Can you get everyone to back up a bit or even move them away?" she whispered. Jeremy's anxiety had ratcheted up with all these people hovering over him.

"Sure thing."

Quickly, he and Dan Löwe, the Westen team's coach, started dispersing the crowd, while she focused on her patient.

"Jeremy, I'm going to hold your leg and foot steady. Do you think you can try to move just your foot a little?"

He blinked away some tears and nodded.

She felt his calf tighten slightly in her hand, but he hissed and turned his face into his mother's side. The little whimper that escaped him tugged at Dylan's heart. The nine or ten-year-old boy was trying to be brave in front of all the people.

"Okay, Jeremy. That was good. I know it hurt, but you were very brave for trying. You don't have to do that again." She nodded at Callahan, who stood behind the boy and his mother, watching for her signal. Thankfully he knew what she meant, pulled his phone out of his pocket, and walked away to call 911 for the EMTs.

She wiggled into a sitting position so her thigh was under Jeremy's calf to free up her right hand, then slowly pulled back his sock to the ankle, wiggling it carefully away from his skin where blood oozed from an apparent abrasion. Hesitant to remove his cleat just yet, she looped the sock over the heel to keep it out of the way.

The leg was oddly shaped, but no bones protruded through the skin so she ruled out an open fracture and relaxed. However, the ankle and lower leg were already swelling and turning a dark purple. She slid her hand up and gently pressed on the oddly-shaped area and felt the crunchy part of bone, known as crepitus, beneath her fingers. The action elicited another quiet whimper from Jeremy. It wasn't an emergency situation, but he would need to go to the hospital for the x-ray and the leg would need to be stabilized for transport.

"Here, Doc." Lorna was suddenly there handing her a bag of ice and a dish towel with her café's logo on it.

"Thanks, Lorna. Could you wrap the towel around the ice bag for me?" she asked, not wanting to move Jeremy's leg more than necessary. Sirens sounded in the distance, coming closer.

Lorna did as she asked and handed it back. "There you go."

"Thanks." She took it and made eye contact with her patient again. "Jeremy, this may hurt just a little and be really cold, but it will also help it feel a little better after a few moments, okay?"

He nodded and she pressed the wrapped ice bag on his leg. He hissed and clenched his mom's hand tighter but didn't jerk away.

"Is it broken?" the man she assumed was the father asked.

"Mr.—?"

"Dawson. Hal Dawson. That's my wife Jenifer and Jeremy's our oldest."

She gave him and his wife a reassuring half-smile she'd learned from a doctor during her residency. "Well, Mr. Dawson, I wouldn't give a diagnosis without confirming it with an x-ray, but I suspect there may be a break somewhere in his lower leg.

Which bone or both, again, I couldn't tell without the films." She waited for them to absorb that information, then continued. "We'll get him to the closest hospital where they can get the x-ray done, then the doctors will have a better idea how to proceed. It could just be a very bad sprain."

The last part was said to ease the parents' worry a bit, because she already suspected at least one fracture. One that would probably need surgery.

The sirens stopped and the large red EMT vehicle pulled up in the parking lot.

~

Once the paramedics arrived, Dylan reported to them on the accident, Jeremy's condition, and her suspected diagnosis. She stayed close until they had his leg and foot stabilized in am emergency splint for transport. Jeremy's mother was allowed to ride with him, and his father followed behind in their car.

"I can't thank you enough, Doctor," the coach said, shaking her hand. "I've taken some basic first aid and CPR, but a broken bone is completely out of my league."

"I'm glad I was here to help," she said. Taking a business card and pen out of her bag that Callahan had retrieved for her while she was working, she flipped the card over and wrote on the back of it. "I don't know what kind of sports medicine they have here, but if his parents want to take him somewhere that specializes in sports-related injuries, this is the name and number of a very good doctor in Columbus. They can tell him that Dr. Dylan Roberts referred them."

He took the card with a nod and slipped it into his pocket. "I'll tell them. I'm headed over to the hospital as soon as I get my equipment and team members gathered up."

She walked with him towards the dug outs, then splintered off to where the Red Hawks' fans and families were gathering around for picture taking with the champions. Looking for Callahan, she saw him in front of the team of still very excited kids and decided to hang back while he worked.

Lorna and Melissa stood by the concession stand, so she wandered over to join them.

"How's your patient?" Lorna asked.

"Pretty sure he has at least one broken bone in his lower leg. But he was doing okay when they left. I gave the name of a good ortho guy to his coach. Thanks for the ice pack, by the way."

"No problem. We might be opponents on the field, but no one wants to see a child injured in a game."

Melissa nodded. "It's one of my fears with Lexie and Sadie playing. The boys aren't much bigger right now, but when they hit the teen years, one of them plowing into our girls could really hurt them. Thank goodness you were here today, Dylan."

"I'm glad I was, too. Are Lexie and Sadie planning to try to continue to play ball when they're in middle school?" she asked, happy to turn the subject away from her. Helping Jeremy was instinctual and not heroic. It was simply her calling.

"We've already talked to Lexie about switching to girls' softball, but she'll have to learn how to pitch for that. It's different than baseball."

"She'll be good at it. What's going on here?" she asked with a nod to the group of kids and parents near Sean.

"The newsman is trying to get a group picture for the paper," Lorna said.

"Can you kids all get together so we can get a picture?" one of the mothers, standing closest to the kids and coaches, yelled out over the noisy group as the team tried to calm down after winning their first game in the playoffs.

It was like watching someone trying to herd squirrels on a nut scavenger hunt into two stationary lines.

"I don't think Nora is going to get her way this time," Lorna muttered.

"Is she always this..." Dylan paused to look for a diplomatic word.

"Pushy?" Lorna said with one brow arched.

"Persistent?" Melissa said with a bit of a smile teasing the edge of her lips.

"Yes." Dylan would let them figure out which one she meant. "What's her story?"

"She blew in like a spring tornado two years ago and started a real estate business with her husband," Lorna said.

Dylan nodded. "Smart move, considering all the people moving into the area."

"And they've been instrumental in helping with the remodeling of some of the older homes and businesses in the older part of town," Melissa said.

"I did notice there are more businesses in the center of town. Two clothing stores, the barbecue, Italian and Thai restaurants." She turned to Lorna. "Are they affecting your business much?"

The crayon yellow curls bounced as she shook her head. "Nope. With the number of newcomers to town, not to mention the tourists staying at both the Westen and Country Inns, there's more than enough hungry people to go around. Even the pizza place hasn't cut into our business. I have to admit I wasn't thrilled with Nora's approach of high tides float all ships when she pitched it to the town council a few years back but bringing more traffic to the downtown area and away from those big-box stores setting up shop on the outskirts of town really paid off."

"So, pushy is good?" Dylan asked.

Lorna just shrugged.

Dylan turned to Melissa on the other side. "And persistent?"

She shrugged. "Nora seems to think that whenever we need to do a fund raiser—like for the new uniforms for the team for the playoffs—I will have plenty of time to cook and co-chair each event with her because my work has me at home all day."

"I can see her point. Running a home for at-risk kids, counseling them and others, while having a young daughter who is a star pitcher and ballerina-in-training isn't much work."

Melissa elbowed her in the ribs. "Don't forget, I'm the coach's wife, so it's my responsibility to organize all the parents to provide snacks for practices and transportation to the away games for the kids whose parents can't make those."

"Yeah, I can see how you have more time than anyone else to bake."

"I don't mind baking and Lexie loves to help." Melissa let out a little sigh watching the realtor woman maneuver the kids so a boy with the same shade of light brown hair as hers was front and center, moving the two girl players to flank him. "I just wish Nora didn't see the need for so much...attention, especially from *my* husband."

Dylan narrowed her eyes to study the scene playing out before her. The short curvy brunette realtor didn't just tell the kids where to stand but grasped both Coach Dan and Coach Joe by the biceps, grinning flirtatiously with both to put them where she wanted them in the photo.

"She thinks she's a friggin' movie producer," Melissa muttered beside her.

Dylan sputtered and stared at her friend a moment. It was so out of character for Melissa to curse, even mildly.

"What? She flirts with every man, married or not. See?" She nodded at the group again. "Nora really loves Mr. Callahan. Probably hopes he'll give her free advertising in the paper."

Biting back a grin at how disgruntled Melissa sounded, she shifted her gaze back to the group photo-op again. She was right. Nora seemed to be very touchy-feely with Callahan. Not that she could blame the woman. With his broad-shoulders, lean hips, thick wavy brown hair, green eyes, and charming smile, he drew women to him like ants to a picnic. They'd been friends since her sister Bobby's wedding to Gage.

She stood on the edge of the crowded room, watching all the townspeople interacting with each other. It was her sister's wedding and she felt like a stranger in a strange land. She knew some of the people, like the big deputy Cleetus and the owner of the café, Lorna Doone, but once again, just like in school and college and medical school, she was the outsider. Even her other sister Chloe had made herself at home among these people. She tilted her head to the side to study her sister closer as she leaned in to talk to the ruggedly handsome deputy Wes, who poured both of them a drink from the bottle of whiskey on their table. Perhaps Chloe was making friends with that bottle more than others in the room? Maybe she should go rescue her?

"Can I interest you in a dance, Doctor?" a deep voice said behind her.

Turning, she recognized the man introduced to her earlier as the newspaper editor. What was his name?

"Sean Callahan," he said, answering her unspoken question.

Wait? She didn't ask that out loud, did she?

"Wow, I guess I didn't make much of an impression earlier when your new brother-in-law introduced us," he continued as if disappointed she didn't recognize him or his name. The puzzled look she always wore when trying to think what embarrassing thing she'd done this time probably gave him that impression.

She forced a relaxed smile to reassure him that she did indeed remember meeting him. "The newspaper man. I remember. I'm just lousy with names when I've met more than one person at an event."

"And I bet you've been introduced to everyone in town today."

"Well, at least everyone who knows my sister and brother-in-law."

The music turned to a slow romantic dance number.

"Would you mind if we got something to eat?" she asked not wanting to turn him down for a turn on the dance floor, but not wanting to start out knowing him with intimate contact either. "I've been dying to try the buffet."

They'd spent the evening laughing and joking with people who stopped by their table, danced a few fast dances—including the chicken dance which Dylan always thought was great fun. After Bobby and Gage left for their honeymoon, Sean escorted her back to the Inn when Chloe disappeared with the deputy.

Now, watching this other woman smile at Callahan and stroke her hand up and down his arm as they moved back to take pictures of the softball team, an uneasy feeling washed over her. Did he have to smile back and act like it was okay for a married woman—whose spouse Melissa had pointed out was just across the parking lot glad-handing with the men of the local Elk's club—to be practically undressing him in public?

For some reason the whole tableau irritated her, and her stomach soured. She turned her back and began gathering her bag and water bottle. Suddenly, she stopped.

Crap.

While she'd been talking with the paramedics, both her pregnant sisters and their families had left for home, and Callahan had offered to give her a lift back to Westen. Riding with him after watching him flirt with another woman didn't sound near as fun as it had earlier. Now how was she supposed to get home?

She glanced over to ask Melissa, who was surrounded by her husband Coach Dan, their daughter Lexie, three of her four foster brothers and two newer residents of the half-way house they lived in. She didn't think they could squeeze another body in their van.

Maybe Lorna?

Nope, the Peaches 'N Cream van she drove everywhere was already pulling out. And so was her last option.

"Ready to go?" A familiar deep voice asked behind her.

Sean. Great. How did she act natural and friendly when inside she wanted punch him for letting the realtor run her hands all over him? And wasn't that resentment stupid? She had no claim on him personally. Their relationship had always been just friends. So, what had her so irritated? Because the woman was married? Or because Callahan hadn't rebuffed her attention? And worse, why did she care so much? It wasn't like she planned to live here. She was only in town long enough to be sure Chloe and Bobby's deliveries went off without a hitch and she'd get to see her new nieces or nephews.

Swallowing her irritation, she plastered on a pleasant smile and turned. "Yep, was just waiting for you to finish your photo session."

"Sorry about the wait." He gave a rueful laugh and shook his head as they walked through the gravel parking lot to his vintage 1960s Mustang.

"Nora can be a little..."

"Pushy?"

"Persistent," he replied, their words mirroring Lorna and Melissa's conversation earlier. "She means well. I think. She's very active on social media, which has brought more awareness state-wide on Westen. In a good way."

"Not in a your-town-almost-blew-up-in-a-Meth-lab-explosion kind of way?"

He nodded as he unlocked the passenger door and opened it for her. "Yes. Much better than that kind of attention."

"Isn't that your job to bring positive light to Westen as the newspaper editor?" she asked after they were buckled in.

"Somewhat. My job is to provide news, good or bad—national, state and local. Weather—especially for the rural residents whose livelihood depends on changes throughout the seasons. Sports—local school and independent teams like the little league champs today. And of course, local events—fairs, festivals and holiday happenings." He put the car in gear and spun a little gravel as he pulled out of the lot. The powerful engine growled and rumbled around them as they flew down the country road.

Dylan laughed as the summer wind whipped through the open windows. She glanced at Sean. The grin on his face told her he enjoyed the freedom of the road as much as she did.

"Do you want to head to the hospital where they took your patient?" he asked.

"Nope. He's in good hands and since I'm not on staff, no one will give me any details anyways."

"You did a great job with him," he said with a glance her way.

"Thanks. I usually assess my patients in an ER or hospital room, not on a baseball field."

"Well, no one would know. Calm, collected and very kind was what you were."

She smiled at him in thanks, then looked out the passenger window. For some reason, she hated getting praise for simply doing her job. It always made her feel uncomfortable.

Instead of heading to the highway, Sean chose to drive them through the scenic back roads of Ohio farmland. Rows and rows of nearly six-foot high stalks of corn were broken up by flat pastureland dotted with dairy cows, the occasional horse or donkey, and farmhouses and barns reminiscent of a painting from the middle of the last century.

The peacefulness of the picturesque drive relaxed Dylan more than the hours of yoga and meditation her friends at the hospital insisted would relieve the stress she'd been under the past year ever had. Her handsome companion singing to old rock songs with the radio only added to her improved mood.

They drove through one of the small towns on the edge of Amish country filled with small shops of local craft goods for tourists similar to the ones popping up in Westen. Only here, many of the parking spaces on this Saturday were filled with black horse-drawn buggies.

"Hungry?" Sean asked as they stopped at a light.

"Yeah. All I had at the game was cotton candy with my nephew and the other little kids." And now that he'd mentioned it, she was suddenly ravenous.

"I know," he chuckled. "It was fun watching Gage give you the stink-eye as he wiped down Luke with wet wipes and the little bugger kept trying to escape to grab more sugar from you."

She laughed. "Sometimes it's so much fun being the aunt who spoils him. Irritating my brother-in-law at the same time? Added bonus."

He drove further through town then turned into a parking lot filled with cars and RVs.

"Dutch Country Inn." Dylan read the sign as she climbed out her side of the car. The converted two-story farmhouse had a large extended addition, complete with outdoor seating and Edison bulb lights strung across the pergola covering. "Looks charming."

"Food's even better than the ambiance," Sean said as they maneuvered their way through the lot to the main entrance.

A young woman dressed in a pale pink Mennonite dress with the little white cap on her head smiled as they entered. "Welcome. Dinner? Or are you checking in?"

"Just two for dinner," Sean hurried to say. If Dylan didn't know better, she'd say he was a little embarrassed by the girl's innocent question.

The hostess smiled again, grabbed two menus, and escorted them to a table with four chairs. There were longer tables filled with six to ten people and all the food appeared to be served family-style.

"You can order your food family style or separate plates," Sean said after they were seated. "I highly recommend the chicken and dumplings."

"How did you find this place?" Dylan studied the laminated menu, her mouth watering and stomach growling over some of the offerings.

"When I first moved to Westen and took over the newspaper, I wanted to get to know not only our town and the local residents, but other towns in the general area. So, I traveled around looking for interesting places and people I could feature in the news when things might get slow in Westen."

Dylan looked over the top of the menu at him. "From what I've heard from my sisters and brothers-in-law, there's never a dull moment in Westen."

"I have to admit to having more exciting news than I originally thought when I bought the paper," he chuckled. "But I should have paid attention to the clues."

Before she could question him further, the waitress came back, and they placed their orders for chicken and dumplings.

"What clues did you ignore?"

"First, would be the low purchase price I paid for the company, all the equipment and office space."

She grinned at him. "When a deal is too good to be true, it usually has a catch. What other clues did you ignore?"

"There was the large crater on the Southwest corner of town where all the new construction has been happening."

This time Dylan nodded, all amusement gone. "Meth lab explosion in a former Underground Railroad safe house, literally buried underground. That's where Gage almost died, and my sister crawled into a small hole to help rescue him." She paused, playing with the fork on the table. "She was terribly claustrophobic at the time but crawled into that hole nonetheless."

"I know. Bobby was one of the first interviews I did, when I took over the paper."

She looked up to see tenderness in his eyes. "I remember. You captured my sister perfectly. Strong, but unassuming. The person who steps up and does what's needed, despite her fear."

"She kept telling me about how Gage had gone in after the crazy former paper owner. She insisted he was the real hero of the town. And of course she pointed out how Deke, Wes, Aaron and all the town people helped to rescue him, never really thinking taking that oxygen tank down to him was the reason he actually survived the whole ordeal."

"No, to her, she was just doing what she could for the man she loved. Just like when she quit college to come home and raise Chloe and I after our parents died." She lifted the corners of her lips in a loving smile. "That's my big sister. She cares about people and does anything to protect the ones she loves."

"Probably why the whole town loves her," he said as the waitress returned with their meal.

The tempting aroma of the food tickled the back of Dylan's throat and triggered her stomach to growl in happy anticipation. "This smells amazing."

"Wait until you taste it," he said with a grin.

Dylan scooped up a spoonful of the thick gravy and took a taste. Closing her eyes, she let out a little moan.

The look of pure ecstasy on her face hit Sean smack dab in the middle of his chest and quickly went southward. A little on the shy side, Dylan had always been a sensual person to him. She loved good food, great music, dancing, laughter. She used all her senses to connect with the world around her. It wasn't a surprise to him that she'd become a doctor and a surgeon.

"OMG. You weren't kidding."

He chuckled as she dug into her meal, once more moaning as she ate a big thick dumpling. "I did a long interview with Mrs. Lehman, the main chef about her food and particularly how she made this dish. All the recipes have been handed down for centuries, mother to daughter. I got this chicken and dumpling recipe, and she did tell me the chicken is slow roasted on a spit in the smoker outside. She says they use nearly fifty chickens every week the dish is so popular."

"You know she probably left out one ingredient."

He paused with his spoon halfway to his mouth. "Why do you say that?"

"Because of Lucy Cabrini's Nona," she said and continued with her meal.

"Who is Lucy Cabrinis Nona?"

Dylan laughed. "Lucy Cabrini. Her grandmother, or as she calls her, Nona."

"Who is Lucy Cabrini? And what does her grandmother have to do with Mrs. Lehman's chicken and dumpling recipe?"

"Lucy was one of my only friends growing up. Her family lived in the same apartment building we did. When Chloe had to stay after school or work at the grocery store down the block and Bobby was at college on a night class, I would go over to Lucy's house for the evening. Her Nona lived with them, and she made the best Eggplant Parmesan. I mean you didn't even think you were eating a vegetable. It tasted like some sort of meat. Anyways, one day she told us she had to give the recipe to her oldest friend, who kept bugging her for it." Dylan stopped and grinned at the memory. "Then she told us it would never taste as good as hers. And when I asked why." She leaned in real close with a twinkle in her eye. "Nona said, I left out an ingredient, so mine is always the best."

With a giggle she sat back, took another bite of her food, and wiggled her eyebrows at the secret she'd just shared. Her sense of humor was one of the things he liked best about her. It was at times wicked, sometimes irreverent, but always heart-felt. Despite all the tragedy and obstacles she'd had to overcome in her life, she saw the absurdities and comedy in the world.

~

"So, did you get some good PR photos of the Red Hawks today?" Dylan asked after they'd finished their food and ordered dessert. She'd been pretty full from the meal, but when Sean insisted she shouldn't pass up the late summer peach cobbler, she'd given in. Growing up, Chloe had existed on junk food and coffee. Sweets, on the other hand, had always been Dylan's go-to comfort food. Thank goodness at nearly six-feet tall she had the metabolism to handle the extra calories.

"Let's take a look." Sean pulled out his digital camera and scooted into the seat catty-corner from her so they could look at the screen together. He pushed a few buttons and up popped a crowd scene of the stands behind their team. "I started out with just some background shots. You never know what fun pictures you'll get of the crowd."

"I know. I've seen some of your online articles about Westen."

"You have?"

His surprise that she'd noticed his work made her like him more. In her work as a doctor, she'd been exposed to more than her fair share of arrogance from colleagues—both male and female. It was refreshing to hang out with someone who didn't recognize their own talent.

"Well, I do have to keep up with what's happening in the town my entire family lives in," she teased him, then continued. "But I've noticed that not only do you write factual stories about what's going on in town, but the human side of the story too, both happy or sad. You also have the eye of a photographer, Mr. Newsman."

A little blush filled his cheeks and he stared into her eyes a moment longer than usual before he focused on the camera screen again, breaking the odd connection of the moment.

"Here's a fun one," he said after a few pictures rolled by.

It was an image of the sheriff looking highly disgruntled as he tried to clean dried blue sugar from his son's face.

Dylan laughed. "You publish that, and you may find yourself with a mountain of traffic tickets all of a sudden."

Sean shook his head with a grin. "No. Your brother-in-law is too much a by-the-book lawman to ever take revenge out on me that way."

"You're probably right. He'd find some other way. Maybe take you out hunting or camping and leave you lost for a week."

He leaned back and raised one brow her direction. "Oh, you don't think I could survive a week in the woods around here on my own?"

"You are from the big city. I mean how often did you go camping in Central Park?" she teased again.

"I came to Westen from New York City, that's true, but I didn't grow up there."

Surprised, she blinked. "You didn't? I never knew that. Where did young Callahan spend his youth?"

"Born and raised near Utica, in upper New York state, not too far from the Adirondack Mountains. Spent lots of summers and fall weekends hiking and camping with my dad and brothers up there."

"That's right, you have three younger brothers. You guys must've driven your mother crazy."

He grinned. "Yes. She insisted on every dog we had over the years being a female because she couldn't take anymore testosterone in the house."

"How's she doing since your dad died?"

"It's been nearly three years now and I think she's starting to come out of her funk. She was just so angry at him for dying. Said they'd had too much still to do, and he wasn't supposed to go yet." He shook his head. "We were all worried she was going to be stuck in that stage of grief forever."

"Grief is such a personal thing. There's no real right or wrong path for people to follow. I remember Bobby trying to explain it to me when I was a kid. Chloe stayed in anger more than we did." Sadness swept over her once more as her own grief reared its ugly head. The pain of losing Bulldog seemed to reach out at the oddest times and slap her. She blinked hard, willing the unshed tears to reabsorb before Callahan could notice, then pointed to the camera. "What else you got in there from today?"

Without commenting at the abrupt change of topic, he scrolled through more pictures. One of Nora's son sliding into home for a scoring run. Another of an outfielder catching a fly ball as he fell on his butt. They both laughed at the memory of that play. Then there was the new mayor's daughter, Sadie Landon, throwing the ball from her position as shortstop to the first baseman for an out. Several shots of the team members at the plate batting and finally one of Lexi pitching.

"Those are all great and tell the story of how the team worked together to win the championship."

"I'll try to use as many as I can on the website. For the physical paper I can probably fit in two plus the team picture." He pushed the button and up came the group photos Nora had choreographed. She tried to get Maggie Landon to be in the pictures, but the mayor had declined saying it was all about the kids, not a political op for her. Dylan like her more and more.

"That's a good one," she said, stopping him from going on to another.

"Yeah, but if I use it, I'll have to do some editing on it."

"Why? All the kids and coaches look great in it. No rabbit ears and no crossed eyes."

"True, but there's this." He enlarged the picture and scrolled to show the left-hand side where Twylla could be seen talking to Lorna in the background. "I'll have to edit Twylla out of the picture."

"Why? She's hardly noticeable in the larger picture."

He shrugged. "I promised her not to put any pictures of her in the paper or on the internet ever."

"Did she say why?"

"Nope. It was when I first took over the paper and wanted to do a feature on her place. I mean, who wouldn't want to find out about the town's beauty shop, especially one named The Dye Right?" He turned off the camera as the waitress brought their desserts. "Anyways, she seemed so serious and adamant about no pictures..." He paused, his brows furrowed. "Not just serious, but afraid, that I promised her and have always edited her out of them."

As they ate their cobblers and then all the long drive home, Dylan pondered the mysteries of Twylla's past.

CHAPTER 4

The image flashed on the screen so fast he almost missed it.

He paused the computer and slowly scrolled backwards, one image at a time until it reappeared. There in the background. She held her right arm across the front of her chest to rest over her heart. Whenever she'd done that, he'd told her she was pledging allegiance.

Instead of accepting his criticism positively and trying to improve herself to his standards, she'd cried. She always cried. Even though she knew it angered him and he had to teach her the lesson over and over, she still reacted like a child that needed disciplining.

He slammed his fist on top of his desk.

For years after her disappearance, he'd searched all of New York to find the bitch. Even hired a few private investigators to find her trail. They all came up with nothing. No report of her in any hospital in the New England area. No unclaimed body in the morgues of any major cities matched her description. It was as if she'd been snatched off the earth by aliens. Worse, there was no trail on where she'd hidden what she'd stolen from him.

That betrayal was why he'd never quit looking for her. Why, now with the internet, he spent every morning searching for images of her. Why when he found her, he'd get the information he needed, before he killed her.

Picking up his cell phone, he selected the first number in his list. "Ricky, I want you in my office, now."

Then he hit the off button.

It had been nearly twenty years, but now he'd get his justice.

~

The phone went dead.

Rick Saunderson stared at it a moment.

What the hell had put a burr up Myles' ass now?

Just getting home from the Long Island estate and the negotiations with their biggest rival, he slumped into his chair. Rubbing the spot between his eyebrows, he reached for the bottle of Scotch he kept in the bottom drawer of his desk along with the headache medicine he seemed to need on a regular basis lately. He should've left when he'd had the chance.

Had he ever really had a choice to leave though?

He swallowed two tablets from the medication bottle and downed them with a healthy swig of the alcohol, then leaned back in the chair and closed his eyes, thinking about that night all those years ago.

"Please come with me," Meredith begged.

"We talked about this Meri. You'll only be safe if I keep him following false trails." He stared down into her deep blue eyes, her hands trembling in his as they stood at the bus terminal exit door.

They'd left an airline ticket receipt for California in the bottom of the waste basket in the room Myles Compton had provided for her in his compound as a false lead. Myles' search out west kept him off her trail long enough for her to make it north by bus into the New York countryside and hide until the bastard's temper and need to strike out at her had cooled. They'd thought it would only be a few weeks or months at the most then Rick would be able to join her. Who knew Myles anger would not only take a long time to cool but would coalesce into ice cold vengeance?

Eighteen years.

"I can't do this without you."

He cupped her face with both his hands when she started shaking it no. "Yes, you can. You're strong. Remember the night you walked out onto that stage to fill in for the star of the play and belted those songs so perfectly that you got the role permanently?"

She nodded. "That was the night you and Myles were in the audience. The night my life changed."

"You were strong then."

"But then I let him hit me. I let him berate me and convince me I couldn't be a Broadway Star."

"But now you're here. You're leaving him. That takes courage and you can do this. With or without me."

"I have to tell you something. Meredith isn't my real name. It's—"

With a finger to her lips, he stopped her from saying more. "Don't tell me. If I don't know it, he can't get it out of me."

"Albany!" the bus driver called. "Last call for Albany!"

Rick pulled her into his arms and held her, careful not to squeeze her frail bruised body too tightly. "Get on the bus Meredith. Stay safe, remember, no credit cards. Only cash."

He watched her climb on board and take a window seat, his eyes never leaving hers until the bus pulled out.

That was the last time he'd seen her beautiful face. It had taken all his efforts not to go back and kill Myles. He'd wanted to, but the man was connected to too many gangs—supplying drugs, weapons, prostitutes, whatever was needed and hard to get—that he was nearly untouchable. Better to stay alive and keep him off Meri's trail. He couldn't protect her while she was with the bastard, but he could keep her hidden.

He took another swallow of the Scotch, then shoved himself out of his office chair. No use wishing for things to be different. Wherever Meri had landed, she was safe. Myles had no clue because *he'd* had no clue. And that made putting up with the life of crime and suffering Myles Compton spewed onto the world worth it.

But if he didn't get back to the estate ASAP for whatever new crisis his boss had, there'd be hell to pay.

Snatching up his phone and his keys, he headed back to his car.

CHAPTER 5

"Thanks for meeting me here, Dylan." Maggie Landon reached out to shake hands as she approached the bench in front of the new Westen Mercy Hospital a week and a half after the softball game. "Let's have a seat and chat a bit. It's too nice a day to spend inside."

The early September sun shone down on her face as she sat next to the town's mayor. "By the way I never got a chance to congratulate you on your re-election win last fall."

"Thank you. I never thought I'd run for public office, but when Tobias Rawlins talked with me about his plans to run for Congress and asked if I'd consider running for mayor so he wouldn't worry about leaving the town in someone else's hands, I thought to myself, well, why not?"

"Why not," Dylan concurred. "I suspect that's how a lot of people end up doing things they never thought they would. Like my sister Bobby becoming a private investigator and then a deputy sheriff. Sure surprised Chloe and me."

"Your sister shook things up around here. She brought a lot of change with her, that's for sure. We're lucky to have her in our community."

"I'm just glad she found a good man, son and this coming baby to love. She deserves a happy family. Having a job in a town that loves her almost as much as Chloe and I do? That's a bonus."

"Chloe's fitting in nicely, too. How much longer before her baby is due?"

"About three weeks. She's planning to deliver here with the new OB doctor she's been seeing." Dylan paused trying to recall her name. "Paulson, I believe her name is."

"Eileen Paulson. She's been out of her residency at OSU a few years and decided she wanted to extend her practice out here in an area growing with young couples just starting their families."

"Smart move on her part. Especially having a new state-of-the-art hospital like this one," Dylan said, turning to look at the large three-story brick building behind them. She had an idea why Maggie wanted to meet her here, might as well let her get on with her sales-pitch.

"Would you like to take a look inside?"

"I thought it wasn't open until next week?"

There was a big opening day ceremony and town celebration planned for the next weekend.

"It won't be open for patients until after the opening dedication ceremony, but there's a lot going on inside. The units have all been staffed and those nurses, techs and other support personnel are working hard to prepare to hit the ground running from the moment we cut that blue ribbon." Maggie stood and Dylan followed suit.

"I'd love to see the inside."

They entered through the front door and were greeted by a cheery smiling sixtyish receptionist at the large square desk in the center of the lobby. "Hello, Mayor Landon."

"Hi, Catherine, how are things going?" Maggie shook the other woman's hand and smiled.

Catherine literally beamed, whether because she was thrilled to be talking about the progress being made to get the hospital ready for opening day or that the mayor knew her by name. Dylan had to admit, Maggie wasn't just a politician and businesswoman—she ran the guest shop out at the Christmas Tree farm she and her husband owned outside of town that had customers coming all year long—but she also seemed sincerely interested in the other woman's opinion on the state of the hospital's progress.

"We have the computer system up and running. The secretaries and techs from all the departments, as well as the nurses have gone through the training," Catherine said. "It was a bit of a learning curve for someone my age, but with some practice I've gotten the knack of finding patient rooms and locations in the various units or service departments."

"I'm sure you'll be teaching us all," Maggie said with a wink. "When do the doctors take their classes?"

"Well, Doc Clint wanted them to start before everyone else, but Harriett put the kibosh on that idea, real quick." Catherine nodded with a change in her demeanor. "She said the physicians were the last people who needed to know how this place worked." She gave a little giggle. "She said they'd just muck it all up."

Maggie laughed and so did Dylan, who'd learned her first week out of medical school how little she knew about the workings of a hospital and its staff. She also learned not to piss off the night nurses if she ever wanted to get some sleep on call nights.

"Well, if anyone can get Doc Clint to listen to them, it's definitely Harriett," Maggie said.

Catherine nodded. "She did the same thing with his uncle, Doc Ray. I don't think there's a person in this town who would cross that woman." She leaned closer and whispered as if the tenacious nurse might be able to hear her. "They say she used to work for the CIA."

"I heard it was a dark ops unit during the Vietnam War," Dylan said.

Maggie laughed. "Catherine, this is Dr. Dylan Roberts, sister to—"

"Deputy Justice and Mrs. Strong," Catherine said, then her cheeks filled with a light blush. "Oh, I hope you don't think I believe all doctors are underfoot or muck things up, I was just repeating what Harriett...oh dear, now I sound like a gossip."

Dylan smiled and laid her hand on the older woman's. "Oh, don't worry about it. I've been hearing about Harriett ever since Bobby first came to town. And honestly, she's right. Doctors do muck up the working of a hospital. I usually just go where the nurses tell me."

"Speaking of places to go, I'm going to give Dr. Roberts a little tour," Maggie said. "Is there any place we shouldn't be going? Construction or meetings going on?"

Catherine tapped on the computer's keyboard and leaned in close, tracing her finger down the screen. "Other than the kitchen getting their new refrigeration units installed today, the hospital is good for a tour. You're not planning on checking out the kitchen, are you?"

"Except for a sample of the food in the cafeteria later, I think we can avoid the actual food prep area, don't you, Dylan?"

She nodded. "As long as they're not making powdered scrambled eggs, I think we're good."

"Oh, I don't think they use the powdered kind," Catherine hurried to reassure her.

"That's too bad," Dylan said with a wink. "I got addicted to them in college."

"You're kidding me? They served those in the hospital when

I had my kids, and I couldn't stomach them." Maggie gave her a disgusted look.

Dylan laughed. "That's the same look my friend Bulldog gave me whenever we'd have breakfast at the end of a long night shift. He said I wasn't a normal human being. And I don't just get one helping, I get two."

Maggie made a gag look. "He's right. You aren't normal."

All three of them laughed, then she and Maggie thanked Catherine for her help and headed down the hall. Dylan expected to be sad after talking about Bulldog, but for the first time since she learned of his death, the memory of his reaction to her secret addiction to hospital eggs made her smile inside. She guessed the old adage was right, *time heals all wounds*—well, at least it softened them.

Besides trying some very tasty samples in the cafeteria, they visited one of the patient care wings, the surgical admission unit and a quick tour of the operating room. She got to talk with the unit managers and meet some of the staff—which was a mixture of what appeared to be experienced nurses and green, fresh-out-of-school graduates. Everyone seemed excited about the new hospital and the chance to build and organize it to their specifications.

"One of the things the town council wanted to do was make this facility fit the community," Maggie said as they relaxed in the staff lounge in the surgical wing. "Not just the town of Westen, but the medical community, doctors, and nurses. Especially nurses. This is their environment. They know better how things run, what works, what doesn't. Harriett pointed that out at our first planning meeting on which architect to hire."

"That's a smart idea," Dylan said, sipping on the bottled water they'd found in the refrigerator.

"That's why Harriett was on the planning committee, along with Lisa here," Maggie said with a nod to the brunette seated at the table. Lisa Tapp was the Chief Nursing Officer for the entire hospital.

Lisa gave her a thank you nod. "First thing we did was meet with the different architects to determine who would be the best fit for designing not only an aesthetically pleasing facility, but an efficient one for the staff. Harriett and I both believe that nurses bring the functional needs to the design process. That's why the units aren't separated by long hallways."

"I did notice how radiology and the lab are in close proximity to both the emergency and operating rooms, which are both very close together, too," Dylan said.

Lisa nodded. "That's intentional. Those units need results fast and sometimes a patient's condition necessitates we need to move the Radiology equipment to the patient rather than transporting them, so having all the departments close by provides not only timely use but prevents wear and tear on our staff moving them."

"What about the other units, like post-op and regular patient care units?"

"We took into consideration how to increase their productivity, too," the pleasant nurse said, enthusiasm shining in her brown eyes. "We installed a tube system to send blood draws to the lab, small pharmacy stations with pharmacists and trained pharmacy techs on each floor to quickly process and dispense medications. And obstetrics is only one floor up, directly over the OR suites. Again, quick access to the ER, radiology and the lab."

"I noticed you've taken the *bullpen* mode of patient care," Dylan said, slowly rotating the bottle of water. It was very interesting to hear how the hospital was designed and how the staff was involved in the planning of it.

"We took a tour of some newer hospitals and were very impressed with the bullpen design of the nurse's station placed in the center of a unit and all the patient rooms surrounding them," the CNO said. "It keeps the patients at a closer proximity to the nursing staff, and also helps the staff work as a cohesive unit. We interviewed nurses working in that system, and they had positive feedback."

"I'm impressed," Dylan said.

"Impressed enough to consider joining our staff?" Maggie asked.

There it was. The proposition she knew the mayor had intended by dangling this state-of-the-art hospital in front of her. It was tempting. Start her private career in a brand-new hospital, help establish protocols, choose her own surgical staff. Sadness filled her. No matter where she landed, here or a big city practice, her surgical team would always be missing someone. Bulldog.

"I really haven't decided what I'm going to do after Chloe has her baby," she started to say, then Maggie held up her hand.

"Before you turn me down, let's take a walk down to our ER and have a look around. I was saving it for last." She scooted her chair back and shook hands with Lisa. Dylan followed suit and let herself be escorted to Maggie's ace-in-the-hole.

They entered the twelve-bed emergency room lit with both natural light from skylights above and florescent lights in each patient care bay. Like the other nursing units, this one was set up like a wagon wheel—the nurse's station in the center, patients' rooms and adjacent storage closets extending out in a circular fashion—and the staff gathered in the center for a meeting. The speaker, a man dressed in a sports shirt and jeans, probably some sort of tech support, paused at their approach and all heads turned their direction.

Dylan forced a pleasant expression onto her face, something she'd learned to do right after her parents' deaths. She did it at the funeral home after she heard someone say how terrible it was for the three girls to be orphans now. When she walked into middle school and was taller than all the boys. In college when sorority pledge week came and went, and she'd happily not made any of the houses. Medical school when not only did she have to fight the male dominant faculty, but other girls who thought she should've gone into modeling at nearly six-feet tall and blonde, rather than take up a spot another girl might want in med school. Yes, she hated to be the center of attention, that was Chloe's job in the family, and as the possible new surgeon being escorted around the hospital, here she was again sticking out.

Movement across the room caught her attention. Leaning against the doorjamb to one of the patient care bays was Callahan, who grinned at her, one hand loosely holding a professional looking camera. She gave him a little smile then turned her attention back to the others

"Hey, Mayor Landon." A mid-thirtyish looking man stood from the circle of staff dressed in scrubs of various colors. "Is there something I can do for you?"

"Hi, Josh," Maggie said, walking forward to shake his hand. "We didn't mean to interrupt anything, I'm just giving Dr. Roberts a little VIP tour of the facility. Dylan, this is Josh Turnball. He's the nurse manager for the ER."

Dylan shook the man's hand. He had a firm grip. One that said I am confidant and know I'm in charge of my crew, but not overpowering.

"Glad to meet you, Dr. Roberts. We're having a training session for the new IV pumps we'll be instituting in the hospital. Don, here," Josh said, indicating the man dressed in street clothes, "is the rep from Erwin Medical Corp. He's going to give three in-services today so all the staff can get up to snuff on how these work."

Dylan stepped closer to see the pump with several IV lines

attached. "I've seen these in use in the ICUs on some of my post-op trauma patients. I have to tell you I'm always amazed at how much technical and electronic chops nurses have to have in order to use all the equipment you deal with on a daily basis." She smiled at the group. "If I had to know all this, my patients would be waiting a long time to get their meds."

Everyone laughed and the tension in the room dropped by ten degrees.

"We don't want to keep you," Dylan said, taking a step back.

"You won't be," the nurse manager said. "Don can go ahead and finish with this group while I give you a tour. I'll sit in on another one later."

"Then lead the way."

"Mind if I join the tour?" Callahan asked, moving from his spot of observation to join their trio. "I could use the information about this unit for one of my articles about the hospital."

Josh nodded. "Sure. We're proud of this unit and want the community to know how the state funds and their own donations were spent, what we can do, and what care we hope to provide them once we open."

For the next half hour, Josh showed them the unit from one spot to another, especially referencing how they'd set it up to eventually be a level two trauma unit.

"Why not try for a level one trauma unit?" Maggie asked.

"A level one unit provides programs for teaching and research," Dylan said. "Usually, it's a hospital associated with a medical school program. Interns and residents train in trauma care. They also do research to enhance trauma units to function better and some in ways to improve patient outcomes from trauma care. Some have fellowship programs for intense training in trauma surgery and post-op care."

"Like the one you took in Columbus this past year?" Sean asked.

"Yes." She wasn't surprised he remembered she'd done the fellowship. Moving to the state capital to do the fellowship meant she was less than an hour away and spent most free weekends visiting her sisters there or here in Westen. "I figure in this field the more training, experience and knowledge you have the better the possible outcome is for the patient."

"So the educational aspect of trauma is the only thing keeping our hospital from being a level one unit?" Maggie asked.

Josh nodded. "And I don't see us opening a medical school anytime soon in Westen, do you?"

Maggie laughed. "All the state funding went to expanding the K through twelve school system and improving the existing facilities. No higher education in the plans."

"I noticed the helipad on the south side of the hospital," Callahan said, taking notes on his tablet as they talked.

"We built it there for easy access, yet out of the way of normal traffic by the public." Josh walked them over to the exit door of the unit, opening it so they could step outside and see the covered walkway connecting the hospital to the helipad. "For now, we'll use it to transport stabilized patients to hospitals in Columbus, but we're hoping as we grow and become designated to care for more critical patients, we'll be the hospital smaller, more rural facilities choose to transport their trauma patients to."

"So, you're thinking not just for community care now, but for the future of Westen," Sean said, taking notes on his phone.

"We have to," Maggie answered. "In the past six years this town and the whole area has doubled in size, both structurally and census-wise. With the new micro-chip production company, the natural gas mining industry growing in our area, and other manufacturing we hope to coax our way, we'll continue to see growth for at least the next decade."

Sean grinned at her. "Starting to sound like a politician, Mayor."

She gave him a pointed-look. "This is my home. I'm raising my family here. My business is here. My friends are here. Promoting Westen isn't politics for me, Mr. Callahan."

He held his hands up palms out, phone clutched in the left, in surrender. "Just joking, Maggie. I know everything you do for Westen is because you love this place and the people in it."

"Good. Just make sure you say that in the paper," she said with a wink, then she glanced at the clock on the wall. "Now, I have to get to the office to meet with the planning commissioners. Thank you for the tour, Josh." She shook his hand. As he returned to his nursing staff, she turned her attention to Dylan. "Before I go, I figure you know why I wanted to meet you here today."

"You want me to stay and start my surgical practice in Westen."

"We really could use someone with your skills. You'd be working in a state-of-the-art facility with a well-trained staff."

"My sisters and Doc Clint have already pointed this out to me." Dylan gave a hesitant shake of her head. "I'm just not sure what I plan to do."

Maggie laid her hand on her arm and squeezed gently. "You take your time. If you decide to stay that would be fantastic for everyone, but you have to go where your heart leads you, otherwise you won't ever be happy." Her phone rang, and she retrieved it with a wink and wave at Dylan and Callahan as she turned on her heel and strode for the front of the hospital. "Yes, Leslie, I'm on my way. Should be there in ten minutes or so."

"How does it feel to be the number one recruit?" Sean asked.

"Shut up, Callahan," she said and started for the visitor entrance of the ER. Of course, he fell in step with her. "Is it too early for a drink in this town?"

"It's after noon, I bet we can get something over at the Wagon Wheel."

"Good. I need one. Meet me there?" She paused at the door and looked at him.

He grinned. "Never let a friend drink alone. Besides, I haven't had lunch yet."

"As I recall, they have good burgers there, don't they?" she asked, her stomach suddenly reminding her she hadn't had more than granola and yogurt for breakfast.

"Second best in town." They walked out into the late summer heat.

She pulled her sunglasses off her head where they'd been holding her hair back and slipped them onto her face. "Let me guess, the best burger would be at the Peaches 'N Cream?"

"Yeah, but the hardest drink you're going to get there is coffee or extra sweet tea."

She stopped at her car. "Wagon Wheel it is. Still out by the county line road, right?"

"Yep. Meet you there," he said and jogged off to find his car.

Dylan climbed in, turned on the engine and hit the air condition button, staring out at the park just to the side of the hospital. A calm place for staff to take a break, and for visitors and patients to get out of the medical facility on a nice day. She had to admit the town council and hospital planning committee certainly invested the funds to produce not only a modern medical facility with plans to carry it into the future of health care, they thought of the aesthetics—inside and out—for the patients, staff and public.

The question was, what did she want? Did she move to Westen to be close to her family? Would there be enough work for her to keep her trauma skills sharp? Or did she join one of the many inner-city practices courting her in the three major cities in Ohio—Cleveland, Cincinnati and Columbus—where there would always be trauma cases for her to work on, but keep her from spending time with her sisters and their growing families?

Her head began to throb.

She leaned back and slowly rubbed her temples. For most of the past year she'd been on automatic. Work, sleep, work. Numb since the day her brother-in-law Wes came to her apartment to break the news about Bulldog's death. His mission had been classified and no formal acknowledgement of the loss of his or any of his team's lives would be made public. So Wes, who'd been the one to put Steve Janowski, aka Bulldog, in her life to act as her silent bodyguard years before, realizing he'd become her best friend, took the time and risk to inform her.

With Bulldog gone and since finishing her trauma surgery fellowship, she'd felt...adrift.

Sitting up, she buckled herself in and put the car in gear. What she really needed was protein, alcohol and some good company in that order.

~

Sean leaned against the hood of his SUV in the Wagon Wheel's parking lot and waited for Dylan to pull in beside him. When she climbed out of her silver BMW, the wind whipping her honey-gold hair around her face and shoulders, as he had the day he met her, he once again marveled at how stunningly beautiful she was. The woman could've strutted down the runway of any fashion show in New York or Paris with her long, graceful body. As their friendship grew over the years, so much more than her looks held him enthralled.

Dylan was smart. Not just book smart, she had a good amount of common sense. But the thing he loved the most about her was her sense of humor and her laugh. God, that laugh. It wasn't a tee-hee kind of laugh of a little girl or the polite soft chuckle of someone who doesn't get the joke. Nope. She had a from-the-gut, spontaneous laugh. Along with it she had an ornery wit at not only a good joke, but the absurdity of life and how ridiculous people could be.

"Did you think I'd get lost?" she asked, walking right past him.

He straightened, thrusting his hands into his jeans pockets and matched her stride for stride to the tavern's front entrance. "Nope. Figured we'd been here enough you could maneuver through the newer subdivisions to find the old county road here."

"Good thing I knew where it was. My GPS didn't have some of these newer roads on it yet," she said, pulling off her sunglasses as he opened the door and held it for her.

The fresh scent of lemon wafted over him as she passed by. He swallowed hard. Every time they were together, he had to remind himself they were just friends. She'd been in town two weeks. By now he should've had more control over his desire for her.

"How many?" asked the college-age young woman standing at the newly added hostess station.

"Two," Sean said.

She smiled at them, picking up two laminated menus. "Booth or table?"

Sean looked to Dylan, already knowing her answer.

"Booth, please," she said, and they followed the younger woman through the tavern.

At their table, Dylan slipped into one side and immediately slouched back against the wooden seat. He'd asked her a few years back why she always wanted to sit in a booth. Her answer had been, *people didn't stare at you when you were in a booth*. At the time he had no reply and the subject changed. Afterward, he realized it showed another side of Dylan, the vulnerable, shy side she worked very hard to hide from the world.

Dylan picked up the menu, then paused to look around the inside of the tavern. "Is it my imagination or has this place grown?"

"Just like most of Westen. Hank had to grow to accommodate all the new citizens flooding the area. He added more seating up front," he said, perusing the menu like he planned to eat something other than his usual.

"Did he get rid of the pool tables then?" she said with a disappointed pout in her voice. "I loved playing pool in here."

Sean laughed. "Don't worry. He added on to the back and moved the pool room there."

"Oh good." She grinned at him, and the room seemed to take on more sunlight.

After the waitress took their orders, burgers and fries for both of them with IPA beers, he leaned back and studied her. "So, what did you think of the new hospital?"

"Off the record?"

"I left my reporter hat in the car. You're an expert on hospitals, do we have a good one?"

The waitress returned with their beers.

Dylan took a long drink of hers. "Damn that's good."

"Hank also increased the variety of beers he offers now. And you're avoiding my question."

She stared over his shoulder long enough to make him think she wouldn't answer, but he'd been a reporter a long time and waited for her to continue. "It's a beautiful, state-of-the-art hospital. The town should be thrilled and proud of what they've built."

"But...?" he prompted.

"A good hospital isn't just all the newest gadgets, bells, and whistles. The best ones are full of the best people. The staff—

doctors, nurses, techs, everyone down to the cooks and housekeepers—both older experienced personnel and fresh out-of-school full-of-enthusiasm people, that's what the heart of a good hospital staff consists of. Some work better than others."

"How?" he asked as the waitress returned and set their food in front of them. He thanked her with a smile.

"Take the OR for example," she said, squeezing ketchup over her fries before biting into one, the look of pure joy filling her face. "Man, I love double fried fries."

Grinning at her, he took a bite of his burger. Another thing he loved about her was her ability to enjoy a good meal, be it a fancy steak or a plate of fries.

They ate for a few moments, then she took a drink and stared at him. "Like I was saying. Take the operating room. When you have the A team working, it's like an intricate ballet full of prima ballerinas. Each member of the team knows their function, knows what needs to be done and often they function with limited verbal communication. They've worked together so long they never miss a step, even if a problem arises. Even if a scared new surgeon steps into the mix."

He swallowed and wiped his mouth. "What if it isn't the A team? Is there a B team?"

"No." She laughed then finished off her food and sat back. "Often there are combinations of the staff, with majority knowing what they're doing or work together enough to function well, and maybe there is a new graduate or hire mixed in. Things work okay, it's just not perfection." She leaned in, propping one elbow on the table and her chin in her hand, and let out a big sigh. "Unfortunately, sometimes communication lapses can place the patient in jeopardy."

"How do you prevent that from happening?"

"I'm not in nursing or hospital administration, but I suspect it takes lots of training. It's one of the reasons I went through the trauma surgery fellowship this past year. I figure the more practice I have under my belt, the more diverse cases I see, the quicker I can make decisions when something odd happens in a case."

"Does that happen often? Oddities?"

She shrugged. "The human body is a quirky thing without the stress of trauma. Put it through a car crash, a shooting or stabbing? Anything can happen. In a car crash, you can have a head injury, broken legs or hips or arms, internal injuries—or all of them at once. In a shooting, not only do you have an entry wound, possibly an exit wound, but the bullets can bounce around inside and nick any number of organs and blood vessels. Stabbings are always interesting."

"Interesting?"

"There have been times when a patient presents to the ER, alert, articulate, vital signs stable. The only way you would know there was something going on is a kitchen knife is buried hilt-deep in their chest."

"You're kidding me?"

She shook her head. "The reason they were so steady is the blood vessels that have possibly been severed by the initial thrust of the blade into the chest have tamponade."

"Tamponade? As in cardiac tamponade?"

Her eyes brightened that he'd actually heard the term before. "That's one kind. Tamponade means to compress by pressure to stop the blood flow through a vessel. In this case the body itself presses against the blade of the knife and seals off the cut vessels."

"That's why in Western movies they'd tell people not to pull out the arrow?" he asked.

She chuckled. "I don't know about that, Hollywood has their way of telling things that aren't always true, but if people historically realized leaving the arrow in place would prevent them from bleeding out, then yes, that would be a tamponade. The reason we leave them in place nowadays is to keep the patient stable until we can sono the area around the blade and determine how to approach the removal surgically with the best possible outcome."

"How do you do that?" he asked, unable to hide the awe in his voice.

"Remove the knives? Surgically," she said with a *duh* look.

He laughed. "I figured that smartass. I mean how do you talk so matter-of-factly about what amounts to life-and-death situations?"

She shrugged. "I have to. Especially when I'm in the moment. What Bulldog called the zone."

"The zone?"

"It's that period of time when every move is critical. You don't have time to let your emotions take over. You have to observe the situation, gather as many facts as possible as quickly as possible, plan a course of action and move forward. Sometimes it's minutes, sometimes only seconds. You compartmentalize the emotions and focus."

"So, do you ever give into the emotions?"

She nodded. "Everyone has to. It's the adrenaline release. Everyone handles it differently. Some break down in tears almost right outside the OR doors unless they have some task to focus on. I've seen them hug and tell dark-humor jokes."

"Dark-humor?"

A little lift to the corners of her lips. "The kind that have to do with blood and body parts. It's a medical thing. Only people who deal in the life-and-death arena really appreciate the joke and can laugh at them. It helps to break the tension, release the adrenaline. To decompress."

"And how do you decompress?" he asked, praying it didn't sound like a sexual innuendo.

"For a time, I would focus on getting post-op orders written, then escape into the OR's doctors' lounge. I'd go into one of the bathroom stalls and have a long private cry, especially if the patient didn't make it through the surgery." She paused to stare out the window into the early evening light. "It was the best place for privacy for a young surgeon. Tears scared the male surgeons away and the females didn't want to get involved in my meltdown. Then one day I was in there after a particularly bad case, indulging myself, when suddenly someone was banging on the stall door."

"Who was it?"

"That's what I asked," she said with a little lift of the corners of her lips. "It was the new surgical tech that had assisted me in the case, Steven Janowski. I found out later he was a member of Wes' dark ops team and went by the codename of Bulldog."

"The guy who was with you when your sister had a stalker?" He'd heard the tale from Wes and Chloe.

Dylan nodded. "Bulldog earned that name. He kept knocking one of those big fists of his on the stall door until I opened it and asked him what he thought he was doing."

"What did he say?"

"Nothing, he just held up a bottle of beer and said he needed someone to help him get pissed and since I was off duty, I just got volunteered."

Sean chuckled. "That's a new way to hit on a woman for a date."

"He wasn't asking for a date. He really did want to get drunk. Besides, I already knew he was gay."

"Bulldog was gay?" Sean was stunned by the revelation. Not so much that a gay man could have a rather hardnosed nickname, but that his good friends Wes and Gage had known this and not filled him in. They'd left him thinking that Dylan was heartbroken over the loss of a lover, not just a good friend.

Dylan nodded, finishing off her beer and signaling the waitress for another. "He was also the best surgical tech I ever worked with, a great friend who could discuss fashion and listened to my heartache over cases I couldn't save. He also taught me self-defense moves and how to fire and maintain my Glock. I miss him every day."

CHAPTER 6

"Why did you have to make your hair appointment so freaking early in the day?" Dylan asked Chloe the next morning as they drove into the heart of Westen and pulled up out front of the Dye Right salon. She'd ended up playing pool and drinking beer with Callahan until he'd followed her back to her sister's house in the middle of the night to be sure she'd gotten home safe. "I'm supposed to be on vacation, sleeping in, not getting up at the butt-crack of dawn."

"How did you ever get through med school, let alone your residency with your hatred of early mornings?"

"It helps if mornings come right after an all-nighter of studying or working. Sane people do not get up while it's still dark outside," Dylan replied, exiting the car and waiting for her sister.

Chloe wiggled her way out from behind the steering wheel, then stood, straightening and slightly arching her back, the way Dylan had seen many pregnant women do over her years in medicine. Intellectually she understood all the changes that happened with the female body during pregnancy, but seeing her beloved sister suffer through them made her ache to find some way to ease her discomforts.

"Is there a massage studio in Westen?" she asked as she held the door open to the salon.

"Oh, I wish there was," the pixie hair stylist Sylvie said from the reservation desk just inside the door. "I would've been there weekly while I was pregnant with Sunshine. Poor Cleetus hated hearing me moan so much he went online to learn how to do massages at home."

Chloe stopped dead in her tracks to stare at her friend, and Dylan grasped onto her shoulders to keep from plowing into her.

"Cleetus gave you massages?"

Uh-oh, her sister's tone made it clear that her brother-in-law Wes was failing the supportive spouse role in the massage arena.

"Lord, yes," Sylvie said, pushing buttons on the computer in front of her. "That man has those big old hands for a purpose. The spots he could find on my back were heavenly. But what was better was the foot massages. Made me moan like I'd had an orgasm. Now that I know he has that talent, I ask him for one every night after work."

Thank goodness all the noise in the salon from the women chatting and hairdryers blowing prevented everyone from hearing that comment. Everyone in town knew that tiny Sylvie had her giant of a husband wrapped around her finger. The man would find a way to bring her the moon and the stars if she asked, so of course he learned to massage her aches and pains.

"I think someone is going to have to go on the internet tonight to learn about prenatal massages or he's sleeping on the couch for the next few weeks," Chloe said, looking over her shoulder with a sparkle in her eye.

Dylan shook her head. Cleetus wasn't the only one who would jump through hoops for his wife. Both her brothers-in-law felt the same way. Wes would not only be searching for instructional videos on back massages, but which oils and creams were safe to use in pregnancies.

It was rather refreshing to know there were men in the world who not only protected their wives but cherished them, too. In her line of work, she'd run across all kinds of men—some who wore chauvinism like it was a trophy, some who treated their wives and families like punching bags, some who openly ignored their loved ones. Then she thought about the women in those relationships, some were willing to be doormats, others whined and complained to get attention, and some couples were the reverse of misogynistic with the woman brow-beating the man into submission until he exploded in dangerous anger which resulted in someone needing her services to save one or both of their lives.

"Sylvie raved so much about her massages," Twylla said, stepping up to the reservation desk, "I'm considering adding a licensed pedicurist who can also do foot massages."

"Is that why you're expanding again?" Chloe asked.

Twylla peered over the upper rim of her glasses at the sisters. "And what makes you think I'm expanding the Dye Right?"

Chloe didn't blink under the question, something Dylan always admired in her older sister. "Twylla, you know as well as I do, that your salon is second only to the Peaches 'N Cream for good gossip. That the news impacts this bastion of small-town harmony, well, wasn't hard to hear the whispers."

Twylla closed her eyes a moment, shaking her head, then grinned. "You can't fart in this town without everyone getting wind of it."

Dylan choked on her laughter at the salon owner's pun.

"Let's get you two started before someone confides in you what size bra I ordered last week." Twylla winked at them and motioned for Sylvie to take them back into the business part of the salon. When she'd expanded two years earlier, Twylla had decided to not only add more styling chairs and shampoo sinks, but set the front up like a comfortable lounge, still in pinks, white and black. They had an espresso machine, as well as a refrigerator with bottled water for guests.

"I'm going to be your stylist today, Doctor." Sylvie giggled, then paused at a shampoo chair in the rear of the salon, while Chloe went to the spot right beside her and slowly lowered into the seat.

Dylan settled into her chair. "Sylvie, it's just Dylan."

"I was just practicing," the little pixie of a woman said as she turned on the water, letting it run over her hands to test the temperature. "We just had a seminar on how to act in the workplace. We want to make our clients feel comfortable, but still have a professional persona."

"Memorized it, did you?" Dylan said with a chuckle. The last sentence out of Sylvie's mouth sounded just like a webinar pitch, not the usual southern charm she'd brought with her from her home in Appalachia. "And I like the water hot," she said, leaning back in the chair to rest her head in the wash sink. She nearly moaned at the feel of the hot water and Sylvie's strong hands working over her scalp.

"Well, since Miz Twylla paid for us to attend the workshop, I figure I'd best try to use some of the training. Of course, no matter how professional we sound or act, the ladies in here love to gossip. It's like mother's milk to some of them. And it's not just the regulars who've lived in town for decades. How do you think everyone knows Miz Twylla's thinking of expanding the shop?"

"Sylvie!" Darcy whispered beside her as she washed Chloe's hair.

"Well, it wasn't us, it was that real estate lady, Nora." Sylvie lathered on some gardenia scented shampoo and worked it into

Dylan's hair. "She couldn't keep a secret if her life depended on it."

"You just don't like her because she flirts with Cleetus," Darcy whispered, helping Chloe sit up.

Sylvie finished with Dylan. "Well, she does flirt with him and every other man she comes into contact with. Well, except for Deputy Strong. I don't think he gives her the time of day."

Chloe laughed. "No. My husband is impervious to flirts of any kind."

"I bet that changes if you have a little girl," Sylvie said as they all walked to the front chairs for the rest of their styling. "Sunshine has Cleetus wrapped around her fingers and she's just two months old."

"Do you still not know what you're having?" Darcy asked as she began combing and clipping Chloe's signature short shag cut.

"Yes. Wes and I wanted to be surprised. When our OB asked us if we wanted to know during the sonogram, we said we wanted to know that everything was okay with our baby, but not to tell us the sex. She said we were a rarity these days."

"Y'all have better self-control than Cleetus and me..."

And now the conversation drifted off into the world of pregnancies and babies. As much as she loved her sisters and their families, this wasn't a topic she had any experience in other than in a clinical fashion. So, she happily relaxed with her eyes closed, letting all the feminine chatter turn into background noise as Sylvie toweled out and combed her wet hair.

"How much do you want me to cut off?" Sylvie asked, holding out one section of her hair.

Dylan opened her eyes and studied it. "Just an inch. I like to keep it long enough to wear in a ponytail at work. It's easier to get into the scrub hats that way."

"Oh, I would think short hair like mine or your sister's would work better for that," Sylvie said peeking over her shoulder, her red hair looking like little spikes of fire.

"Not for me. Sometimes, I'm in surgery for hours and I sweat under the hot lights and all the extra sterile clothes I have to wear over my scrubs. So, short hair would just end up plastered to my face. Medium length hair also ends up sticking to my face or my neck. Below the shoulder length that I can pull up into ponytails is my answer."

"Well, now that makes a lot of sense. I never would've thought of that for a surgeon. I'll have to mention it to some of my nurse clients if you don't mind?"

"Feel free to share."

"Good. I've had several new ladies come in who are going to be working at the new hospital when it opens."

Dylan waited patiently for Sylvie to ask the question about her future plans with the hospital and was surprised when instead she started singing along to the instrumental version of George Gershwin's *Summertime* playing over the salon's sound system. Thankful that Sylvie might listen to gossip but wouldn't put her nose into someone else's business unless asked, she exhaled and closed her eyes again.

Listening to Sylvie sing and having her hair done like this reminded Dylan of when she was a little girl, and her mother did her hair. Fresh from a bath and in her pajamas ready for bed, she'd sit on the floor in front of Mama, who'd slowly work the comb through her hair after rubbing it real hard with a thick towel. Then Mama would part her hair down the middle, slowly plaiting each side from her temple to the ends of her hair. Usually about half-way through the first braid, she'd doze off, her head bobbing as her mother hummed to some church hymn.

The blow dryer started, and Sylvie began working her hair with it and a large round brush.

Mama loved singing in the choir and often sang hymns at home while cooking, cleaning, or doing her daughter's hair. Bobby had been old enough to do her hair for as long as Dylan could remember. Chloe hated having long hair, insisting hers be cut short even back in elementary school. So, Dylan had been the beneficiary of their mother's efforts. Dylan would sleep in those wet braids, which stayed in place all the next day and night. The second day, Mama undid the braids, and her hair was a huge wavy mass. Daddy called it her lion's mane.

"What do you think?" Sylvie asked, pulling Dylan out of her memories.

She blinked back the tears pooling in her eyes.

"You okay?" Chloe said beside her, concern lacing her voice.

Dylan nodded, pulling on those tactics she'd learned the day of her parents' funeral to put her emotions in a lock box and present the world with a smile and positive attitude. "Still getting over my late night and too much beer."

Refusing to let Chloe cross-examine her, she focused on the mirror and saw the subtle volume Sylvie's efforts had given her hair. Reaching to the ends of the front strands on both sides, she nodded at the acceptable length. "It looks great, Sylvie. Thanks."

She managed to keep her sister's inquisition at bay until they were outside the salon. Chloe stopped to arch her back once more, her hands in the small of her back. The mid-morning sun shining through the leaves of the old oaks that lined the sidewalk in almost perfectly uniform distances warmed their faces. "So, what had you near tears in there?"

Dammit. Her sister knew her too well and she was also a very good lawyer. When she saw a string of truth, she'd pull it like a French bulldog with a ball of yarn until she got to the center. Years ago, she learned to pick her battles with Chloe.

"Nothing to worry about." Dylan slipped her sunglasses in

place. "Just memories of when I was little and Mama would do my hair."

"I remember that. You'd fall asleep while she braided it and Dad would have to carry you up to bed. I was a little jealous."

Dylan turned to stare at her older sister. "You were jealous? You hated long hair."

"I was jealous of the attention you were getting. But I hated hair on my neck more. I'm not sure why remembering something you enjoyed made you tear up like that."

"Possibly because unlike you and Bobby, I have fewer clear memories of Mom and Dad since I was only six when they died. You had two more years with them, and Bobby had a whole decade longer than either of us."

"You're right. I get all teary every time I think of Dad teaching me to box. Who knew it would come in handy when I had to punch Cindy Seacort's nose for picking on you back in elementary school?" Chloe turned to stroll up the street. "Let's go for a walk. I'm feeling a little restless."

They wandered up to the corner and turned onto Main Street. Dylan chuckled.

"What?" Chloe asked as they passed the bank.

"Westen is so much the quintessential small town, they actually named the main street of the town, Main Street."

"The town has existed since before the time of the Underground Railroad, so what did you expect them to name the street? Sunset Strip?" Chloe laughed, but Dylan heard the little bit of defensiveness she had for her new hometown. "Not only small towns have a Main Street. Big towns do, too. Cincinnati has one."

"True. Columbus does, too. But they aren't the main throughfares as this one is. And I'm not being judgmental. I think it's charming, just as I think the whole town is charming. The only thing Westen is missing is a town square."

"That's because it started out as a coach and inn stop between Cleveland and Columbus back when there weren't even any railroads."

They stopped at the corner just across from the Peaches 'N Cream café.

"Hungry?" Chloe asked.

Before she could answer, the door to the sheriff's office opened and out walked Bobby. Walked was being kind. All of five feet four inches tall, Bobby carried her baby out front. The hormone Relaxin allowed her hips to spread wider to cradle her baby, thereby giving her a distinct waddle in her third trimester.

She waved at them and pointed to the café.

Her stomach took that moment to growl loudly, reminding her she hadn't had more than coffee before Chloe had dragged her to the salon. "I guess we're having lunch."

CHAPTER 7

"Glad you all could make this security planning meeting for next weekend's festivities," Gage said to the group gathered in the conference room at the courthouse. "Even you, Callahan."

Sean leaned back in his chair and grinned. "Wouldn't miss it."

The room was full of safety-security people, medical types, and shop owners from downtown, including Lorna Doone, whose café provided the buffet lunch they were enjoying.

"We're expecting a huge influx of visitors next weekend, so I've put all my staff on duty and on call for their off hours," Gage continued. "I've also requested extra manpower from the State Highway Patrol, some off-duty officers looking for overtime."

"We've earmarked money for extra manpower out of the funds from the state." Colm Riley, a town council member and county treasurer, tapped his pen against the legal pad in front of him. He looked over at Deke Reynolds. "Same for the fire and paramedics, Chief."

"Good to know. Thanks, Colm," Deke said.

"My deputies will be spread out at various areas starting

Saturday morning at the ribbon cutting at the hospital," Gage continued. He turned to address Donald Sanderson, the CEO of the hospital. "Bobby and I'll be at the hospital for the ribbon cutting ceremony, and she'll stay around until the health fair is finished."

"That's one way to be sure your wife gets her way to keep working and also see that she doesn't over-do things," Mayor Maggie said.

Gage gave her a half-grin and a shrug. "And if she does, I figure all the medical staff will be happy to get her off her feet."

Chuckles filled the room.

"To add to the fun, as you know, Tobias will be here for the ribbon-cutting ceremony," Gage said, just barely concealing his sarcasm.

Sean had to give him credit for not making an exasperated look—well at least not one more frustrated than the average civil servant having to provide security for a visiting dignitary, like State Representative Tobias Rollins. Three years ago, Tobias decided after serving as the town's mayor for two terms to seek higher political clout and run for the State House. Although Sean didn't know all the details, he'd heard rumors that before the Meth lab explosion occurred, he'd been almost a caricature of the spoiled rich boy wielding power and influence over his former classmates, including Gage, who was the new sheriff at the time. They'd been antagonists since high school.

However, when Gage was trapped in the explosion, something clicked in Tobias. He helped in Gage's rescue, took charge of the aftermath of the explosion, worked with the state to get funding, and convinced the board to use the monies the town was receiving as reparation for the DEA's sloppy handling of the situation into a fiscal trust fund to help the community grow, yet keep its small-town charm. From what Sean could determine, the bills he introduced or supported all seemed to have some positive aspect for the people of not only Ohio, but the Westen area in particular.

So, Gage and Tobias' relationship, while not good-buddy friendly these days, was on very good terms.

"I got word from the head of his security detail that unlike his usual visits where he comes alone, they will be accompanying him for the hospital dedication. Along with the governor's people, since she will be attending, too."

"The governor's coming?" Sean asked, adding that fact to his notes "I hadn't heard that."

"Believe it or not, I can keep a secret, unlike some people." Mayor Maggie grinned at Gage. "It was supposed to be a surprise. Tobias called last week to give us the heads up. Apparently, she wants to see how the money they gave us is being used. I'd appreciate it if it didn't leave this room or show up on the news' website."

Sean nodded. "I can manage that."

"Will she be visiting the downtown while she's here?" Lorna asked.

"God, I hope not," Gage muttered.

"And why not?" The café owner leaned forward and pierced him with a glare. "You don't think we're good enough to host a governor at our places?"

Gage quickly held up his hands in mock surrender. "Lorna, you know I don't think that at all. She should be honored the people of this town would want her to visit them. It's the security of it all that has me grumbling, that's all."

"Well, it better be," she said, settling back into her chair. "Sure would hate to ban you from the Peaches 'N Cream, otherwise."

"What's your plans for the downtown area?" Sean asked, hoping to diffuse the tension.

"There's going to be lots of visitors. All our rooms are booked for the entire weekend," Ida Tumbolt, who ran the boarding house with her sister, said. She turned to Adele Carlisle, who owned the Westen Inn. "You're full, too, right?"

Adele nodded. "We filled up early. Some of our regulars who come for the Saturday farmers market decided to be here for the whole weekend because of the festival, the hospital dedication on Saturday and the barbeque dinner and dance Sunday night."

"And I was talking to Mary Lou the other day," Ida said. "She said she and Walt are all full and that the new motel two miles down the highway is also booked up."

"What are we going to do for parking?" Harold Russet, the county civil engineer asked.

Suddenly, everyone was talking among themselves. Sean watched the room with a smile. It was one of the things he loved about life in a small town. Everyone had a stake in how things should be governed. They showed up for town council meetings, school board meetings, emergency weather briefings, and weren't afraid to add their opinions on any and all subjects.

Gage gave them time to chat, then stood up to get their attention—and at six-feet-five inches tall, he got everyone's attention fairly quickly. He held up his hand and everyone quieted down. "We're planning to use the parking lots from both the middle school and senior high school at the east end of town. Parking for all day will be five dollars and all proceeds will go into the school maintenance funds. The football and baseball teams will be manning the ticket booths at both sites with fathers of team members rotating in and out to keep things secure. We'll have my deputies and the patrol do hourly drive-bys to check on everyone.

"The farmers market will have its usual parking, and of course we'll suspend the parking meters in the downtown area for this weekend only."

"Won't we be giving up a lot of revenue on those?" Andre

Danner asked. He'd started out as a member of the road construction and maintenance crew years ago, gotten his degree in civil engineering and moved up the chain of command in his department to the position of County Road Supervisor last year. He'd proposed that the income from the parking meters on the main throughfares of town be ear-marked for road maintenance on those roads and the county board had agreed.

"We considered that, Andre," Mayor Maggie answered. "But the idea is to get people walking throughout the downtown area, into the shops, to the market, eating at the restaurants. If they don't have to worry about the meter every two hours, they should spend more money in the town. And..." She paused, slowly looking at everyone. "...if this works well, we can hope to see an increase at the market craft fairs this fall and at the Jubilee in December."

Andre nodded. "A meter holiday to increase future revenue is good thinking."

The meeting continued until all the questions on security plans for all the events, as well as patrolling the downtown stores and businesses, were answered and everyone had finished their lunch. Sean gathered up his pad and pen, intending to head for the door.

"Where do you think you're going, Mr. Newsman?" Lorna called to him.

He froze, recognizing that tone in her voice, the same one his mother used whenever she expected help in the kitchen for a family dinner. No one escaped it. Carrying his things, he walked over to where she was loading her dishes back into a large cooler. "Is there something I can help you with, Lorna?"

Grabbing up two bags of paper supplies she'd brought with her, she nodded at the cooler. "You can carry this out to the van for me and we'll have us a chat."

Great. Somehow, he was in trouble. He set his tablet on top of the cooler, grabbed the handles, and hefted it up, wondering what he'd done to fall under Lorna's displeasure. "What are we going to chat about?"

She didn't answer until they were out by her van with the highly decorative advertising covering it. "You've been hanging out with Dylan a lot since she came to visit," she said, standing with her keys out but making no move to open the van door for him to slide in the cooler.

Nope. Not going to be interrogated on Dylan or what they talked about. He set the cooler down. "We're friends. We usually spend some time together when she's in town."

"Don't get your shorts in a twist," Lorna said, pushing the unlock button on her key fob. The door opened and Sean lifted the cooler and slid it inside. Grabbing his tablet, he stepped back, faced Lorna and waited. She pulled her sunglasses out of her bag and slid them on. "I just wondered what your thoughts were."

"My thoughts on what?" For years back in New York he'd spent enough time pushing people to give him information, even if they didn't know they were divulging things, to know when he was being pushed.

"On how long she's going to be visiting." She closed the van door without taking her eyes off him.

Translation: Is Dylan planning on moving to Westen to start her medical career? While he wanted her to move here for his own personal reasons, he hadn't breached the subject with her, and he even if he had, he certainly wouldn't pass that information on to the head of the town gossip network.

"All she's said is she's here until Chloe and Bobby have their babies. Nothing more." He stared straight into the tinted lenses of Lorna's glasses. "But she's said that to everyone she knows, including you."

She nodded. "Today's meeting has me thinking. We have this

new, state of the art hospital, highly trained staff, a growing neighborhood. Are we going to have enough smart doctors to fill the need?"

"That would be a question for the hospital's board of directors and Doc Clint, wouldn't it?"

"Humph," she said with her lips pressed together in that skeptical way she had that spoke volumes and climbed into the driver's seat, closed the door, snapped her seatbelt, and rolled down the window. "They have one reason for wanting her to move here, but I thought I was asking the man who might have another interest for her to stay. If you don't give her a reason to have a second thought now, you might not get another chance."

Before he could reply, she drove out of the lot.

Slowly, he wandered back to his car, mulling over that last statement. For years he'd been patiently Dylan's friend, content to spend time with her when she visited, knowing how much commitment it took to finish her residency and establish her career. Had he waited too long?

CHAPTER 8

After lunch with her sisters, that had been both relaxing and fun, she'd been on her own. Chloe went to her office to meet with a new client, while Bobby had to finish up her shift at the sheriff's office. So, she'd strolled down Main Street, doing a little window shopping, stopping into the child's boutique to buy newborn outfits as gifts for her sisters after they had their babies. The new general store, that looked very much like one out of the nineteenth century on the outside, drew her attention. The inside surprised her. Everything on sale was some sort of local craft item—pottery, handblown glass items, quilts, rod-iron decorations made by an actual blacksmith—and artisanal food items, such as cheeses, preserves, baked items and sausages. She ended up getting a sampling of everything edible.

Still feeling at a loss of direction, she continued strolling down the street until she came to the stone and white clapboard covered church with the green, neatly trimmed lawn and tall oak trees with their golden leaves. The door was propped open, seeming to invite her inside.

The cool interior enticed Dylan in from the late afternoon heat of early autumn in Ohio. The light filtering through the stained glass windows mirrored the changing leaves on the trees outside the church. Halfway up the nave, she slid into a pew and set her bags beside her. She didn't know why she was here. It wasn't like she was a particularly religious person. As a child her parents had taken her and her sisters to church every Sunday and she'd enjoyed Sunday school lessons. But after their death, Bobby hadn't pushed them to attend, probably because suddenly not only raising her younger sisters was stressful, but she also had all the other responsibilities of work, home, and finances.

When she'd stepped into the world of surgery, she'd put her trust in her training and the skills she had to heal her patients. Which, when you were doing scheduled, elective cases, was easy to see how those things were enough. It gave her ego a boost, then seemed to feed it. It carried her into those trauma cases that required concentration, quick reactions and occasionally thinking outside the norm for solutions. Protocols and algorithms worked for most cases, but not all bodies reacted to trauma within pre-set conditions, and the surgeon had to go with their gut and act accordingly.

Sometimes, no matter what you did, the patients didn't make it.

Those were hard cases. Often, especially after Bulldog came into her life, she'd get a little drunk and sulk for a day, but because the person was older, or perhaps their own actions had been the cause of their injury, she'd accept the outcome as fate.

Then she'd lost five-year-old Taylor.

Such a beautiful little girl. She'd been outside playing with her friends when a car pulled up and three gang members fired their illegally bought guns into the car where Taylor's uncle sat watching his niece play. He'd been killed instantly. Bullets pierced the metal car frame and slammed into Taylor. One in her leg, one to the abdomen and one in her upper chest. Despite her team's best efforts and several transfusions of blood, the little girl died.

For once Bulldog didn't recommend drowning her sorrows in a bottle of vodka. Instead, he'd driven them to a small country church outside Cincinnati.

"What are we doing here?" she asked, anger swelling inside her.

"Because we need to give this one up to God," he said, cutting the engine and turning to face her, compassion in his eyes and sadness softening his features.

"Why? Where was God when I was digging around for that bleeder? Where was he when we were trying to save her life?" She faced him, spewing out all the anger inside. "What good does it do pray to God now?"

Steve set his hand on her fist clenched in her lap. "I asked my mother once why she prayed for things and they didn't turn out better? You know what she said?"

She shook her head.

"She said that sometimes the answer is no."

"That doesn't freaking help," she muttered.

"At sixteen, I didn't think so, either. But I've had to come to terms with it over the years." He leaned in until she could only stare into his eyes. "We can't save everyone, Doc."

"I know that. It's just she was so young and had so much of her life still ahead of her. Why take her?"

He shrugged. "Don't know. And you may never know. But when this happens and I don't have the why, I give it to God. Figure he had a good reason for telling me no or for taking someone too soon, and the best I can do is pray for their souls to find peace."

She opened her mouth to protest that she would rather have done more.

"Did you do everything you possibly could have done?" he asked as if he read her mind.

"Yes."

"Could you have done anything different?"

"I don't think so."

"I was in the OR with you, Doc. You and I both know there was nothing more we could've done to save her. So, now you have to give your anger over to God. Accept that some things are out of your control."

"How—"

"If you don't, you won't be able to save the next person. And God gave you those skills and that wickedly smart brain for that purpose."

They'd sat there in quiet for a few minutes watching the big fat snowflakes float down onto the windshield. Then he'd climbed out and patiently waited for her. Finally, she'd followed him inside the church like a sulking, sad child, just like she had Bobby and Chloe on the day of her parents' funeral to try to make sense of things.

And damn him, he'd been right. Sitting in that church, giving her anger and frustration to something, someone more powerful than her had eased her pain. Funny thing was it had changed how she approached her surgeries. In that tiny moment of aloneness before she entered surgery—the three-minute surgical scrub required before getting garbed up under the sterile gown and gloves in the OR—she'd started saying a prayer that God would have her do what was best. Simple. And it always steadied her.

After Bulldog had been killed, all the fears and frustration returned. She'd worked so hard to become a doctor, someone who could save lives, but once again someone she loved died in a remote place without adequate medical help without her.

It had taken her a few weeks of self-pity and wrestling with her own feeling of inadequacy to wander into that church and sit just like this, giving her grief and anger over to that higher being. It's what her friend would've wanted.

Was that why she was here today? Looking for answers?

"Hello, Dylan," a pleasant voice said from in front of her.

She opened her eyes to find Suzie Miller, the pastor of the church's wife, standing in the aisle two pews ahead of her, her hand resting on the slightly rounded top of her belly. "Hi, Suzie. I hope it's okay that I came in. The door was open."

"Of course it's okay. In fact, the door is always unlocked during the day for anyone. Mind if I join you?" she asked, heading to the pew in front of her, then she paused. "Unless, of course, you want to be alone."

"No, please take a seat."

She smiled as she settled in, then turned and stretched out her feet. "I've been helping out with the preschoolers today, and those little buggers have kept me busy running around."

Dylan laughed. She'd never heard a preacher's wife complain about anyone and certainly not children, which she was pretty sure Bobby's son was one of that group today. "Luke wears me out when I watch him, and he's only one little guy."

"Yes, he and my Billy are two of the most rambunctious. Stereotypical."

"How so?" she asked, not quite sure what Suzie was talking about.

"The preacher's kid and the sheriff's kid causing the most chaos." She grinned. "Growing up, I was that kid."

Dylan grinned, too. "So, the good news is they'll turn out to be good citizens?"

"I pray that's the case." She paused and shifted her weight. "You'd think after three previous pregnancies, this would get easier."

"Bobby is saying the same thing, and this is only her second."

"You must be tired of hearing pregnant women complain right now."

Dylan shrugged. "You all may complain, but it's always

followed with a smile like the one you have right now. And seeing my sisters happy? *That*, I could never get tired of."

Quiet settled between them. Not a strained one, more like a pause.

"So, what brought you in here today?" Suzie finally asked.

"I had lunch with my sisters. They both had to work this afternoon and since I rode into town with Chloe, I decided to do a little shopping," she said, nodding at her packages on the seat beside her. "I wandered this way and just felt drawn inside."

Suzie nodded, like that happened to everyone who passed the church doors.

"When I was in my residency I started going to this little church when I had a particularly bad outcome on a case looking for some answers as to why or how to keep going."

Again, the pastor's wife nodded.

"The quiet always seems to help me."

Another nod.

"I guess, I thought I'd find some answers today."

Suzie straightened in her seat, then stepped out into the aisle. "Then I'll let you have some of that quiet."

Dylan blinked. "You aren't going to ask me what I need answers to?"

Suzie laid one hand on her shoulder and squeezed gently. "That's not something I need to know. You came in here for a reason and getting my opinion on whatever is bothering you isn't it. But quiet time in God's house might help you find your answers."

Dylan watched her move to the altar and then out a door near the choir loft. Once again, she was alone.

For years she'd been alone. The little sister who felt like a burden to her older sisters, even though they showered her with love and laughter whenever they were together. The geeky girl who didn't fit in at school, even through med school. A woman trying to find a spot in a field predominantly held by men—men with big egos. Other women assumed she got her spot because she must've slept with someone because it had to be her looks and not her brains or skills that got her where she was.

Come to think of it her two best friends were men. Bulldog and Callahan. One was buried in Arlington Cemetery—she'd gone there and wept for the loss of his friendship and wisdom. The other was happily entrenched here in Westen.

And why was he here? That was a question she'd never really asked him. Weren't journalists supposed to want to be in New York or Washington or some other metropolis fighting to unearth the truth? He'd done that. Lived that life. They'd talked about his time in New York, but never why he'd left. Why he'd really come to Westen to put down his roots like her sisters had.

Roots seemed to grow here. Deep ones.

Was that what she was looking for? A place to put down her own roots? But to do that she'd have to give up the career she'd worked so hard for, her life's goal, saving people from dying in the horrific accidents like the one that snatched her parents out of her life.

That was her dilemma. Her work, while fulfilling, required her to be alone in an urban setting. Coming to Westen where she could be close to her family required her changing her career some, tweaking it to fit in to the more sedate environment and not fulfilling her goals.

She closed her eyes and cleared her mind. What was the answer?

Her phone buzzed in her bag beside her. She pulled it out and answered. "Hey, Chloe."

"I'm about done here, if you want to meet me over at the salon to pick up my car." She paused. "What have you been doing? I thought you'd pop in here a while ago."

Chuckling, she gathered up her things. "Just wandering around town. I'll be there in a few minutes."

She clicked the off button and slipped it back in her bag as she headed for the front door. Outside, she slipped her sunglasses back on, then paused, listening to a very soft sound coming from the side of the church where the centuries-old cemetery lay. Cautiously, she walked to the corner of the church and peeked around the corner, not wanting to disturb whoever might be visiting a loved one's grave.

In a far corner of the graveyard cordoned off by a white wrought-iron fence stood a lone figure. Twylla. She'd recognize that signature bright pink sweater anywhere. It was the same color as the smocks she wore at her salon and the color of two of the wingback chairs in the waiting area. Pink and black. Twylla's colors.

As she stood there, she heard the beautiful sounds of an old song. Twylla was pulling up weeds and placing flowers at one grave site. Perhaps it was her mother's.

Not wishing to disturb her, Dylan inched back from the corner and wandered back into town, the haunting sound of Twylla's song tickling a memory of her own mother crooning to her as a very young child. Why would Twylla be singing a child's lullaby in the graveyard?

CHAPTER 9

When Dylan arrived at the salon, Chloe once again stood in profile against the car, holding the lumbar area of her back with her hands and once again stretching out her spine. Slowing her stride, she squinted at her sister. "How long have you been doing that?"

Chloe turned to look at her. "About a minute."

Dylan shook her head. "No, how long have you been having to stop and hold your back today? How often?"

"I don't know. It started out once or twice this morning," she said, opening her car door and wiggling behind the wheel.

"And now?" Dylan asked, sliding her bags into the back seat before climbing into the passenger seat, wondering if perhaps she should insist on driving?

"I guess my back's been hurting off and on all afternoon. Why?" she asked, buckling up her seatbelt.

"Is it regular?"

"Regular, how?" Chloe fixed her with a brows-drawn-down look.

"Like every hour? Every half hour? Every five minutes?"

"I guess about every ten minutes or so." Those brows shot

up. "You think this might be labor? Wouldn't that be in my abdomen?"

Dylan shrugged. "Not if it's back labor."

"That doesn't sound good," she said as she put the car in gear.

Not wanting to stress her out more, Dylan chose her words carefully. "It's not necessarily a bad thing. It's been a while since my obstetrics rotations during my residency, but a lot of women start off their labor with back pains."

"Why?" Chloe asked as they cleared the downtown area and headed to the outskirts where her, Wes and Wöden's cabin sat. The old-growth forest was dense back there. Not someplace to have your baby in case of an emergency.

Maybe they should give Wes a call.

"Because the back of the baby's head is pressed against your spine."

"Why is that?"

Again, Dylan tried to choose her words with care and keep her voice calm and steady, even though inside her worry ratcheted up the further away from town and the hospital they drove. It had been years, but she could deliver this baby if she had to, as long as no complications arose. "Because it's probably early labor and the baby hasn't turned into the correct position."

"You think it's breech?" her sister asked as she pulled into the drive to the cabin.

"No. Your last sonogram had your baby head down. He or she is just facing the wrong direction—for the moment. Usually," she said as they parked, "the baby turns during labor and the back pain eases, but the abdominal pain gets more intense."

Chloe took a deep relaxing breath and let her head rest against the steering wheel.

"You okay, Chloe?" Dylan asked, leaning forward and laying a hand on her sister's arm.

She nodded and sat up straighter. "Yes. I just needed to know this was normal and not a problem." She unfastened her seatbelt and opened the car door. "I guess we better give Wes a call if this baby's decided to be a little early. Figures."

Dylan hurriedly got out of the car. "Figures what?"

Chloe laughed as she waddled up to the porch and patted the big wolf-dog who'd come out to greet her. "The man's motto is that if you're on time, you're already late. Of course his child would come three weeks early." She paused to press her hand against her back again. After about a minute, she shook her head. "Dammit."

"What?" Dylan asked, coming up behind her.

"I guess we'll have to go into Columbus since the new hospital isn't open yet."

For once, her very professional, grown-up and self-assured sister sounded a little nervous. Dylan relaxed and laughed a little. "They'll have a nice place for you at the hospital in Westerville. It will be okay."

∼

"Any news yet?" Sean asked, flopping down onto the sofa beside Dylan and plopping a paper bag in her lap.

"Other than Gage and I ganging up on Bobby to get her to go home and get some rest before she ends up in the labor bed next to Chloe? Nope." She opened the bag and inhaled, closing her eyes a moment in pure bliss. "You got burgers."

"With cheese, pickles and mustard," he said, trying not to grin at the look of pleasure on her face.

She opened her eyes and smiled at him, the kind that made your insides go soft and your heart do an extra beat that you gave her such pleasure. "You remembered."

"How could I forget? You're the only person I know who has

two standards for her burgers. How did you say it? Oh yeah, *If you're eating the burger hot off the grill at home or in a restaurant, then mayo, onions and tomatoes are the best. If you're getting it to go and might be a while before you eat it, then mustard and pickles.*"

She giggled as she pulled one of the two burgers out of the bag. "I don't think I can eat two of these. They're huge."

"Good. The other one's for me."

"Oh, so, which one has mustard and pickles?"

"Both," he said, snatching the bag back and fishing out the second sandwich. Then he opened a second bag, this one from a local grocery store and handed her a bottle of water. "Something to wash it down with."

"My hero," she said just before sinking her teeth into her burger.

They ate in companionable silence as two other families, who'd been waiting for their loved ones to give birth, left.

Finished, Dylan scooped up the garbage and put it in one of the trash bins near the door. She stretched her arms high over her head and then bent down to touch her toes, letting out one the sexiest groans he'd ever heard outside of a bedroom.

Swallowing hard, he adjusted his seat and crossed one leg, with the ankle on the other knee. With a glance at the clock at almost midnight, he asked, "Does it always take this long?"

She straightened and twisted her body from side to side. "First babies can be a long time. The mother's body has never done this process before, and each person's labor is different. That said, the last time I checked she was finally completely dilated and would begin pushing."

"And how long will that take?"

"Depends," she said, coming back to sit beside him and leaning her head back against the headrest and closing her eyes. Despite all the stretching she'd just done, he could feel the tension in her body where it touched his side.

"On what?"

"How big the baby is, how it's positioned, how exhausted Choe is from the labor."

"Okay, let's assume everything is in good order, what's the usual time you, as a doctor, would expect her to do this in?"

She shrugged. "First baby? Between one and two hours. She's got good muscle tone and is tall, so that should help."

"Height helps?" he asked, turning to look at her.

She opened her eyes and met his gaze with a grin. "It's been a long time since I delivered a baby, but I remember this real experienced nurse name Teri tell a new nurse that women in good shape who had tall frames could pull their knees back to their ears and push like champions."

He choked out a laugh. "Well, that's an image I can't unsee."

"It shortens the birth canal and helps get the baby through."

They sat studying each other. "Why didn't you go into obstetrics? Sounds like you know a lot about it."

She blinked, breaking the connection, and went back to watching the door to the waiting room. For a moment he was sure she was ignoring his question and he could kick himself for asking it.

"I did like my rotation in obstetrics. I liked it so much I actually did a second one, which was unusual, but I felt it would help me if I ever had to do trauma surgery on a pregnant woman."

"Seems like a smart move."

"They even tried to recruit me into their program, but it wasn't my calling. Trauma surgery was."

"Why?" he asked.

"My parents both died from a drunk driving accident when I was six."

He knew she'd been young when her parents died, and her

sister Bobby had raised her and Chloe, but didn't know drunk driving had been the cause."

"Daddy was a professor of engineering and had been invited to speak at the University of Kentucky in Lexington. Since it was their anniversary week, Mom went with him, leaving us home with Bobby. The second night there was a banquet and awards ceremony, which my parents attended. Since it was only a two-hour drive, they decided to come home rather than spend another night away from us." She paused and swallowed, blinking hard—probably to fight back tears. "A sudden rainstorm hit, the kind that pops up out of nowhere, making the roads slick before anyone realizes it. A drunk driver plowed into them from behind and sent them over the edge of the highway into an embankment of trees."

"Oh, man." Really wishing he hadn't asked that question, he laid his hand over both of hers clenched together in her lap.

"They'd both been transported to a local hospital, but it wasn't a trauma unit, there weren't many back then. Mom died of blood loss by the time they'd gotten her to the hospital. Daddy held on long enough to get taken to surgery, but only a general surgeon was available and due to the massive injuries, I suspect the doctor was well out of his league, and Daddy died on the operating table."

"And that's why you became a trauma surgeon."

She nodded, releasing the clench of her hands and slipping the one closest into his. "I know my being a trauma surgeon won't bring them back, but maybe, just maybe I'll be able to stop some other little six-year-old girl losing her parents someday."

"I think you're going to do that for a lot of people." He squeezed her hand. "Thanks for sharing the story with me. I know it wasn't easy."

"Thanks for understanding. I'm not sure my sisters do."

"They may understand more than you think they do."

"Since I've been in town, they keep pointing out how much Westen has grown and how Doc Clint was looking for a partner. How there's a new hospital. I just don't know that there would be a real need for someone with my skills out here. Be a general practitioner like Clint? Yeah, I don't know that's for me either."

Before he could press her for more, the waiting room door opened and in stepped a weary but happy looking Wes.

"It's a boy!"

Dylan flew off the couch to hug her brother-in-law.

"Come on, you have to see him." The usually serious new father beamed with joy.

Sean watched the two of them disappear out the door, then Dylan stuck her head back in and grinned at him. "Aren't you coming?"

CHAPTER 10

The motel room was as inviting as an empty meat locker and just about as warm. He set his room key on the desk and dropped his duffel bag on the chair before sitting on the edge of the bed.

Damn, he was exhausted.

Ever since he got that call from Myles a week ago, he'd been traveling. *When he arrived at the compound, Myles had shoved his tablet in his face.*

"Look!"

He hated that the old man had a tablet now. Instead of losing interest in Meredith and moving on to the next shiny object like he usually did, the internet's possibility of hunting her down had heightened his interest and spurred his anger. The tablet let him continue his obsessive pursuit of her anywhere he wanted, even sitting on the toilet.

So, when he took the electronic device, he couldn't identify anyone in the image at first. Then he saw her standing in the background. He enlarged the area.

"It's her!" Myles spat out, his voice dripping with venom.

He didn't argue with him. She was older and had gained some weight, a healthy amount compared to the nearly emaciated skeleton she'd been when she fled. But he'd know her stance anywhere. He'd watched her from afar so long, that she was etched in his brain—even after eighteen years.

"You found her," he said, almost as a whisper.

"Damn straight I did! I told you she wasn't going to hide forever."

His eyes locked on her silhouetted image, he asked, "Where is this?"

"Some place in Ohio. A baseball tournament or something." He poked one meaty finger at her on the screen. "But that's the bitch, for sure. You go to Ohio and find where she's at."

"Now?"

Myles grabbed him by the shirt collar and pulled him in tight. "You've been looking for her for eighteen years. Yes tonight!" He let go of his shirt with a little shove.

He took one step back, but that was all the space he was going to give. "You don't even know what city she's in."

"Start in one of the big ones. I don't care how long it takes. You turn over every fucking rock until you find her. Then you let me know. I'm going to take care of her myself."

So, the first thing he did was get a flight to Cleveland. About a month after Meredith got on that bus, he'd gotten one postcard from her with a picture of the Rock & Roll Hall of Fame on it. *Arrived safe* was all it said. After that, he never heard from her again. Now, he had to find her before Myles lost patience and sent others to find her.

Once in Cleveland, he went straight to the local library to research the baseball tournament listed in the image they'd uncovered. The image was posted by a real estate agent in a town called Westen, but the tournament was in Howard, a town east of Mount Vernon, and teams from other small towns all over the area had participated. Meredith could be living in any of them.

After eliminating her living in Howard, Mount Vernon, or

any of the closely surrounding towns, he was moving further south. He'd check out Martinsburg tomorrow, then he was heading to talk to the lady who took the picture, one Nora Hendrix of Hendrix Realty. Hopefully, she could shine some light on where Meredith lived.

His phone rang. Myles' ringtone.

He considered not answering, but his boss would just continue to call until he did. Best to get the conversation over with, then he could take a hot shower and get some sleep.

"Hello, Myles."

"Any news?" *And hello to you, too.*

"Nothing yet." He held the phone away as Myles yelled a string of curses. Once the other man took a breath, he continued. "I've eliminated a lot of places. There's two more towns in this area to check out, then I'll head into Columbus."

"She's there somewhere, dammit," Myles ground into the phone, some of the starch taken out of his voice.

"And she's had years to hide and is probably very good at it."

"Bitch is probably living off my treasure."

For years, Myles accused Meredith of taking something from him. He'd never told him what it was. When he'd put Meredith on that bus, she'd only had her backpack of clothes and toiletries. Because of his viciously angry rants, he'd continued to work for the crime boss just to keep an eye on him and protect Meredith.

"You find her this time, Ricky, or I'm sending in Carver to do it." And the connection went dead.

He clenched the phone in his hands between his spread legs and bent over, weary from the fear he'd been carrying for nearly two decades.

His time was running out.

∼

"You want me to wait until you're inside?" Sean asked as they pulled up beside her car parked next to her sister's in front of the cabin. Where the headlights shone, a large white mass slowly arose on the porch. Wöden. The wolf-dog stood at the top of the steps, blocking access to the front entrance. "Will he let you inside?"

Dylan yawned as she fished Chloe's house keys Wes had given her back in the hospital room out of her bag. "He's just a big puppy."

"A big puppy that could rip someone's throat out if provoked."

She turned and grinned at him. "Then don't provoke him. Just walk behind me."

"Behind you?"

"You do want to come inside, don't you?"

He glanced at the dashboard clock. "It's nearly three in the morning."

She stared at him. "I'm not a coward, but I'm not real comfortable sleeping out here in the woods by myself, even with Wöden on guard. Please stay with me."

He wasn't sure exactly what she was asking, but a trace of fear was in her eyes and if sleeping on the couch made that go away, he'd be happy to do that every night. "Okay. But you have to tell your roommate I'm harmless."

Surprisingly, as soon as Wöden saw her climb out of the car, he started wagging his tail and moved to the side of the porch.

"Hey, boy. It's okay," she said, scratching him behind his ears.

"He lives here full time?" Standing back so as not to give off a threatening vibe to the half-tame animal, he waited for Dylan to get the door unlocked and opened before moving. Wöden sniffed him as he walked by, wagged his tail, and followed them inside. "I must've passed muster."

She laughed. "I suspect he smells Wes on you, since you guys did the 'bro hug' in the delivery room."

"Way to burst my male ego. Here I am thinking I'm cool enough to get the approval of a wolf."

"Half-wolf and you are cool," she said, flopping her bag onto the table. Opening the refrigerator, she retrieved a jug of milk. "And yes, he does live here full time. According to Wes, from the moment Chloe moved in, so did Wöden."

Wondering what she was up to, he turned the lock on the door behind them, then leaned one hip against the kitchen counter and watched her pull out a pan and a box of expensive powdered chocolate. "You do realize there's one of those single cup coffee makers behind you?"

"Yep. Reminds me of being at the hospital. I prefer my hot chocolate made the old-fashioned way." She pulled two mugs off the open shelves flanking the sink, filled one with milk, poured it into the pot on the stove and repeated the action, then turned on the gas flame. Next, she opened a jar and scooped some chocolate chips into the bottom of each cup. Then she spooned the sweetened cocoa powder into each cup, tested the milk with the tip of her little finger and deciding it was just hot enough, filled each mug almost to the rim. "Can you get me the can of whipped cream out of the door of the fridge?" she asked as she stirred the cups of hot chocolate.

He retrieved the whipped cream and set it on the counter next to her, thoroughly enjoying her movements. "Aren't you worrying about the caffeine in the chocolate keeping you up the rest of the night?"

"Nope. Hot chocolate actually helps me sleep," she said, foaming whipped cream into both mugs, then handing him one.

"Really?" he asked, following her over to the leather sofa and sitting next to her. Wöden curled up on the rug by the front door.

Kicking off her shoes, she took a drink of hers then licked the whipped cream that clung to her lips. Damn how he wished he could've licked them for her.

"Yes," she said, and he wondered if he'd said that lustful thought aloud. "It's the warm milk. My mom tried to get me to drink it when I was little, so I'd go to sleep. My mind was always whirring with thoughts, and I'd stay up long past my sisters, but I hated the taste of warm milk. To this day I prefer it ice cold. So, to get me to drink the warmed milk she put some chocolate in it. I drank it down and slept the night away."

Relaxing next to her, he took a long drink of the hot chocolate. "Damn, that's good."

She grinned at him. "I know. Over the years I've tried all kinds of combinations. Sometimes, I drizzle Caramel ice cream topping over the whipped cream, but Chloe doesn't have any."

"I bet that combination tastes great, maybe with a little sprinkle of sea salt."

She giggled. "Great minds..."

They continued drinking, even scooping out the melted chocolate out of the bottom. She took both mugs and set them on the coffee table. Then she pulled the afghan off the back of the couch, spread it over them both and laid her head on his shoulder.

"For a newborn, Benjamin is a cute little fellow, isn't he?" she asked, then yawned.

He stretched his legs out in front of him and closed his eyes, enjoying her snuggling up beside him. "I'll take your word for it. To me all babies look like toothless little old men."

Another giggle escaped her. He smiled. He liked that he could make her relax. She worked too hard in a world of life and death.

"Well, I'm glad he's here safe and sound. The death of a baby can be so devastating. I wouldn't want that for Chloe and Wes.

Or Bobby and Gage..." She paused, a soft shudder going through her. "Or anyone."

And there it was. The seriousness of the world she lived in on a daily basis.

He turned his face resting against her hair and kissed her forehead. She lifted her head to stare into his eyes and parted her lips just enough to tempt him. He'd wanted to kiss her for years and here she was, offering him the chance. His mama hadn't raised a fool.

Lowering his head, he took her lips with his. Softness. Heat. Chocolate. She tasted of comfort and decadence all at once.

She laid her hand on his chest and tilted her head, her lips pressing back against him. Reaching for her face, he cupped it in his hand and deepened the kiss as his thumb stroked the soft skin along her jaw line. The moments ticked by as he enjoyed his first taste of her. He wanted more but didn't want to break this new bond they'd formed. She was too important to him.

Slowly, he released his pressure on her mouth, still stroking her with his thumb, their lips clinging for the briefest of seconds before they parted. He watched as her eyelids fluttered, then opened. The light they'd left on over the sink gave him just enough vision of the heat in her golden-brown gaze.

He'd put that there.

And didn't that make him want to jump up and shout to the world with a giant fist pump?

Instead, he pressed her head back against his shoulder and leaned his cheek against her hair.

"You tasted like hot chocolate," she murmured. "I love it."

Her words hit him hard. Did she simply mean she loved the taste of hot chocolate? Did she love the taste of hot chocolate on him? Did she mean she loved him? Was he reading too much into her words?

Before he could screw things up and ask her those questions, a soft little purr escaped her.

She'd fallen asleep.

Reaching over, he pulled the afghan over her shoulders and slid just a little more into the leather sofa so she wouldn't be in an uncomfortable angle while she slept. When he walked in the cabin, he hadn't known what to expect. It certainly wasn't this, but right now there wasn't anywhere else he'd want to be.

~

A low growl cracked through the foggy mist of Dylan's sleep. She tried to snuggle into the warm cocoon surrounding her, but the pillow behind her wouldn't budge and the one in front of her wouldn't either. Then it moved.

Her eyes snapped open.

In the early morning light, she took stock of where she was. Chloe's cabin. The living room. Stretched out on the leather couch...with...she slowly lifted her head to find Callahan staring down at her.

"Good morning," he said, his husky voice rumbling against her ear.

How had they ended up like this? The last thing she remembered was drinking hot chocolate and then resting her head on his shoulder. When had he maneuvered them to sleeping stretched out and cuddled up together? Or had she done that?

Another low growl sounded near the front door. She peeked up over Sean's chest to see Wöden standing at the door. He wasn't growling at her and Sean. No, his attention was focused on the outside of the cabin.

"Do you think he wants out?" Sean asked, his attention on the wolf-dog, too.

"I think there's something or someone out there."

"Would it be Wes?" he asked, slowly unwrapping his arms from around her.

She wiggled back to give him room and then they both sat up. "I don't think so. He was planning to stay with Chloe until she and the baby were discharged."

Sean rubbed his face, stretched his arms, then stood. Dylan fought off the urge to giggle. He was like a grumpy bear coming out of hibernation. Slowly, he walked over to the door.

"What's up boy?" he asked Wöden, who wagged his tail and let out another growl. Holding his hands out like he was calming a would-be attacker, Sean inched his way close enough to look out the window. Then jumped back. "Shit."

"What?" Dylan jumped off the couch and hurried over, just as he opened the door.

There stood Harriett, all four-foot-ten of her, with a paper bag and a box of donuts from the Yeast & West bakery.

"Gonna invite me in?" she said, and Dylan was sure she was talking to the wolf-dog. He wagged his tail and moved back.

The septuagenarian marched past all three of them to the kitchen and deposited her parcels on the kitchen counter. "Go get changed, Doc. We have rounds to make."

"Rounds?" Dylan asked, half-opening the lid to the donuts. "I hate to tell you this, Harriett, I'm on vacation. And I don't have a practice here. Unless Clint is ill over at his clinic?"

"Nope. Doc's fine. It's Wednesday," she said, pulling a small package out of the paper bag. She unwrapped it to show a pile of raw stew meat, which she walked over to Wöden's bowl near the door and dropped it in.

Dylan waited for the taciturn nurse to finish her explanation, but nothing further came from her. She looked at Sean, who simply shrugged, then finished opening the box of donuts and snagged one of the chocolate-iced ones. She followed suit, selecting the caramel and apple crumb-topped one, because obviously she needed her blood sugar up to deal with Harriett.

"What does Wednesday have to do with anything?" she asked, then bit into her donut.

Harriett pulled out a chair at the table and sat. "Second Wednesday of the month I visit the Amish families in our county. You need to come with me."

Dylan swallowed her mouthful. "I don't know anything about rural medicine."

"Nonsense. Medicine is medicine."

"And I'd be totally useless."

Harriett just stared at her with those steely blue-grey eyes of hers. Dylan crossed her arms over her chest and stared right back.

"Coffee?" Sean asked, turning to the one-cup coffee maker.

"She likes diet pop," Harriett said, pulling a cold bottle of one out of her brown bag.

Dylan narrowed her eyes at her as she took the bottle and opened it. "How did you know?"

"I'll meet you outside in fifteen minutes." Harriett rose and went to the door. Opening it, she let Wöden out, then paused. "Wear jeans and good walking shoes or boots."

Still staring at the door after Harriett's departure, Dylan took a long swig of the diet soda. "How did she know I don't like coffee?"

Sean came to stand next to her. "She knows things."

She swiveled her body to face him. "But how does she know them?"

He gave a skeptical shrug. "No one asks."

"Everyone is scared of her?"

He nodded.

"Even my brother-in-laws?"

"I'd say Gage and Wes have a healthy respect for her. Rumor

has it she used to work for the CIA before arriving in Westen twenty years ago. Most of us don't argue when she suggests we do things, either. She usually has a reason."

She fished another donut out of the box. "I'm going to make country rounds, aren't I?"

"Yep. You have about twelve minutes to change."

Shaking her head, she started for the guest room to change. Suddenly, Callahan grabbed her upper arm to stop her. "What?"

"This." He leaned in and kissed her again.

God. He tasted so good. Not just chocolate this time, but the masculine salty taste of his lips, and the heat he gave off—from his mouth, his breath teasing her face and his hand on her arm. Then he broke the contact but eased the loss with a little smile. "Thought I'd best do that in case Harriett has nefarious plans for you."

"Gee, thanks for that piece of positivity. If I wasn't a little scared of her before, I am now." She made an exasperated face at him and continued on to the guest room.

No time for a shower, she quickly changed into another pair of jeans, a t-shirt and finally, pulled on a lightweight sweater. She finished her second donut, brushed her teeth, and pulled her hair that had come loose while sleeping against Sean back into a neat ponytail once more. Finally, remembering Harriett's admonition about her footwear, she put on her hiking boots.

"By the way," she said to Sean, who was standing near the front door waiting for her as she stopped to grab her bag from the table, "do you know anything about the Baptist church's cemetery?"

His brows dropped down in confusion. "The one here in Westen?"

She shot him a what-other-cemetery-would-I-be-asking-about look.

He laughed. "Just checking. Westen was established in eighteen-thirty. The Baptist church was built two years later. Oldest tombstone is for one Josiah Davis who died in eighteen-thirty-two. Why?"

"There's an area marked off by a white fence. What is that?" she asked as she locked the door behind them, and they headed down the steps to where Harriett sat in her refurbished WWII-era Jeep with the motor running, parked next to his car.

"Not really sure. Why?"

She paused and lowered her voice so only he could hear. "I was near the church the other day and saw Twylla in that part of the cemetery, singing."

"Singing?" He looked as intrigued as he sounded.

Dylan nodded and they continued to the cars.

"That's very curious. I might have to check that out."

She climbed into the Jeep, buckled up, and closed the door, rolling the window down. "Let me know what you find out."

As Harriett reversed out of the parking area, Dylan caught a glimpse of white fur disappearing into the woods beside the cabin. In the side mirror she watched Sean following them out the gravel road to the highway. Harriett turned left out towards the farmland east of Westen while Callahan headed back into town.

She looked at Harriett. "So, who are we seeing?"

"Asa Miller."

"What's Mr. Miller's ailment?" she asked, knowing that Doc Clint's biggest issue with his nurse was having to pull information out of her. She treated words like a limited global commodity.

"You'll see."

CHAPTER 11

"We're going to have to make some changes to our roster and scheduled hours with Wes out," Gage said, glancing over the top of his computer screen at his wife.

Bobby was sitting with her feet elevated, scanning through pages of arrest statistics she'd printed up earlier. Despite how happy she was about this second pregnancy, he worried that she wasn't getting enough rest this time around. Chasing a three-year-old certainly didn't help things. Convincing her to get off her feet for an hour every morning and afternoon at work was all he could do to get her some rest. She'd balked the first time he'd suggested it, forcing him to go into boss mode. Either she agreed to the time off her feet, or she'd go to half-shifts this last trimester.

One of the things he loved about his wife was how much she loved her job and the people of Westen. Facing the possibility of losing time at work or helping others, she'd acquiesced and now planned her work so that she was occupied mentally while off her feet. Mornings were spent with her feet up, doing paperwork. Afternoons, she stretched out on one of the empty cots in the old jail cells—the new jail below the courthouse housed prisoners now and the three cells at the sheriff's office were for the staff when doing double shifts or Earl when he needed a place to sleep during inclement weather—for a short nap.

"He'll be on paternity leave for the next two weeks, won't he?" she asked, resting the papers in her hands over her rounded belly.

"Yes. That was the plan we'd discussed. But I'd hoped it would happen after the big hospital opening and the town's fall festival this weekend." He folded his hands behind his neck and leaned back in his chair, stretching out his legs.

"Daniel can step in as second-in-command, can't he?"

"Sure. We've already discussed that happening if Wes and I were both out." He paused and winked at the disgruntled look she shot him. "And you, of course."

"You'd better have included me, since your child and I are the reason you'd need paternity leave."

"I'll put everyone on ten-hour shifts," he continued, "to overlap each other and cover as much of the work as possible."

"You know," she said, pausing and biting her upper lip the way she did whenever she was considering a problem and possible solution, "the town is growing so much, perhaps it's time to do some more hiring? I know it won't help solve this particular problem, but in the long run the town is going to need more trained people to provide safety and security to the community."

He grinned at her.

"What?"

"That's exactly what I was thinking."

"So, what do you have to do to make that happen?"

Standing up from his chair, he walked over to lean one hip against the corner of her desk. "It's not what *I* have to do. It's what *you're* going to have to do."

"Me?" she narrowed her gaze at him, laying all her papers on her desk.

"Yes. I'm delegating this project to you. You'll need to determine how many new hires you think we'll need, including office help. What each salary should be, including raises for Wes, Daniel and Cleetus, as they'll be getting promotions. Then make a proposal for us to present to the town council."

"Us?" Of course, the work volume didn't surprise her, but the fact he considered her his partner in obtaining the funds from the council did.

"Yes. I figure we'll present it in two months to the council. You should be back from maternity leave by then." He reached over and ran his hand over her face and then laid it on her belly. "That is if everything goes well again."

"It will." She laid her hand over his, reassuring him all was well with her and their second child.

"Will that be enough time for you to get this project ready?"

She gave him a gentle smile. "It will."

He leaned over and kissed her softly, thanking daily for the day she'd literally landed in his arms and changed his life and the lives of all the people in Westen.

The front door to the office opened as they broke apart.

"Hello Sheriff, Mrs. Sheriff." Earl, the town's resident homeless man stood in the doorway, holding a handful of flowers in his hand.

"Hello, Earl," Gage said, going over to shake hands with the white-haired old man. "What ya got there?"

"I was helping out setting up some booths for the farmers market and Maggie had some flowers she cut from one of those pretty arrangements she makes, so I asked if I could have them. Thought Mrs. Sheriff might like them." The sheepish smile the older man gave his wife made Gage grin at her.

"I would love them." Bobby wiggled out of her chair and

came to take them, planting a kiss on Earl's tanned and wrinkled cheek. "Daisies always make me smile. Let me get something to serve as a vase."

"How are things going over at the market?" Gage asked, sitting back down on the edge of Bobby's desk.

"Lots of busy people. Lots of work to get done," Earl said, shuffling from one foot to the other.

"Did you eat today?" Bobby asked, coming back in with a travel mug full of water. She set it on her desk, took the stems from Earl and cut the ends so they'd fit before arranging them in the make-shift vase.

"Yes, ma'am. Joe Gillis has me helping him build some extra booths. We had lunch from that new barbecue place in town. Pretty good brisket and the sauce had a little kick to it. Reminds me of ...when I was a kid in..." He drifted off, as he often did when trying to remember something from his past.

Earl suffered a head trauma sometime before arriving in Westen back at the end of the Vietnam War. He had little memory about his past, only small flashes like today. Gage's dad had contacted the military, but because his fingerprints had also been burned off at some time in his past, there'd been no real way to identify him. Gage considered doing DNA testing when he first became sheriff, but Earl seemed so happy here. He never posed a threat to anyone and actually helped stop the stalker that tried to kill Wes and Chloe so, he decided why put him through that and nixed the idea.

An idea popped into his head. "You going to be at the market and festival this weekend, Earl?"

He nodded. "Joe said they'd need some help doing cleanup. I like helping with that."

"Can I ask a favor?"

"Sure thing, Sheriff. Whatever you need."

"While you're walking around town, picking up trash or

cleaning up any messes, if you see anyone doing anything you think isn't right, can you come tell me or one of the deputies?"

Earl nodded with his whole body. "Sure thing, Sheriff. I always keep my eyes open. Never know when the enemy might sneak up on you."

"I know and I appreciate how much you watch over the citizens of Westen," Gage said, laying his hand on the older man's shoulder, stilling his movements. "But remember, there will be a lot of strangers coming to town this weekend and most of them are friendlies we've invited."

"Joe and I were talking about that. Lots of people visiting the town and buying stuff will be good for everyone."

"That's right. So, you'll have to be very careful. I only need to know if you see something very, very out of the ordinary."

"Like that waitress carrying the sniper rifle a few years back?"

"Exactly." Gage leaned back on the desk once more. "You gonna need a place to sleep this weekend?"

"Might take you up on that starting tomorrow. Think I'll go out to the bridge tonight to catch up with some friends."

The old Wilson covered bridge that spanned the creek on the north side of town was a favorite place for homeless traveling through the area in the summer months. His deputies increased their patrols of the area when the weather turned warm. They watched for drug dealers and at-risk teens. But there were also regulars of more experienced homeless who were like modern-day nomads.

"That's good. Can you do one more thing for me?"

"Sure thing, Sheriff. Whatever you need."

"Can you let the regulars know that if they need a meal, Pete always has some extra meals after breakfast and dinner for anyone at the back door of the Peaches 'N Cream? They should go there and not bother the owners of the festival booths."

"Will do," he said, nodding again, which set off his physical shaking again. "Might head over and see old Pete before I go out to the bridge."

This time Bobby laid her hand on his shoulder to ease some of his shaking. "You be careful out there, Earl, and thank you for my beautiful flowers."

His cheeks turned bright red, and his elderly eyes welled up just a bit. "You take care of that little one, too, Mrs. Sheriff."

He turned and shuffled out of the office.

"His shaking is getting worse," Bobby said after the door closed behind Earl.

Gage nodded. "I know. Clint suspects he may have Parkinson's and has asked him to come into the clinic, but Earl keeps ignoring the invitation."

"Well, the wrong person is asking him," Bobby said, heading off to the cot in her favorite cell—the one he'd locked her in the first day they met—for her afternoon nap. "Have Harriett tell him to come in. He'll show up. No one argues with Harriett."

~

"Where are we going now?" Dylan asked as Harriet drove them down the gravel road from the Miller farm.

When they'd arrived at the Miller's she'd been surprised to see the fields full of workers piling hay high up on old-fashioned wagons pulled by teams of work horses. It was like stepping back two centuries. The door to the two-story farmhouse opened and out came the matriarch of the family, Catherine Miller, dressed in her long dark dress, black apron and kerchief hat on her white hair. Her dress sleeves were rolled up over her elbows and she was drying her hands with a dishtowel. Two toddler-aged boys and several school-aged girls came out on the porch behind her.

Harriett called one of the tallest of the girls over and whispered in her ear. She nodded and ran out into the field to where the wheat was being loaded.

Catherine greeted Harriett and Dylan, happily ushering them into the kitchen where two younger women cooked and canned green beans, while two teenaged girls peeled apples. Dylan quickly realized that three generations of Millers lived on this farm. While the women worked, she found a place out of the way and observed Harriett do quick check-ups on the smallest children—the two toddler boys, an infant girl and the four school-aged children. Apparently, she did this once a month and all the family was comfortable with the usually taciturn nurse.

By the time she'd done these quick check-ups, the kitchen door opened and an older man with leathery wrinkled skin, a long white beard and balding head entered and greeted them. What surprised Dylan wasn't that a man his age had been out in the fields harvesting hay in an old-fashioned way, but that he was missing the lower half of his left arm.

"I was hoping you wouldn't mind talking with Dr. Roberts about how you lost your arm, Asa," Harriett said as they all took a seat at the table.

Dylan blinked her surprise and started to protest.

"Ya, I can do that, Miss Harriett," he said, leaning back into his chair a bit. "It happened about ten years ago. I was riding the thresher when something jammed. I went down to check what the problem was when a copperhead bit one of the horses. They bolted, and the blades sliced me up." He rubbed the bottom of the stub as he remembered.

"They brought him to the clinic to see Doc Ray," Harriett said.

Doc Ray was Clint Preston's uncle and ran the town's medical clinic before he retired and Clint took over the practice.

"The arm was pretty mangled by that time. Doctor Ray did his best to save it."

"Ya. He tried to put it back together," Catherine said, taking a chair and pulling one of her grandsons into her lap. "My poor Asa was in such pain and there was so much blood."

Asa reached over and patted her shoulder.

"There were no emergency vehicles to get him to the closest hospital, which was nearly thirty miles away at the time," Harriett said, taking over the conversation. "Doc Ray wasn't trained in repairing such extensive damage to regain function of the arm and Asa had lost about two pints of blood already."

"So Doc Ray had to amputate to stop the bleeding as best he could and save his life," Dylan finished.

Over the course of the day, they'd been to several Amish homes for check-ups on the children, removal of stitches on wounds, observing the progress of someone in a cast. All of them had some story to tell about how a faster and more modern approach to trauma treatment might've saved a loved one's life or prevented the loss of a finger or limb.

Now she knew why Harriett had wanted her to come with her today. While her sisters and brothers-in-law had already pressed the need for a surgeon in their new hospital on her during this visit, and she understood on paper the growing community's concerns for medical care, Harriett intended to put some faces to the conversation.

"Ruth Johnson's next on my list," Harriett said, turning off the gravel road to a paved one. "Doc changed her blood pressure medicine last month. Need to do some follow-up care to be sure there's no side effects."

"What's Ruth's story?" Dylan asked. Might as well be prepared in case this was another amputee.

"Widow. Lives on her family farm with her daughter and son-in-law."

Dylan waited for more. None came.

For a town full of gossips, Harriett was a like an armored safe. You'd need explosives to get information out of her unless she wanted to tell you something. So, Dylan just stared out the passenger window at the passing scenery—more farms with men and boys in black pants, white shirts and straw hats, harvesting hay or wheat. She wasn't sure. Groves of trees, maple and oak and birch, all turning colors. The occasional brick farmhouse that had cars or trucks parked outside—and wondered if this was really a place she could live and work, or was she destined to live in the city and join a practice where her skills would be used daily. Lives changed because of her abilities.

She'd always been the weird girl. The geek. She'd always known what she wanted, where her life would lead her. Other people had job choices, career choices. She'd had a calling. But ever since she walked out of the OR after ten hours working on trying to patch up a teenager caught in a gang shooting who was still not out of the woods, to find Wes waiting for her with the terrible news about Bulldog, that calling seemed to be a faint whisper.

Harriett pulled into a long drive up to a classic two-story white clapboard house with a huge front porch. Cornfields on one side of the drive seemed to go on for the length of a football field with a tractor harvesting the furthest part. On the other side was a garden of different vegetables.

"Daryl, Ruth's son-in-law, and her daughter Heather are harvesting right now, so we're doing a home visit," Harriett said as she parked the car.

"So they don't have to take time from the harvest to drive her to town." It wasn't a question. Dylan understood that life out here was different than what she was used to. She climbed out of the car and followed Harriet to the front door.

"Miss Harriett." The grey-haired woman dressed in jeans and a blue linen blouse hand-embroidered with wildflowers on the shoulders smiled as she opened the door and the scent of baked bread and cinnamon wafted out. "Come in, come in. How are you today?"

"Doing fine Ruth. This is Doctor Roberts," Harriett introduced her as they entered the farmhouse.

"Deputy Bobby's sister? It's so nice to meet you." She led them into her kitchen. The table was covered in loaves of bread, some resting on tea towels to cool, others packaged into zip-lock bags.

"Getting ready for the market tomorrow?" Harriett asked as she set her nurse's bag on an empty chair. The look she gave the other woman made Dylan want to defend her right to bake bread.

Ruth just grinned. "Heather has a booth and we're hoping to sell out. I haven't been on my feet all day, I promise."

"You know God doesn't like people who lie," Harriett said, motioning for Ruth to have a seat. "Let's see what your blood pressure tells me."

Dylan leaned back against the kitchen counter as Harriett checked her patient's blood pressure then asked her questions about the new medication she'd started taking, any side effects she'd noticed and how she felt. Ruth gave her all positive answers.

"Would you like some tea?" she asked once Harriett was satisfied that all was well with her.

Before Dylan could decline, Harriett said, "Yes, we'd love some and maybe a sample of what you're selling at the market?" She motioned for Dylan to take a seat as she pulled out her own chair.

Whatever it was that Harriett wanted her to learn from Ruth was going to happen now, so she sat and politely took the cup of iced tea and the slice of the warm cinnamon bread. She tore off a chunk and ate it.

"Oh, that's delicious."

Ruth smiled. "Thank you. It was my Nathan's favorite."

"Your husband?"

She shook her head and looked at the bookshelf behind her where pictures filled the space of all the shelves, except the top one. Ruth pointed at the one picture on that shelf of what Dylan would guess was a school picture from the early nineties of a young teenage boy, twelve or thirteen. "That's Nathan."

Her body seemed to sag just a bit as she stared at her son's picture, and Dylan's heart ached for her. She'd seen that exact posture on mothers sitting in the waiting room when she'd enter to give them bad news. They seemed to collapse into themselves as if the words they anticipated would cause them physical injury. And in a way they did.

"He died the summer after that picture was taken," Ruth said, slowly turning back around. She took a long drink of her tea and set the glass back on the table. She looked at Harriett, who nodded for her to continue. "He'd been riding his bike into town to visit some friends. When he wasn't back by dinner time, I knew something was wrong. Harold, my husband, and I drove the roads he'd usually take, since he wasn't allowed on the main highway. Not with all those trucks flying by. We drove slowly, looking for any sign of him or his bike."

There was another long pause and Harriett laid her hand over Ruth's where it lay on the table. The other woman blinked a few times, then continued. "We found the bike on the side of the road above the rocky and steep embankment of the stream. Nathan was about a hundred feet down stream."

Dylan fought back her own tears at the story, forcing her

emotions into that box in her mind where she hid them whenever listening to a patient or their family give details about the trauma. Later, when the emergency was over, the patient treated as best she could and she was alone, she'd pull those emotions out to examine and sometimes give into them.

"He was alive. Harold slid down the embankment to get to him. We don't know why he was off the bike, but his leg was twisted under him, and he had bruises all over his body."

Fractured femur? Bruises from the fall. Possible internal bleeding.

"Harold managed to get him back up to me and ran to bring the car closer. I held him, listening to his labored breathing and praying that we'd found him in time. I wanted to take him to Doctor Ray, but Harold said he needed more attention than the doctor's clinic had available, so we drove down to the bigger hospital in Newark. A good hour's drive on the roads back then.

"When we got there, they whisked him into the emergency room, his breathing sounding raspy."

Broken ribs. Punctured lung. Possible fat embolism from the fractured leg.

"It seemed like they worked at warp speed. Then everything and everyone slowed down. The doctor in charge of everything shook his head and said something about calling it."

Time of death.

"And then Harold and I had to say goodbye to our son."

Dylan managed to control her anger at Harriett through the remainder of the visit, even accepting a loaf of the delicious bread from Ruth to take home. She waited until they were off the Johnson's property.

"I don't know how many more people you have arranged to tell me their stories, but you don't need to take me to see anyone else, Harriett," she said, trying to sound firm without giving into her anger at having been manipulated by the nurse, possible spy.

"Figured you'd get the message."

Dylan shot her a narrow-eyed look. "I didn't get through med school, residency and a fellowship by being stupid."

"Didn't say you were," Harriet answered as she maneuvered the jeep onto the road back to town.

"But I also don't like being manipulated. You didn't just take me to those homes to watch you do health checks. You pre-arranged for them to tell me the stories you knew would affect me. Twist my emotions. Play on my empathy."

"I didn't pre-arrange anything. Their histories are with them every day. I knew they would talk about them with you. And you needed to put some faces to the needs of Westen. Take it out of the abstract. The town's addressed the problem of a facility. Now they need trained people to make it work."

"Yes, they do. I know the hospital board, Mayor Landon and Doctor Preston have been interviewing surgeons from some very prestigious schools."

"True. But you have unique skills, training and something extra."

"What are you talking about?"

"You have a connection here. A bond. Family." Harriett pulled up outside Bobby and Gage's home.

Dylan looked from her to the house and back. "Did my sister put you up to this?"

"No. She doesn't know anything about it."

"Then why are you dropping me off here?"

"Because you need to see her."

Dylan waited for more information. Was something wrong with Bobby? Her baby?

Nothing came.

In complete exasperation, she climbed out of the jeep, slung her bag over her shoulder, held onto the top of the vehicle and leaned inside. "You could drive someone to drink."

An enigmatic smile was her only response.

"Arg!" Whirling, she stomped up the driveway and around the house to the backdoor. She was still grumbling under her breath when she walked into the kitchen and was hit in her knees by the full force of her nephew Luke running to her.

"Aunt Diwwon!" he said, hugging her tight. And all her frustration at the annoying nurse dissipated.

She dropped her bag on the kitchen counter and scooped him up into a fierce hug and bussed him with a noisy kiss to his neck, causing him to giggle.

"He's been asking for you ever since we walked in the door this afternoon," Bobby said, standing at the stove stirring what smelled like spaghetti sauce in a big pot. "I tired to call you to invite you over for supper. What have you been up to?"

Switching her nephew onto her hip, she wandered over to see what was in the pot and got hit with a hard whiff of tomatoes and garlic. "Spaghetti and meatballs?"

"I had a craving for Mama's sauce."

Dylan studied her oldest sister. "You look a little tired. Why don't you take Luke and let me finish making dinner?"

At first, she thought Bobby was going to protest and go all motherly on her, but then she acquiesced, traded her spoon for her son, and pulled out a chair at the table. She scooted a coloring book and the box of big crayons over for him to scribble some art for her.

"Did you make the meatballs, too?" Dylan asked, stirring the pot to be sure nothing was sticking to the bottom.

"No, I picked up a bag of them from Martelli's on our way home from visiting Chloe and the baby this morning."

"I got's a baby cousin," Luke announced from his seat on his mother's rather full lap. How she could manage him with the thirty-six week baby inside her was a miracle to Dylan.

She checked the large pot on the other burner to find it boiling. "Did you already salt this?"

"Of course. The spaghetti is right there on the counter. Add all of it," Bobby said, nodding at the extra-large bag of pasta.

"All of it? That's a lot of spaghetti for just three adults and one little boy," she said, already following her oldest sister's instructions to drop the entire package of pasta into the water. She'd learned long ago not to argue with her as she always had a reason for doing things a certain way.

"I made extra to freeze for leftovers as baked spaghetti and meatballs."

"With melted American cheese on top?" One of her favorites from when they were kids. Bobby never wasted anything and created ways to make leftovers taste just a little different.

"Of course. I'm trying to stock up on meals we can pop into the oven the first few weeks I'm home. But there are going to be four adults for dinner, not three."

Just as she turned to question her, the backdoor opened and in walked Gage and Callahan. Sean smiled at her and she went warm knowing that seeing her gave him as much pleasure as it did her. Bobby wiggled out of her chair and headed to the dish cupboard, feigning innocence on Sean's presence in the room. Dylan knew she should be angry at her sister for playing matchmaker when her own life plans were so up in the air, but his company wasn't unwelcome. In fact, he made her feel very wanted.

"Daddy!" Luke ran to his father who scooped him up into a big bear hug.

"Hello, little man. Have you been a good boy for your mama today?"

"Yeah. I wearin' my dinosaurs," he said, holding out the bottom of his shirt to show his father.

"I can see that. Can you say hi to Mr. Callahan?" Gage said, turning so Luke could see who he was talking about.

"Hi," he said, then hid his face in his father's neck.

Dylan laughed, then turned back to the food on the stove.

"I brought garlic bread from the bakery," Sean said, coming up beside her.

"Not wine?" she asked with a grin.

"Yeah, didn't think it would be a great idea to drink wine at the sheriff's house then drive home."

"No need to worry about that. I'd just breathalyze you before you left," Gage said, setting his son on the floor, then going to lock his weapon in the gun safe in the top of the pantry.

"Yeah, right." Sean chuckled, laying the box from the bakery on the counter.

Dylan leaned in closer to him and whispered, "He's not kidding. There's one in the pantry with his gun."

Sean looked at Luke. "That poor little guy's gonna have a sucky adolescence."

"No, he's not. He's going to have a safe one, because he has two parents who will be sure it is." Bobby reached to get plates out of the cupboard.

"Let me get those," Gage said as he returned to take the plates out of his wife's hands. "You need to get off your feet."

"Seriously? I'm not a fragile flower." Bobby pouted as she walked back to the table. "Tell him, Dylan."

"I'm not getting in the middle of this." Dylan went back to finishing the sauce with a cup of Parmesan cheese, then handed the container to Sean. "Can you put this on the table, please? And try to stay away from the combatants over there."

He took it and leaned close to whisper. "I'll try, but frankly your pregnant sister scares me more than he does."

"I grew up with her. You're right to be nervous," she whispered back.

"Is the pasta ready, Dylan?" Bobby asked from her seat at the table.

"That's my cue to pay attention," she said to Sean with a wink.

Dinner proceeded with good natured ribbing of Gage going from undercover cop who rode a motorcycle to the soon-to-be-father of two and the possible need for a minivan. Then they switched over to Chloe, Wes and their baby. They also discussed the upcoming weekend's festivities and plans.

"And what plans do you have for Harriett? Up on the courthouse watching with a sniper rifle in her lap?" Dylan asked before she slipped a spoonful of peach cobbler Bobby bought from the Peaches 'N Cream Café between her lips.

Sean choked back laughter while Gage seemed to pause with his spoon halfway to his mouth as if actually considering the idea.

Bobby, feeding Luke from her dessert, shot him an incredulous look. "You aren't seriously thinking of doing that, are you?"

Gage shrugged and ate his last spoonful of dessert before sitting back in his chair. "Your sister might have a good idea. We could post her up on the top of the hospital. I'm sure she's had sniper training."

"Gage! You don't know that." Bobby stared at her husband.

"You didn't see her shoot Wes in the backside four years ago. Perfect through-and-through. An inch to the center and she'd have shattered a bone. Too far inside he could've bled out from the femoral artery. It was a perfect shot on a moving target."

"She probably has her own Gilley suit," Callahan said.

Gage nodded. "Wouldn't doubt it."

"You spent the day with her today," Bobby said to Dylan as she cleaned Luke's face and hands. "What did you do?"

"Besides the fact she'd arranged her country rounds to

patients who had some sort of traumatic accident so I could put faces to reasons I should move my practice here?"

"She didn't!" Bobby said, and the look on her face confirmed Dylan's belief that her sister hadn't put the other woman up to it.

Dylan nodded.

"Harriett is very protective of Westen and everyone living in it. She probably sees you as an asset we need in our town," Gage said.

"An asset?" Dylan asked, narrowing her eyes at Gage.

"You know what I meant. Someone who would add to the overall community." He nodded towards Bobby. "You know your sister and I would love for you to move here but only if you think it's what's best for your life."

"Good. I hate being thought of as someone to be used. An asset sounds like…"

"Spook talk," Sean finished for her.

"That!" She pointed her spoon at him. "Is it true she used to work for the CIA?"

She looked from him to Bobby to Gage. Each one of them just gave her a shrug.

"No one knows," Bobby said.

"No one's done a background check on this woman?" she asked Gage.

Again, he shrugged. "I asked Dad about her after she'd been in town a few years. He said sometimes people come to Westen to get away from their pasts and we should respect their privacy."

She switched her attention to Sean.

"Hey," he said, holding up his hands. "The woman is scary. I'm not interested in having her pull some dark ops maneuver on me in the dead of night."

Nervous laughter came from all of them, as if what he said might have a possibility of occurring.

"You know," Dylan said after a few moments, "this town really is filled with some interesting characters with mysterious pasts, like Harriett."

"Like our brother-in-law, Wes," Bobby said with a nod. "I have to say, I'm glad he's let us know some of his secrets, but I suspect there's still things he'll never share, even with Chloe."

"Somethings don't need to be examined," her husband said.

Dylan knew some of Gage's own history as an undercover narcotic agent and how his first wife nearly got him killed by blowing his cover. A shiver ran over her. That same ex-wife tried to kill her in a sick psychotic attempt to get revenge on Bobby and Gage right before their wedding.

Sean's warm hand landed on her arm. "You okay?"

She blinked and gave him a little reassuring smile, and he slipped his hand back off hers. "Yeah, just thinking of someone else who hid their past in town."

"Moira," Bobby said, making a disgusting face. And Gage scooted closer to put his arm around her shoulders.

"While I have to admit not everyone who shows up in Westen is harmless, I mean we let Callahan stay," he said, and they all laughed.

"After your last newspaper owner, you're lucky to have me," Sean said in his own defense and Dylan grinned.

"But," Gage continued, "if someone doesn't want us digging into their lives because we're just being nosey, I say they have the right to that privacy."

"And if they have dangerous or nefarious reasons for being in town like that waitress who ended up being a stalker of Wes's that nearly killed him and Chloe?" Dylan asked.

Gage shrugged. "Well, then all bets are off."

"So, who would you say are the harmless people with secrets?" she asked.

"Earl," Bobby answered, and Gage nodded.

"He's been here as long as I can remember. Dad tried to do some preliminary background on him when he first arrived, and Doc Ray assured him the old guy's memory loss was real but had no luck learning anything."

"Have you tried DNA testing?" Sean asked.

"Considered it, but this is his home now. As far as I know he has no other family but the people of Westen."

"And he's a harmless sweetheart," Bobby said with a tender smile.

"You just love him because he calls you Mrs. Sheriff," her husband teased.

"Well, yes, and he helped save Chloe and Wes."

"He did?" Dylan asked.

"Sure did," Sean said. "Seems he was out before dawn that morning and noticed the new waitress dressed in white snow gear similar to what he'd been trained to wear in the Army, and she was carrying a bag made for sniper rifles. Went over to your brother-in-law's office early that morning and told Gage all about it."

"Bout the same time, Harriett called to let us know she'd heard shots out at Wes' place," Gage said, taking up the story. "So, we headed out there in time to help stop his stalker from completing her mission."

"Wait." Dylan held up her hand. "This happened the day after the blizzard happened, right?"

"You know it did," her sister answered.

"Then what was Harriett doing out there to hear the shots?"

"She lives just up the road from Wes and Chloe's cabin and deeper in the woods."

Dylan flopped against the back of her chair. "Well, that's just great!"

"What?" Bobby asked, exchanging a confused look with her husband.

"I'm staying out in a cabin with an elderly sprite of a woman who's possibly a spy with sniper skills, and no one warned me?"

"Surprise."

Gage ducked as Dylan tossed a slice of garlic bread at his head.

CHAPTER 12

The last of the clients left and Twylla locked the front door behind them, flipped the sign on the Dye Right's front door to closed and turned off the lights in the front of the shop. Behind her, Molly and Darcy chatted along as they cleaned the hair washing stations.

Each stylist was required to keep their regular stations clean and organized, but the extra jobs—washing towels and client smocks; washing and sanitizing scissors, combs, brushes, curlers; and organizing the color and curl room where all the chemicals were stored—she assigned those jobs on a rotation basis, along with working the early morning or late evening shifts. When she first opened the salon, she learned very quickly that being the boss and treating all her people equally kept squabbles to a minimum.

The only area her stylists didn't have to keep clean was the foyer and scheduling desk. Those were her domain to maintain. As she straightened the magazines and cleaned up the waiting area, she looked around it with pride. She'd wanted to introduce something chic and inviting for her clients, the women in her town. Something to make them feel special and pampered when they came to get their hair done, like she'd felt in some of the salons she'd gone to in New York.

The first thing she'd done was choose the pale pink, black and white color palate for the walls, the floor, the furniture and the décor. The black and white photos of the Eiffel Tower, the Arc de Triumph and Louvre were all framed with pale pink matt boards and thin black frames. There were also images of models in nineteen-fifties fashion salons and outdoor French cafés.

Next, she considered what else might make her clients feel pampered. Beverages and something to snack on while they were having their hair or nails done. So, she'd approached Willie Mae at the Yeast & West Bakery to provide pastries—at first just simple cookies, but then Willie Mae tried her hand at madeleines, miniature croissants and even macarons—on a daily basis and installed a cold beverage refrigerator. When specialty coffees like espressos and lattes became more popular, she'd invested in a high-quality machine to provide those for her patrons.

Four years ago, she'd expanded back in the shop to open more stylists and stations for the influx of families to Westen and the surrounding area. She and Molly set up a website and social media accounts for the salon, with strict instructions to keep her photo off all of them, and the salon had become a destination for not only the town's residence and regular customers, but for tourists in the area.

Now she had the opportunity to expand into the space next door that had been vacated by the old craft consignment store that moved into a new building on the other side of the downtown business area resembling an early American mercantile, but full of crafts and specialty food items by the town's local artisans.

She sat down at the desk and opened the paper scheduling book and the computer screen for the electronic schedule for tomorrow. Molly teased her about her choice of using paper in a digital world. She didn't mind. A long time ago she'd learned to be careful in what and whom she placed her trust.

Inhaling, she paused as the memory of how she'd learned that lesson invaded her thoughts.

Myles.

"You have a very sexy voice."

Startled, she looked into the dressing room mirror to see a ruggedly handsome man standing between her and the closed door of the tiny dressing room she shared with another understudy. Taking a breath to calm her sudden nervousness like she did before stepping out on the stage, she slowly turned to face him.

"Why thank you," she said without demanding how he'd gotten into the room and who did he think he was to feel free to do so. She could tell by the cut of his suit, the Italian loafers and the expensive watch on his arm, he was a man who routinely did what he wanted.

"I'd like to take you to dinner," he said, moving closer.

A shiver of wariness skittered over her. She'd had a few followers approach her, mostly semi-drunk college boys or wannabe actors looking for a hook-up that might promote their own careers, but never someone who exuded confidence, maturity and success. It thrilled and scared her.

"I don't even know your name."

He moved closer and held out his hand. "Myles Compton."

"I'm Meredith Clarke," she said, using her new stage name. She slipped her hand into his and was surprised that instead of a handshake, he lifted her hand to his lips and kissed the back of it.

"I hope you'll join me for dinner, Meredith, as a thank you."

"A thank you?"

"Yes, for allowing me to sit in the theater and listen to you sing tonight. It's as if you were singing just to me." The sincerity in his eyes, the charm of his words and the warmth of his hand, still holding hers convinced her there was no harm in one dinner.

What a fatal mistake that had been. His charm continued for the first year, and his words slowly convinced her to change. First, she changed her dreams. They'd gone from singing on the stage to singing just for him and the occasional dinner party for his friends and clients. Then he'd convinced her to stop contacting anyone from the theater, all her friends. She'd also given up calling Mama to keep him from finding out that Meredith wasn't her real name—subconsciously she'd known hiding her real name from him was an escape when she'd need it.

After she'd been living with him for a year, those warm hands that made her feel safe turned into slaps for saying the wrong thing to him. After the first time, he'd quickly apologized and explained it was just a reflex reaction to her sassing him. Instead of storming out and never talking to him again, she'd felt guilty for making him hit her and quickly promised not to do it again.

The slaps turned to fisted punches to the abdomen, arms or legs. Those punches turned to kicks in the same spots. Then her face became a punching bag and his fingers left bruise marks around her neck. Bruises he made when he choked her while raping her.

A shudder of fear ran through her, her skin tingling as if she sensed someone watching her. She'd lived with that feeling for the months she'd been on the run from Myles that first year, certain that any moment he'd find her. It had taken coming home to Westen to shake that feeling, and months for her to finally feel safe.

Scanning the street outside—only moonlight and the streetlight allowing her to see into the shadows, nothing moved.

"Twylla?"

She jumped, clutched her right hand over her heart, and

turned to see Molly standing behind her. "Oh! I didn't know you were there."

Molly gave a little nervous laugh. "I'm sorry. You didn't answer me when I called you from the back door. Darcy and I are finished and ready to go."

The rules were that once the last client left, the salon's front and back doors were kept locked. When her employees finished their cleaning duties for the night, they waited at the backdoor for her to let them out and lock the door again.

She took a steadying breath and gave her a reassuring smile. "It's all right. I got caught up in a little wool gathering and didn't hear you. Let me get my things, and I think I'll leave, early, too."

Usually, she collected the receipts and cash from the drawers and spent time tallying it up after everyone had left, locking the money into the safe in her office to be deposited during the next day's business hours, but tonight she didn't want to be walking out into the night alone. She hurried into her office, locked everything up to deal with tomorrow, and met the girls at the backdoor.

"Thanks for waiting," she said as she let them out, set the alarm code, then relocked the door behind them.

"We don't mind," Darcy said as they walked to their cars all parked in the small lot beside the salon. "Tomorrow's going to be such a big day, we all need to get our beauty sleep early tonight."

The Dye Right was offering free manicures with any cut, color or perm, so they expected extra traffic in the shop for the next three days.

They both gave her a little hug before climbing into their cars. Movement in the alley behind the lot caught her attention, but she relaxed when she saw the white hair above the Navy pea-coat of the man wearing it.

"Hello, Earl. Making your rounds?" she called, holding her

car door open and dropping her purse inside to the passenger seat floor.

"Yes, Miz Twylla. Just heading down to the bridge to check on some friends."

"Not staying in town tonight?" she asked as he stopped on the sidewalk beside her.

He shook his head. "Not tonight. Gonna be in town all weekend, watching things and helping with cleanup. Lots of excitement and lots of people, you know."

"I do. And we all appreciate your help in keeping Westen so beautiful. We all want to put our best foot forward for our guests, don't we?"

"That we do," he said, nodding, his body trembling a bit.

She laid her hand on his arm, which always seemed to steady him. "Why don't you stop by early tomorrow and let me give you a little trim then?"

He grinned and tugged at a lock of his white hair that touched his collar. "Might just do that. Don't suppose I could get a shave, too?"

Smiling, she patted his arm. "Of course. I'll be in by seven, just knock on the back door, okay?"

"Will do. Might go to the Peaches 'N Cream after and make old Pete jealous at my new look."

She laughed and climbed into her car. He stepped back and waited, not moving until she'd pulled out and waved at him in her rearview mirror. Odd how she'd been anxious for some reason tonight, but knowing this old man was watching her until he knew she was on her way, not only calmed her but made her feel safe. That's how all of Westen made her feel. Safe.

∼

He stood in the shadows, watching her leave with the other women. She was just as beautiful today as she was the day he'd met her. Leaving Myles not only saved her life, it had given her a chance to thrive.

After she cleared the block and the older man she'd taken the time to talk with wandered off the opposite direction of the salon, he slowly walked back to the front and studied the business Meredith owned—no her name wasn't Meredith, it was Twylla Howard. He'd learned that from the real estate lady he'd tracked the original picture to. He stepped close to the window and read the fancy script etched in the window.

The Dye Right.

He lifted his lips in a little smile and shook his head at her play on words. Meri, Twylla—how was he ever going to think of her with that name—always had a wry sense of humor.

The insides were very chic. Lots of images of Paris and fashion. She'd also always had good taste, except in men. Myles nearly destroyed her, and he? He'd failed to protect her.

But not this time.

This time, when Myles came to attack her—he was like a predator on the scent of his prey now, so he wouldn't give up the chase—he'd do whatever it took to keep her and the life she created here safe. No matter what.

CHAPTER 13

"You know, tonight was the perfect time for you to ask your brother-in-law about Twylla," Sean said as they walked into the cabin, Wöden at their heels once more. This time he'd planned ahead and brought his backpack with a change of clothes and his laptop, which he set beside the front door. "He did bring up the whole topic about how many people came to Westen and hid their past."

"I know," Dylan said, dropping her bag on the kitchen counter and sounding hesitant as she slipped out of her jacket. "Where Wes and Earl came to town from lives in other places, Twylla left and came back. For some reason, it feels wrong for me to delve into her reason why with him."

"Because it feels like gossip?" he asked as he turned the deadbolt lock and hung both their coats on the peg next to the door.

"Yes!" She grabbed a bottle of red wine from the counter and two wine glasses, then led him over to the couch. "Whatever occurred while she was gone, she came home to Western where she feels safe. She hasn't shared what happened to her during those years. Well, not with anyone we know, because Lorna would've found out long ago. So, quizzing Gage about her, seems a violation of her privacy."

"Gossip," he said, and she nodded.

Sinking onto the leather sofa, he stretched out his legs as she poured them each a glass of wine. She handed him one glass and sat with hers right beside him like the night before. He draped one arm over the couch behind her. This he could get very used to.

"After my parents died," she said after taking a long drink of the wine, "Bobby had to deal with a lot of people who stopped by with food and advice. Friends of our parents from the neighborhood where we lived, some parents from our school and a few from church we sometimes attended. She tolerated it for a while, believing them to all be well-meaning and caring people."

"What happened?" he asked, suspecting those people were far from well-meaning or caring.

"Bobby took us to a baby shower for one of the ladies in the neighborhood. We arrived a little late. The women were all on the back deck and didn't hear us slip out through the sliding glass doors. Bobby went completely still when we heard them talking about us. They were saying how Bobby was in way over her head and we'd be better off in foster care than with a barely-out-of-her-teens sister trying to raise us on her own."

"Damn. What did Bobby do?"

"Well, I thought she was going to go punch someone, and if Chloe had her way, she would've. Instead, Bobby didn't act like a barely-out-of-her-teens girl. She politely stepped in front of them and said something about she might be young, but she'd learned from her mother that you don't talk about other people's problems behind their back, especially when you say different things to their face. She also told them that she was quite capable of raising her younger sisters, and she no longer required any of their help. Then we turned our backs on them and marched out, Bobby telling us to keep our heads held high all the way to her car."

"Wow." He'd always admired how Bobby could smoothly handle not only her alpha-male husband, but diffuse tension that often occurred in the job of a law-officer.

"I know. She was awe-inspiring. She also used their gossipy nosiness to propel her into making decisions she'd been putting off."

"Such as?"

"Selling our family home, for one."

"Was that a wise idea? You and Chloe had just lost your parents."

"That was her reasoning for keeping us in it for a year. But even though my parents had insurance that paid the mortgage off if one of them died, the maintenance and utilities for that house were stretching the budget of her income. But since the house was left to all three of us in the will, she sat us down and had a long talk with us about what keeping it would cost us in the long run. We made the decision together to sell it, however she handled the proceeds alone. She took one third and put in a savings account for living expenses and extras expenditures like vacations so we wouldn't do without those, while decreasing the budget by moving us into a three-bedroom apartment with cheaper utilities. The other two-thirds she invested and used the proceeds to pay for college for Chloe and me."

"Smart sister."

Dylan smiled, the love and admiration for her oldest sister shining in her eyes. "Yes, she is."

"To Bobby," he said, holding his glass out to her for a toast.

"To Bobby." She clinked her glass with his, then snuggled back into his side.

They sat that way, drinking their wine in quiet companionship.

"Speaking of people who came to Westen for a new start, why exactly did you come here?" she asked after a few moments.

"Trust me, it's nothing as exciting as being a former dark ops specialist like Wes."

"Thank goodness," she said with a little shudder of a breath, and he could've kicked himself, knowing he'd just reminded her of Bulldog's death. "But something happened in New York, didn't it?"

Thank God she asked a question and moved past the awkward moment.

"Yeah. I had a disagreement with my boss."

"About what?"

"She wanted me to bury an article I'd been working on for months."

"What were you working on and why did she want you to bury it?"

He inhaled slowly, then took another drink of his wine before opening that particular can of worms. "I'd been given a tip about a construction firm using faulty materials to build an apartment complex in an area being revitalized. They weren't up to code."

She leaned back to give him a puzzled look. "How is that legal?"

"It isn't, but the city inspector and his boss were willing to look the other way for significant kickbacks."

"That's terrible."

"Gets even worse. The city council member for this particular district was also taking money and that's where I ran into the problem with my editor. Seems the two of them went to school together and at one time were heavily involved."

"They dated?"

He nodded. "So, she wanted the story buried so deep it would never find the light of day."

"You told her no."

"I did. She refused to print it."

"So, you went somewhere else with it?"

"I tried. But the editor and her boss had deep ties to most of the other papers in the city. And the ones they didn't have ties to, didn't want to piss them off, so no one would run with the story. And because I refused to roll over and play good little servant, they fired me."

"And they made it so no one would hire you," she said.

"Yep." The anger about that still stuck in his gut like fire. He'd never been fired from a job in his life and certainly not for trying to do the right thing, telling the truth.

"That's when you read about the newspaper in Westen being up for sale."

He smiled down at her. "Who's telling this story?"

She grinned back and shrugged. "I'm good at figuring out plots."

"Remind me never to watch a mystery with you then." He pulled her close for a little hug before continuing. "Despite their efforts to silence me and kill the story, I wasn't leaving town with my tail between my legs."

"What did you do?"

"Luckily, we live in the electronic age. I got in touch with some bloggers, both conservative and liberal. Anyone with a desire and passion to uncover the truth and sent them the entire story on the day I drove the moving truck out of town."

"How many ran it?"

"All of them." He couldn't help chuckling. "The shit storm was spectacular."

"You enjoyed every minute of it."

He grew serious. "Damn right I did. I went into journalism

because I believed the world needs to hear the news. The everyday people deserve to hear the truth about things going on in their world and things people are trying to hide for them. No matter which political party is behind the backdoor dealings, the truth needs to be told. That's the job of the fourth estate."

"You certainly didn't change your beliefs when you came to Westen," she said, then sipping on her wine.

"No, I didn't. The first story I needed to write was about the meth lab explosion and how the sheriff's department was behind the eight-ball on what was going on. Let's just say the town council wasn't happy with that first article, but your brother-in-law actually stood up for me."

"I know."

He cast her a surprised look. "You do?"

"Yep. I think that was the first time I heard Bobby angry with Gage. And with you. She didn't think you should come into town and immediately start casting the department in a bad light, but he took your side."

"He did?"

She nodded. "He said you were just doing your job and you were right. After his father died, he said he'd just been holding the position until the next election with every intent of leaving town ASAP. He said he hadn't been looking for any drug trouble like he'd seen in the big city of Columbus. The laid-back slower pace of his hometown lulled him into forgetting that evil can happen anywhere."

"So, he convinced her to forgive me then?"

"Nope. She was in love and your article felt like an attack of her man, who almost died stopping the crazed drug-manufacturing murderer. Your second article about the near catastrophe cooled her anger, especially when you high-lighted Gage's crazy ex's involvement with the state DEA and how they put the town at risk hiding the facts from Gage."

"That explains a lot," he said with a half-chuckle.

She leaned her head back against his arm to give him a puzzled look. "What?"

"The day after I published that first article, you sister walked into the office with fire in her eyes and that stern look she gives people when she's not pleased with them."

"Her teacher look."

"Yes. That one. Thought I was in major trouble."

She laughed. "Oh, trust me, you were. I'd always been in trouble when Bobby directed that look at me, usually with Chloe."

"Imagine my surprise when she pulled up a chair and slapped a big thick file on my desk, asking me if I really wanted to help the town and get to the conspiracy behind the DEA and the state prosecutor's office to keep the Westen sheriff's department in the dark about what they knew about the meth lab and distribution of the drug locally, I should read it."

"That's Bobby."

"She got me on the path and with the information she provided I was able to write the article that was published throughout the state, and then nationally."

"It was a magnificent piece."

"You read it?" he asked, a little surprised that she'd remember it or had time to read it while in med school.

"Of course. Bobby sent me the link. It was quite an exposé. It's what lit a fire under the collective butts of administrators in both the state government and DEA to pour millions of dollars into the revitalization of Westen and the surrounding area as an atonement for their part in the disaster, wasn't it?"

Heat filled his face at her praise of his work, and he was glad the dim lights kept her from seeing it. A grown man wasn't supposed to blush. "It did help Gage and the town council in their case."

"Oh, I think it did more than just help. The facts you unearthed pointed a direct finger at their secretive handling of the case by one of their agents and one of their assistant attorneys. That resulted in keeping the local police in the dark, giving opportunity for the drug manufacturing to continue and putting the whole town at risk by the volatile nature of meth cooking. It was a very detailed and truthful article."

"Thank you." He liked that she understood that the truth was his ultimate goal when he hit publish on the computer.

"So, you're the reason for all this growth and change in Westen," she teased.

He gave her a rueful chuckle. "Don't say that around any of the old-timers or they'll run me out of town. They're just now beginning to adjust to all the changes."

"Well, I still think you writing an honest article about the sheriff's office failure that pissed off my sister and the second very objective article about the actions of the state officials did what good journalism is supposed to do, at least in my opinion," she said leaning back against his shoulder again.

"And what is that?" he asked, hoping it sounded close to his beliefs.

"I learned in school the press was supposed to be the fourth estate, not a part of government, but to shine a light onto what the three branches are doing for the people to see and thereby hold them accountable."

He hugged her closer. "Yep. That's our job, no matter who is in power."

"I could get used to this," Dylan said, mirroring his own previous thoughts.

"Used to what?" he asked, drinking down the last of the wine in his glass, wishing it was something stronger, like Scotch to steady his sudden nervous tension.

"Relaxing in the evening, with a drink, good conversation..." She paused.

He set his glass on the side table and waited, hoping to hear more.

"...with someone whose company you enjoy."

"A friend." He couldn't help how deflated that sounded, but he was real tired of being in the friend zone with her.

"Well, yes, that." She shifted so she was staring into his eyes. "A friend and something...more."

"More?" Damn, he knew he sounded like an idiot, but he wanted to be completely sure what she was saying.

Stretching across him, her body touching him in ways that sent heat straight to his groin as she set her wine glass next to his. Slowly she sat back, her gaze never leaving his face as she cupped it with her hand. "Sean, I don't know what my future is yet, but I do know that right now, here with you, I'm happy."

She emphasized her words with a soft, tender kiss.

He wrapped his arms around her and pulled her over into his lap, deepening the kiss. She parted her lips with a little moan, and he slipped his tongue inside to dance with hers. He'd wanted this for so long, he tempered his need, afraid it would scare her and the last thing he wanted was for her to reconsider her need for him.

Holding her with one arm, he stroked the other hand down her side to her hip, then back up over her ribs, firmly working the muscles of her back and eliciting another one of those delicious moans from her. She adjusted her position, pressing her breasts into his chest, forcing a groan of pleasure from him. He wanted more from her, but also knew he had no protection with him. The last thing he wanted to do was possibly make her pregnant when she was so unsure of her next step, career-wise.

Slowly, he eased his hold on her and the intensity of their

kisses, but kept stroking his hands over her body, because it felt so good to finally be touching her as a lover.

She blinked as their lips parted and rested her hand against his cheek, then slid it down his neck and to the collar of his shirt. "Why are you stopping?" she asked, and the huskiness in her voice almost made him rethink his decision, his honor be damned.

"Because this is Wes and Chloe's house," he said, dodging his real reason.

"And they aren't here." She stared at him and passion still filled those dark brown eyes. "Don't tell me you're afraid of my brother-in-law?"

He chuckled. "I joined the army out of high school and did two tours in Iraq. I know how to handle myself in a fight or with a weapon, but I'm not sure I want to go up against a guy with years of dark ops training." He paused and pushed a stray lock of her golden hair off her face. "Although you might just be worth it."

The heat filled her eyes again and she leaned in to kiss him, long and slow, then pulled back. "I think that's the nicest thing any man has ever said to me." Then she slid off his lap to sit beside him once again. "I'm not buying that you're afraid of him."

"You're right," he confessed. "The reason I stopped is, as much as I want to take you to bed and make love to you, and believe me I've wanted to do that for a very long time, the truth is, I don't have any protection with me."

"Damn Callahan," she said. "You're honest, noble and chivalrous."

"Don't make me sound like some goody-two-shoes hero. Trust me, I'm not one." To prove his point, he slid his hand into her hair and pulled her around for a hard, thorough kiss to prove just how powerful his desire for her was. Then he released her and delighted in the puffiness of her lips and the increase in her breathing. "You'd better go to bed before I regret being so chivalrous."

She sat back, smoothed her hands over her hair and licked her lips. For a moment, he thought she was going to press the issue and he didn't think he could stand a third assault on his defenses. Instead, she gave him a smile, stood slowly and arched her back in a sexy stretch. "If you're sure..."

"Dylan," he said in a warning not to test him.

She laughed and turned, heading to her room, with a very sexy sway of her hips. Then she paused at the bedroom door. "I'll be in here. You know, if you need me."

He waited until she'd gone in the room before adjusting the large bulge in his pants, then stretching out on the couch. Wöden came over and laid down near the fireplace with a decided "hurrumph" sound.

"Oh, shut up. I know I just did the stupidest thing a man can do."

CHAPTER 14

Twylla pulled the door tight behind her and turned the deadbolt. When she first bought the house nearly twenty years ago, she'd asked Joe Hillis' father, owner of the Knobs & Knockers hardware store back then to install the lock.

"You sure you want to go to all that trouble?" the tall lanky handyman had asked as he stood on the porch. "Hardly anyone in Westen locks their regular locks, much less need one of these fancier ones. Things are safer here."

It wasn't the things in Westen that had her scared. It's what might follow her home. "I've been living in the city so long, Mr. Hillis that I'm just used to having one."

"Well, it's your house. A person should feel safe in their own home."

And she had. Oh, it took her a few years to finally realize that the monster hadn't found her, that she'd managed to get to Westen without him stalking her. The fact that she was still breathing and above ground all these years later was proof of that.

As the Dye Right became more lucrative, even a destination hub for the women and occasional male client, she began to relax. With her friends—Lorna, Harriett, Maggie, Sylvie and now the Roberts sisters—as well as her faithful customers, she'd made a comfortable life. Although when the newspaper changed hands after the Meth lab explosion, she'd been scared her whereabouts would be exposed. Luckily, the new owner, Sean Callahan, had accepted her request not to post her picture in the paper or on any social media promoting Westen. Again, she'd relaxed.

So the odd feeling of being watched today at the shop was unsettling. All the way home, she couldn't shake it. The fear also brought back the memories.

Dropping her bag on the kitchen counter, she walked over to the cupboard and pulled out a crystal tumbler and the bottle of whisky she kept for nights such as this. She filled the glass with ice, then poured it half-full of the golden liquid as she kicked off her shoes. What she'd give to work in more comfortable shoes like her stylists, but she was the owner and face of the shop. If she wanted to give her clients the feeling of being spoiled and fashionable, then she needed to provide high-end care and be an example of classic style. But dang, those heels made her feet ache by the end of the day.

She took a long slow drink and set the tumbler on the counter again. Standing on her tip toes, she reached into the top of the cupboard and pulled out the square box she'd kept there since the day she moved in, only bringing it out once a year to see the contents. Covered in handmade paper with bits of flower petals pressed in the paper, the entire thing seemed as delicate as the memories inside. Carrying it and her drink to the living room, she curled onto the corner of the couch.

Taking another long drink of the whisky, she stared at the small box on her lap. Whenever she looked inside her heart hurt, but a little less each time. Caroline had been right all those year ago when she told her that time would dull the pain.

She set her drink on the side table and pulled the strings of the satin ribbon holding the two flaps of the top closed. With shaky fingers she opened them to see the delicate little shirt embroidered with tiny wildflowers lying on top. Lifting it out she held it to her nose and inhaled, the scent of lavender still lingering in the material. She laid it beside her on the sofa and reached for the small, framed snapshot, tracing her fingers over the image of the little baby. He'd been born six weeks early, underweight due to her months of hiding from Myles and malnutrition. Barely three pounds.

Placing it on the shirt, she let her hand rest over them both, remembering what it had been like to hold him for that brief amount of time, the softness of his skin, how tiny his fingers and toes were, the small tufts of hair on his head. It didn't physically hurt anymore to remember those things, but the sadness still lingered.

The next thing in the box was a plaster cast of two tiny perfect feet. She picked it up and ran her index finger over the ridges and valleys of those feet as if she were tracing them for the first time. Beneath that casting lay the birth certificate with the date, time, weight and length of her little boy. The only thing missing was the father's name. She'd written down anonymous.

She hadn't wanted the box at first when Caroline handed it to her the day she was finally healthy enough to leave the clinic after weeks of IV therapy and emotional counseling from the doctor's kind wife.

"It's okay, Twylla. You don't have to open it now or today, not next week or next month or ever. But you should have it, just in case the day comes when you want to remember him," she said, laying one hand on her shoulder and setting the box in her hands.

"I don't think that day will ever come."

"It may not, but if it does..." Her eyes were full of the compassion

she'd counted on to get her through those horrible days after she stumbled into Westen in the dead of winter.

"Then I will be thankful to have it," she finished and gave the older woman a shaky smile, that garnered one of those special firm, yet loving hugs.

Oh, how she missed Caroline, almost daily since she and Doc Ray moved to Florida. She'd come back to Westen wanting to weep in her mother's arms, only to discover Mama had died and no one had been able to find her for notification. She literally collapsed in Doc's arms at the news only to wake up three days later in labor. Caroline stayed by her side throughout the entire ordeal and aftermath.

Carefully, she slipped the treasures of her heart back into the box on top of the sealed envelope she'd never had the courage to open. It would remain sealed until Myles Compton was buried in his grave. With a swipe of her hand, she brushed the tears that had spilled onto her cheeks away, tied up the box once more and downed the rest of her whisky. The urge to see and touch these things tonight had been so intense at the salon and grew stronger with every mile to her home.

Returning the box to its spot in the cupboard, she set her glass in the sink and double checked the deadbolt once more before turning out the lights. As she headed for bed, she wondered if perhaps she should get one of those new all home electronic alarms being offered by home builders since so many new people were moving into the area?

She went through her nightly routine of preparing for bed—removing her makeup, putting on her moisturizer, brushing her teeth, donning her favorite cotton pajamas—then sat on the side of the bed to open the bedside drawer. Reaching inside, she pulled out the nine-millimeter pistol and checked that it was armed and ready for use, then slipped it back in the drawer.

Gage's father hadn't questioned her when she asked him

about how to buy a gun for protection. She suspected Doc Ray had informed him of her condition when she came home. The sheriff had helped her with all the necessary paperwork to obtain the gun but told her if she wanted to become an accurate shot, he wasn't the person to teach her. That information had surprised her, but not nearly as much as who he chose to be her firearms training instructor.

Smiling to herself, she slipped under the handmade quilt and cool cotton sheets, then turned off the bedside lamp. Curling on her side, she hugged the pillow beside her.

When Sheriff Justice drove her out into the woods that Monday morning for her first weapons training and to meet her instructor, she'd been apprehensive, actually scared out of her mind. Not that being alone with him frightened her, he was like a protective father—the kind she'd never had, since her father left her and her mother when she was a baby. No, it was being in the woods with a stranger, one who knew more than she did about how to use a gun.

They'd driven up a gravel path in the dense forest near the river to what looked like a one-room cabin. He parked the car and gave a honk. A diminutive figure stepped out of the woods. There stood Doc Ray's nurse, Harriett, all not quite five-feet of her dressed in army fatigues and a gun belt fastened around her waist.

Twylla had looked across the front seat of the sheriff's cruiser and he gave her a nod, then explained that Harriett was going to not only teach her how to use her gun, but other ways to stay safe. Then he said he'd be back to get her at the end of the week.

Harriett had lived up to Sheriff Justice's promise and then some. Not only had she taught her how to use, fire and maintain her weapon, the nurse had taught her all kinds of ways to protect herself, including hand-to-hand combat and how to disarm someone wielding a knife, gun or other weapon. Over the years, she'd spent a weekend every few months out in those woods with Harriett, honing her skills and confidence in how to protect herself.

The eerie feeling of being watched tonight might have her on edge, but she wasn't that poor, battered and scared child she'd been when she made it back home to Westen all those years ago. No, if the monster had finally found her, she was prepared to fight back.

CHAPTER 15

The sun shone brightly in the clear blue autumn sky as Sean drove them out of the thick forest around the cabin and onto the country road that split the farms in the countryside. Once again, men and boys dressed in black trousers and white shirts dotted the horse drawn wagons piled full of hay.

"They're working early," Dylan said as they drove past.

"Makes sense," he said. "It's cooler in the morning and the afternoon sun and heat helps dry out the hay. Believe it or not, wet hay stored in the barns can cause fires."

She turned to study him as they drove along. "Really? I would think the drier hay would cause it to be more dangerous like kindling."

"I would've too before we had the arsonist setting fire to half the county nearly five years ago. Deke Reynolds and one of the volunteer firemen John Wilson explained to me that there are microorganisms naturally found in hay. Wet hay over a certain amount can stimulate activity in the microorganisms that makes the temperature rise. The farmers monitor the hay temperature in their barns because if they hay temp goes over one hundred and seventy degrees it causes some sort of chemical reaction that can shoot the temperature to over four-hundred degrees and poof! Big barn fire."

"I didn't know that. Is that what they call spontaneous combustion?"

"It's one kind. Spontaneous combustion is when fire occurs without someone applying an external heat source. Oil-soaked rags, hot piles of laundry, compost piles that aren't aerated properly, and of course the moist hay."

"Wow, who knew you were an expert on fires?" she teased.

He laughed. "I'm no expert. Just a reporter who asks lots of questions and learns from real experts like Deke and John. It's one of the things I like about being a reporter."

"You like asking questions?"

"Yes. Because questions help you learn things. Used to drive my parents crazy with all my questions as a kid. I was always curious. My brothers called me nosy," he said with a grin. "Dragged them into more trouble with my nosiness."

The sound of her laughter warmed him once again. He could spend his whole life hearing her laugh and never grow tired of it.

He turned onto the main highway into town. "What do you have planned for the day?"

"I'm to meet Bobby at the Hopscotch Boutique after lunch. She wants to pick out some clothes for our new nephew, Benjamin."

"How is Benji doing?"

She laughed. "You better check with Wes on that nickname."

He grinned as he stopped at the first light. "It's a great nickname. Especially for a baseball player. I can hear it now, *Up to bat is shortstop Benji Strong.*"

She lifted her brows at him. "Let me remind you, his father is not only an armed deputy of Westen, but can kill you in many ways and hide your body forever."

"Yeah, there is that." He pulled up in front of the newspaper office and parked in the spot reserved just for him. "That's your afternoon, how about the morning?"

"I don't know. I might go back over to the church," she said, turning to unlock her seatbelt. "I'm curious as to why Twylla was there and singing what sounded like a lullaby. Think I'll just look around a bit."

"Want some company?" he asked, his own curiosity piqued. Why was the salon owner singing a lullaby in the cemetery?

Dylan looked surprised. "Don't you have a paper to get out today? What with all the happenings in town this weekend, I'd think you'd be swamped with work."

"That's why I have a staff," he said climbing out of the driver's seat and joining her on the curb.

"You have a staff now?" she said with the mischievous tilt of her lips he always loved about her.

"Yes, I do. Town's gotten bigger and there's more news to cover. Want to meet them?" he asked taking a step towards the office.

"I think I would."

He opened the door and held it for her, the scent of cinnamon from their breakfast once again wafting toward him as she passed. She'd indulged herself in the big icing-covered rolls from the Yeast & West bakery he'd picked up the day before, sharing one with him over coffee and soda. It was the best breakfast he could remember having in his whole life. Not because the rolls were that exceptional, which they were, but because the woman licking the icing off her fingers and eating in pure abandon had been her.

A paper wad flew from one side of the office to the other

right in front of them. He snatched it out of the air. "What's going on?"

Two heads popped up from behind computer screens.

"Hey, Boss!" said a dark-haired young man, probably just out of college.

"Hey, Boss, Dax just wanted the list of activities at the high school this weekend," said the brunette girl coming around her desk.

"Dylan, these are my new reporters," Sean said, tossing the paper to Dax. "Laurel Wingate and Dax Hendrix. Laurel and Dax, this is—"

"Dr. Dylan Roberts," Laurel said coming forward to shake hands. "Did some background on the Sheriff and your sister for a story last month. Glad to meet you."

"Trauma surgery is your specialty, isn't it?" Dax asked, not to be outdone by his partner in crime as he shook Dylan's hand. "Have you gotten a look at the new hospital?"

"I did. Very impressive."

"Impressive to join the medical staff?"

Sean wanted to reach out and slap the boy up the side of his head, but refrained. The kid had a nose for finding facts others overlooked and a doggedness for staying on the trail of a story. He was going to have to learn some smoothness when it comes to small town interviews, as well as what was news and what was incursion into someone's privacy, but that would come in time.

Dylan smiled, the not-quite-happy-but-I'm-too-polite-to-tell-you-to-mind-your-own-business kind of smile. "I'm currently on vacation. Just in town visiting my sisters."

"Oh! Congratulations on your new nephew," Laurel said. "We don't publish births in the newspaper. Boss says it would be too intrusive into people's privacy, what with crazies on the internet these days, but gossip still flies faster than a dragonfly in August around this town. I hope you don't mind me asking."

This time Dylan gave the younger woman a genuine grin and Sean relaxed. He was proud of his reporters and his other staff members but wanted Dylan to be impressed with his paper's growth and how he was running it. Laurel just earned a free lunch.

"I don't mind it at all. Believe me, I know how the gossip mill runs here. But thank you. We think he's pretty special."

"And all babies are special," said the short, salt and pepper gray-haired woman coming in from the break room, stirring a spoon in a mug.

"That they are," Sean said stepping to the side to let her scoot into her desk. "Dylan, this is Marta Gonzalez, the head of the marketing department."

"I'm the only member of the marketing department." Setting down her tea, Marta shook hands with Dylan. "I also run the office, order supplies and try to keep the paper on time. By the way, that list of the weekend activities at the school needs to be online pronto," she said with a pointed look at Dax, who quickly jumped to the task. Then she turned back to her desk to pick up a sticky note and hand to Sean. "Congressman Rawlins called to say he would be in town for the festivities this weekend, if you had time to meet with him and his wife."

Sean took the note and slipped it into his pocket, then perched his hip onto the corner of the empty desk across from Marta. "I'll give him a call later. I want to have a quick meeting with everyone before Dylan and I head back out. What does everyone have in the works? Laurel?"

She picked up her tablet and scrolled on it. "The market opens at noon, so I'm going to go interview some of the farmers and booth proprietors. A human interest piece on how the market helps them sell their wares, crafts and of course the organic, locally grown foods."

"Score me some apple fritters if anyone has any today," Dax said.

"You paying?" Laurel asked. "Because I'm still waiting for you to pay me for yesterday's lunch."

Sean pulled a twenty out of his wallet and waved it at Laurel before their discussion devolved into argument stage. "I'll pay for fritters for everyone and your lunch, Laurel. Dax, pay her for yesterday and what are you doing this afternoon?"

Dax handed some money to Laurel then checked his phone. "I have an afternoon appointment with Dr. Preston at his clinic. Want to get his perspective on what it will be like to finally have a hospital close by and not have to ship his patients to the next county for care."

"Don't be late," Sean said.

"Trust me, I know. Was late for an appointment when I had bronchitis last spring. Harriett gave me that look."

"The one that suggests you're lower than a snake in a hole?" Laurel asked.

Dax nodded. "That woman scares me."

"She scares everyone," Dylan said, and they all agreed.

"Sounds like you two are set for the day. Marta, you have anything?" Sean asked.

"I'm spending the day discussing ad space for several of our usual customers, then I have an online interview with a graphic designer you agreed we needed to take some of the graphic work off my hands."

"Right. We'll meet back here at four to discuss if you think they'll be a fit." He focused on his reporters. "And I want your articles ready for editing." Then he stood, taking Dylan's elbow and escorting her towards the front door again.

"Where are you going?" Laurel asked.

He held the door then winked at his staff. "Secret project."

"That's mean to tease them like that," Dylan laughed as they walked down the sidewalk. "It's going to make them very curious."

"Good. They're journalists. It's their job to be curious, to ask questions."

They walked past the shops opening for the day's business and on to the next block, then turned right on Church Street and headed to the Baptist church at the end of the street.

"Of course, they named this street Church," Dylan said, her voice laced with humor. "Do new businesses have to get their names approved by the town council?"

"I don't know what you mean?" he teased. "Doesn't every small town have interesting names to their stores?"

"Please. The Monkey Wrench car repair shop? The Knob & Knockers hardware store?"

"That's one of my favorites."

She lightly punched him the arm. "Of course it is. It's such a guy thing. Did you help Joe Hillis come up with it?"

"Nope. His father named it that when Joe was a kid. About the time that Lorna's late husband named the Peaches 'N Cream."

"You know what's odd?" Dylan said as they passed into the shade of a giant oak tree.

"That City Hall isn't called Palace of Decisions?"

She laughed and he grinned.

"No, but please don't say that around anyone else in town or they might decide they like it. What I think is odd is that the Peaches 'N Cream doesn't have a signature peach dessert."

"What do you mean? Right now, not only does Lorna have peach pie and peach cobbler on the menu, but homemade peach ice cream. She does it this time every year."

"During peach season. Bobby told me that when we had lunch yesterday. She and Chloe both nearly orgasmed over the ice cream."

Sean choked on his laughter thinking about two pregnant women getting so excited about ice cream. She grinned at him, and he knew she'd said that on purpose. It was one of the things he loved about her. She wasn't afraid to tease him or shock him, in fact she enjoyed it.

"What I'm talking about is a dessert she can serve year round. Something that people will talk about online and will make it a specific destination stop in touring the area."

They stopped at the curb and waited for a middle-aged couple on bikes to pedal past. He waved at them and said hello. Then they crossed over to the sidewalk surrounding the church. "You have a point. She could also ship it to people. I know she's now getting online orders for her t-shirts. For a medical person, you're not a bad marketing pro, doc."

She slipped her hand through his arm and leaned in close. "Don't tell anyone, but one of the things I do to relax, especially when I'm on call at the hospital is to browse online shopping."

He chuckled. "I bet that costs you a pretty penny."

"Oh, I don't buy anything. I just put things in my cart, then never check out. Let's me daydream without the buyer's remorse. And it's a good thing, especially when I'm hungry in the middle of the night."

"Oh? Why is that?"

"Because I'd be ordering deep dish pizzas from Chicago, cheesecakes from New York, and wine from California."

"I have to admit, I've been tempted to order a whole cheesecake delivered from *Junior's* in New York more than once since moving here," he said as they strolled past the church to the walkway into the cemetery. He held the gate open for her and followed her inside.

"It feels a little weird coming here just to look around," she said stopping just a few feet in. "I've only gone to them for a funeral."

He started walking up the main path and she fell into step with him. "I used to walk through them a lot when I was a kid."

"Why? Did your brothers dare you?"

He chuckled. "Nah. It was my mom's passion. She loved to go into cemeteries when we were on vacation and see who could find the oldest date on the headstones. Then she'd write down the weirdest names we could find, making a game out of it. My brother Ian kept the list and uses it to name characters in his books."

"Your brother is a writer, too?"

"In his spare time. He writes fantasy novels when he's not building houses. He's published a few independently and has a small following. They're pretty good." He paused at a very old looking stone. "Look at this one. Cyrus Abercrombie. Born 1803. Died 1862 at the Battle of Shiloh."

"Fifty-nine years old. Isn't that a little old to be serving in a war?" Dylan asked, moving over to read the next one. "This one is Ezekiel Abercrombie. Born 1840. Died 1862 in the same battle. Father and son?"

"Wouldn't surprise me. All able-bodied men fought in that war. Sometimes against a father or brother. Sometimes right alongside them."

They continued past stones in the dappled shade of the old oaks scattered in the yard, stopping to comment on the ones that caught their attention, slowly moving through the timeline of Westen as they walked. Finally, they came to the small fenced-in area.

"This was where Twylla was singing the other day," Dylan said as they passed into the enclosed area.

The stones here were smaller than others in the outer part of the cemetery. Some had angels on them. Sean squatted down beside one and studied the dates of birth and death.

"This was a two year old."

Dylan pointed to the next one. "That one was only six months."

The years varied during the past one hundred years.

"There are quite a few during 1918 to 1920," he pointed out.

Dylan nodded. "The Spanish Flu epidemic."

Then they came to a smaller area with tiny headstones surrounding a pink rose bush. All had first names only and none had dates, although many looked to be decades old.

"What's this?" he asked, slowly moving around the circle of tiny stones.

"I'm not sure, but I'd guess it's a memory garden," Dylan said, bending down to trace the name engraved on one of the stones. "When I did my obstetrics rotations, I had one or two stillborn deaths. The nurses of the unit had a whole program for the grieving parents and one of them was that their baby could be buried free of charge in a small memory garden. Once a year they would have a prayer ceremony for all the children and any parents with babies there could come. I went once. It looked very much like this."

Hearing the sadness in her voice, he stepped closer to her. "You said the song you heard her singing sounded like a lullaby, right?"

Dylan nodded. "It reminded me of one of the songs I remember my mother singing to me as a child."

"Do you think one of these stones belongs to a child Twylla might've had that died?"

"It makes sense. According to Lorna, she was in rough shape when she came back into town. She'd suffered physical abuse and was malnourished. Two things that could prevent her from carrying through to term."

"Does this answer your questions?"

"I think so. Pursuing the mystery any further would mean asking intrusive questions to either the medical people who cared for her at the time, or Twylla herself. I'm not that nosy. Besides, Doc Ray and Caroline are in Florida, not that they'd violate her privacy by talking to me."

"And the only other person who might be able to give you more insight into her history is Harriett."

"And I'm not going to crack that nut."

CHAPTER 16

"I'm back."

Twylla looked up from the appointment desk to see Molly coming through the front door with bags of to-go boxes from the Peaches 'N Cream. It was her turn to get lunch for everyone. Since they often only had half an hour for lunch, they'd take their breaks in the back staff room she'd had remodeled and enlarged when she did the first expansion. Her girls deserved a spot to chill and get off their feet when they could.

"You, Shania and Sylvie go first. Sylvie's already breast pumping back in the break room. Darcy, Linda and Corrin can take their turns as soon as their clients are finished," she said and turned back to the computer to study the schedule for the next day. She always staggered the girls' appointments around lunch time so they could be sure to get a break and only took her meal after they'd all eaten. Her employees were important to her and she wanted them to feel that.

"I'll put your salad in the refrigerator," Molly said as she walked past. "The café was packed with out-of-towners, but Lorna had our food all packed up and ready for me when I got there."

"That's Lorna. Always one step ahead of the rush."

Which was exactly what she was trying to be today. One step ahead. Her day started early with Earl's haircut and shave before the doors officially opened this morning. After her emotional trip down memory lane last night, she'd been surprised by how easily she'd awakened this morning. As soon as the older man left, happily beaming with his appearance, the girls arrived with clients right on their heels. This was the first moment she'd had to catch her own breath all day.

While there was a lull in the customers arriving, she opened the file for charges for the day to get a quick idea how the proceeds were going. While some of her older customers still insisted on checks or cash for payment, most of her newer clients paid with credit or bank cards, which made it so much easier to tally the totals. One of the hardest things she'd had to learn when she first opened was the bookkeeping. It had just been her at first, then she'd started having employees. Which meant payroll, taxes, insurance. Lorna and her husband had taken her under their wing until she understood the business end of her shop.

That's what she loved about Westen. If you stayed here long enough, you were family. Even though she'd returned as the prodigal daughter, they welcomed her with open arms. She tried to do the same for each of the girls she hired.

The doorbell jangled. Not expecting the next scheduled client for half an hour, she looked up to see a teenage girl with two-toned hair of an obvious home dye job, jeans and a tank top standing inside looking around.

"May I help you?" she said, plastering on her best everyone-is-welcome-here smile.

"Uhm. Yeah. I'm supposed to get a job."

Suddenly it clicked. This was one of the teens living at Westen House, a home for troubled teens sponsored by the town, but run by Melissa and Daniel Löwe. One of the rules for the residents of the house was that they had to have a part-time job. Mostly it had been boys living at the house, but in the past few years girls had also been coming to stay. Lorna often hired them as waitresses, or they'd gotten jobs at the bakery or dress shops. This was the first time someone had approached her.

"Are you from Westen House?" she asked.

The light dimmed in the girl's eyes, her whole demeanor going suddenly defeated and defensive. She simply nodded.

Twylla wanted to hug her and tell her everything would be okay, but didn't think it would be helpful right now. Instead she softened her own smile. "Well, Melissa is one of my dearest friends. If she thought you'd like working here, I'd be happy to have you."

"You would?" the girl blinked, her surprise tugging at Twylla's heart.

"Of course, I would, but I need to know something first."

The suspicion flooded back into her eyes. "What?"

Twylla picked up a pen and held it over her note pad on the desk. "Your name?"

"Oh, Mara."

Twylla jotted that down and waited. "Do you have a last name, Mara?"

"Kendal. Mara Kendal."

"Well, I am very happy to meet you, Mara. I'm Twylla and I own the Dye Right." She wrote the rest of her name down, then came around the desk and offered her hand for a handshake.

Mara shook her hand, then once again glanced around the waiting area. "It's nice."

"Thank you. We work hard to make it feel welcoming. If you decide you want to work here, one of your jobs will be to help keep this room clean."

"I get to decide if I want to work here?"

"Sure you do. There are lots of stores and businesses in Westen. Going to a job is much easier when you want to work there."

Mara nodded as she seemed to consider that idea.

"Would you like to see the rest of the salon?"

"Yeah."

Twylla led her into the inner workings of her business. "This is the stylists' stations. Each stylist has her own chair and as you can see some of them have decorations and pictures that personalize their area. We do consultations with our clients here. Haircuts are done at these chairs, so part of your job would be to sweep the area frequently to keep the shop looking clean. The stylists will clean their own spots and chairs."

Twylla was quickly trying to map out a job for a helper she'd never considered hiring before. The more she talked and mentally planned, the more she liked the idea. Later she'd write it all up and make it a real job description.

As they walked past, her girls smiled or nodded in welcome to Mara.

"This is the shampoo station," Twylla said leading her over to one of the sinks. "The stylists have a routine to clean their sinks after each client, so that wouldn't be on your job list, but if we're extremely busy and you aren't busy, you could offer to clean them to help move things along."

Mara nodded as if she thought that made sense.

The stock room was their next stop.

"This is where we keep supplies. It's also where the stylists mix colors and perm solutions."

"Perms?" Mara asked looking at all the different boxes that lined the walls and floor.

"Short for permanents. It makes people's hair curly." Twylla hid her smile. Of course, a teenager wouldn't know what that meant. It wasn't something they had done. In fact, it was rare that any of her clients under fifty had a permanent these days. "We get deliveries once a month, so you'll help me unload, stock and organize things in here."

When they entered the break room thankfully Sylvie had finished breast pumping and was eating with Molly and Shania. Last thing Twylla wanted to introduce a teenaged potential employee to was a new mother using the breast pump. She made a mental note to ask Sylvie to use her office for that function from now on.

"This is the break room. When I have meetings, it happens in here. Sometimes I have speakers come in or we watch videos about new styling cuts which you'll be welcome to be part of. And of course, everyone takes their breaks and eats lunch here as you can see." She turned to her girls. "Everyone this is Mara. She may be coming to work as our part-time support staff." That sounded like a good title. Much better than janitor/gopher. "Mara, this is Molly, my assistant manager. Shania. And Sylvie. Both stylists."

"Hi, Mara," Molly said with a smile.

Shania, who was a bit shy, nodded. "Hi."

Sylvie grinned. "Hey, Mara. You'll love working for Twylla."

Mara nodded in greeting at them all but stopped to stare at Sylvie. "Do you color your hair?"

"Oh, no. The good Lord blessed me with all this," Sylvie said. Looking very much like a fire sprite, patted her bright red spikes and laughed.

"It's really cool."

"Thank you. I hated it when I was a kid. Got called carrots a lot. But then I realized it made me as special as a snowstorm in summer." Sylvie grinned and wiggled her eyebrows. "And my little girl has the same color."

A genuine smile popped onto Mara's face. The first Twylla

had seen since the girl tentatively entered the salon. Sylvie's natural friendliness and optimistic attitude was infectious.

"One of the things you'll be doing if you take the job will be to load the cooler with cold water bottles and pops each morning. They're free to our clients and the staff, but we want to be sure they are cold. Also, do you know how to make coffee?" She asked as they walked around the break room to where the drinks cooler and coffee maker were.

Mara looked at it. "Not really."

"Well, that's something I can teach you. Up front is an espresso machine. Back here is just regular coffee for staff and clients. Once you've learned how to make regular coffee, then you'd regularly check the pot and if it's empty or near empty, make more. And if you want to learn how to make espresso, I'll teach you that, too." She stopped by the sink and spoke loud enough for her stylists to hear the next part. "You will not be responsible for doing the dishes. Each of the girls will clean up after themselves in here."

"Yes, ma'am," Sylvie said and the others nodded along, including Mara.

"Good. There's one last spot to talk about."

Finally, she led the teen into the laundry room. In it was the washer and dryer, a rack for hanging the clean smocks, several different laundry bins, and a shelf with folded towels of various sizes.

"To meet the state's requirements for salon hygiene, we have to do a lot of laundry. This won't be your job only, the stylists will still help, but at least several times a day you'll be washing, drying and folding towels and hanging the clean smocks up for the next use. Will that be a problem?"

Mara looked at the washer and dryer, then shrugged. "I've used these at some of the foster homes I've been in."

"Good. Then why don't you have a seat in the breakroom,

and I'll meet you there to discuss salary," she said leading the way then motioned for Mara to go in the room. "I just need to get some paperwork from my office."

Mara went in and took a chair. The first group of stylists had finished their lunch breaks and were cleaning up before heading out to relieve the other girls. As she hurried to her office, she heard Sylvie tell Mara to get a soda or water if she wanted one.

As she pulled out her new hire forms file from the filing cabinet, Twylla wondered why she was so nervous about hiring this young girl, why it meant so much to her, but it did. She snagged her phone and quickly called Lorna.

"Hey, girl, what's up?" the café owner said.

"What do you pay the kids you hire from the Westen House?" she asked

"Depends. If they've got no experience, I start them out bussing tables, washing dishes and helping stock the shelves. So, I pay them about twelve dollars an hour. They get a free meal while they're on shift, and a split of the tips, same as any of the other kids I hire. If they do well and start waiting tables, they get fifteen an hour, plus tips. Why? Did one of the new kids stop by?"

"Yes, my first one. A girl."

"Bout time. You could start at the twelve dollars an hour and see how she works out."

"Thanks, Lorna," she said and hung up, grabbed a pen and hurried back to the breakroom.

Mara had a pop and was staring out the window at the maple tree whose leaves were turning from green to orange. Twylla paused in the doorway and studied the girl. She was very thin. Of course, living at Westen House Melissa's home cooking would help remedy that. But for today, she could do her part.

"I'm starving, so we'll have to talk while I eat." she said, setting her pen, paperwork and phone on the table, then retrieved her lunch and a water from the refrigerator. She grabbed two paper plates from the stack in the cupboard then took a seat opposite Mara. "By the way, I love Lorna's chicken salad sandwiches from the Peaches 'N Cream café, but there's always more than I can eat. Can you help me out with that?"

Without waiting for the teen to say no, she just slapped half of the croissant sandwich on a plate and shoved it her way. She took a bite of her food and ate. Whether she didn't want to make a scene or she'd decided the food looked tempting, Mara did the same. Once they were done, Twylla discussed the salary and benefits she'd get—one of which was a haircut and style by any of the stylists.

"Have you started school yet?" she asked.

Mara made a little face. "Mrs. Löwe is taking me on Monday. It's the rules."

"It's a good one. If you want to have a way to support yourself, you need to finish high school at least. So, you won't be working during school hours. We're closed on Sundays and Mondays. Tuesdays through Fridays we stay open until eight every night. And of course, we're open and very busy on Saturdays. So, let's start you tomorrow and Saturday for four hours each. Do you think you can be here at ten?"

Mara nodded. "I guess so."

Twylla looked straight into her eyes. "One of the things I will insist on is you being on time. No excuses."

Mara sat up straighter. "Yes, ma'am."

They finished their meeting with Mara signing the tax form and employment forms Twylla used for all her employees and Twylla walked her back to the front door.

"I'm looking forward to you working here, Mara," she said, holding the door open for her.

Mara smiled just a little, then headed out the door in the

direction of the Westen House. As she watched her go, Twylla thought there was a little spring in her step and she seemed to be walking a little straighter.

She pulled her phone out of her skirt pocket and began a text to Melissa. Movement across the street caught her attention stopping her mid-sentence to look. A shiver of awareness skittered down her spine as she caught the glimpse of a man turning the corner and walking further away. Something in the shape of his back reminded her of him.

Turning, she strode down the block, her feet moving faster with every step she took.

It couldn't be him. Not after all these years.

She reached the corner of Main Street and stopped. The sidewalks were filled with people. She strained, standing on her tip toes as best she could in her high heels, but it was impossible to see the man.

If it had been Ricky, he'd disappeared into the crowd.

The weird feeling from yesterday and the night spent going through the memory box had her mind playing tricks on her. That's all it was.

Pivoting, she hurried back to the salon, her afternoon was booked with cuts and blowdrys. Last thing she needed to do was borrow trouble when none existed.

∽

"Have you found her?"

No hello. No how are you. Just straight to the interrogation. Myles was losing his patience.

Rick rubbed his forehead as he held the phone against his ear. "I think I have."

"Where?"

"Small town in Ohio."

"I figured that. You told me you were in Ohio two days ago."

He inhaled and exhaled to keep from telling the bastard to go fuck himself. Pushing Myles' anger at this point would be deadly. He'd already threatened to send one of his hitmen to join him. That's the last thing he needed while he tried to convince Meredith to disappear once more. This time she had more to lose than just her life. He could see that from watching all the traffic in and out of her salon last night and today.

"It's northeast of Columbus," he said, feeding Myles some information. "I have to confirm that it's her." Which he had already but needed to buy some time.

"I want answers tomorrow."

The phone went dead.

Crap. He tossed the phone beside him on the hotel bed and ran his hands through his hair. He'd hoped to have a little time to approach her and ease her into the realization that she was in jeopardy again. The last time he sent her into hiding it had nearly broken his heart. How the hell was he going to do it a second time?

Pulling out his wallet, he flipped open the hidden flap and slipped out the slightly faded photo he'd held secreted away for eighteen years. It was taken the night Meredith met Myles and she looked so young and carefree, her long dark hair hanging over her shoulders, the smile on her face showing her happiness. The short, tight skirt and sequin top accentuating her sexy body. He'd fallen in love with her that night.

A year after this picture she'd been dangerously thin. Her gaunt face—battered and bruised—triggered his rage to the point he almost killed Myles, but it also sparked his fear that if she went back to Myles' compound, she'd be dead. He'd been desperate to get her on that bus, to keep her safe. And she'd been safe for nearly two decades.

For the first few years he'd been on a tight rope trying to

keep Myles in check and his focus on the business, not on Meri's disappearance. Then he'd gotten complacent, his vigilance for signs Myles was still searching for her. Now he felt like things were at a crossroads, a collision on the horizon.

Now she was in danger again and he was going to destroy the life she built here to try and save her once more.

Folding his hands together, he balanced his elbows on his spread knees and leaned over them to pray for some solution, some way to keep Meredith hidden from Myles and some way, short of killing him, to stop his obsession with her.

CHAPTER 17

"May I help you, Doctor?"

Dylan glanced over at the cash register counter where the white-haired gentleman wearing a green apron over his pale blue button down shirt stood. "Hello, Mr. Dubois."

"Please call me Henry, everyone in town does. Mr. Dubois sounds so old," said the man who appeared nearer one hundred rather than fifty as he came over to where she was looking at some fresh flower arrangements.

"Then you must call me Dylan. Doctor sounds so formal," she said shaking his hand. "I'm looking for a welcome home bouquet for my sister. They're discharging her from the hospital tomorrow and I'd like something to surprise her."

"Well, we have some standard arrangements for new mothers," he said leading her over to the glass tower with lovely, dainty arrangements of roses and baby's breath in vases. "Pink for girls, blue for boys."

They were very lovely, very sweet. And so not her sister Chloe.

"I've already got a present for my nephew at the Hopscotch

Boutique," she said pulling the stuffed elephant out of one of the shopping bags she'd gotten from the children's shop. She'd also gotten a few cute outfits. "I wanted the flowers to be for my sister. Bright fall colors and flowers." Then she saw a lovely blown glass vase with vibrant yellows, oranges and dark red sitting on one of the back shelves. "Perhaps in that?"

"It's very beautiful, isn't it?" he said, reaching shaky hands up to bring it down.

Dylan held her breath until the vase sat safely on the counter. She wondered if Henry suffered with Parkinson's or some other disease, or if perhaps it was just essential tremors elderly patients acquired. In any case? She was glad the vase survived the transfer. It was too beautiful to be shattered.

"It is extraordinary," she said, running her hand over the cool glass that so reminded her of fire.

"A young girl brought it in one day last week. Meg took it on consignment," he said bending down to pull a four-inch binder from below the counter and set it next to the vase. "Meg does that for local artisans, if she isn't sure how we can use their crafted items. If we do use them in an arrangement, or in a gift, like those sweet hand-maid dolls that Mrs. Mulligan makes, then the crafter gets paid."

"Where is Meg today?" Dylan asked looking around the florist shop for Henry's very spritely white-haired wife.

"She left early to organize our booth at the market today. We had a load of fresh flowers delivered before eight. Most to the market and some here." He flipped through the colorful images inside the binder. "So, you want a bouquet for your sister. We could do just autumn colors, or we could do a bouquet with special meaning."

Dylan eased onto the barstool on her side of the counter, setting her bags and purse on the floor beside it. "What do you mean?"

Henry gave her a closed lip smile and his eyes brightened. "Flowers all have different meanings."

"Like red roses mean love?" she said looking at the page of roses he'd opened to.

"Yes. But orange roses can mean passion or energy. Yellow are joy, warmth and welcome."

"I didn't know that. What others would you recommend? Choe is so independent, but motherhood is new to her. I'd like her flowers to make her feel confident."

Henry flipped the page. "Sunflowers are for dedicated love. Perhaps the kind she has for her new son?"

"I can see that."

Henry chuckled.

"What?"

"It can also mean haughtiness."

Dylan laughed. "That's so my sister!"

"Gerbera daisies are beautiful in autumn colors, and they mean cheerfulness."

"I do love those. How about mums?"

He flipped a few pages. "Happiness and well-being."

"That would be good."

"Let me get those from the back room and see what we can create," he said, then went through the door behind him.

When she'd wandered into the florist shop, she'd hoped to just find something pretty to cheer her sister up when she came home tomorrow. Now not only was she going to have a beautiful vase, but a bouquet that held a special message for Chloe.

A few moments later Henry emerged with his arms full of flowers and some dried autumn leaves.

"Do leaves have meaning, too?" she asked.

He chuckled. "These are just to add a little bit of fall to the bouquet."

"Oh. I wondered, because olive leaves usually mean peace."

"True," Henry said as he started cutting the stems of the flowers they'd chosen and arranging them in the vase. As he worked, she realized Henry didn't just sell flowers, he was an artist. He picked up a bundle of black-eyed Susans, split them into smaller bundles and filled in the bouquet.

"What is the meaning of those?" she asked.

"Since your sister is a lawyer, I thought these were appropriate." He paused a moment and wiped his brow. "They mean justice."

"That's perfect for her. Do you do this for all your clients?"

He suddenly gripped the counter with both hands and his face paled to the point his lips almost disappeared.

"Henry?" Dylan rushed around the counter to catch the thin man before he fell onto the wood floor, unconscious. She eased him down onto the floor with his head in her lap, then quickly felt for a pulse.

There it was, regular and around sixty. Normal for a man his age.

Leaning to her right, she managed to reach around the counter and snag her bag. She scrambled through it and pulled out her phone. Before she could dial 9-1-1, Henry's eyes fluttered open.

"You're okay, Henry, but don't try to sit up just yet," she said, keeping one hand on his chest, so he would stay put.

"What happened?" He blinked and glanced around as if trying to register where he was.

"You fainted." Seeing his face register that he was in his shop, she helped him into a sitting position, keeping her hand on his wrist to measure his pulse, which was steady, but his color remained pale. "Do you have any heart issues?"

He shook his head. "No, Doc Clint did a heart test on me... you know the kind with all those wires."

"An EKG?"

"That's the one. He did that when I went in for my checkup last month. Said my heart was ticking away just fine."

"Have you ever fainted like this before?" He seemed quite cognizant, so she didn't think he'd had a stroke episode.

"Only when my blood sugar is low."

Ah-ha. Diabetes. Explains the tremors.

"When did you last check your sugar?"

"This morning before breakfast. Meg always makes sure. Won't let me eat until I do and take my medicine."

"That's because she loves you," she said with a smile then glanced at the clock. Almost two. "Did you eat lunch?"

"I meant to, but then we had some customers come in," he paused. "Meg isn't going to be happy I forgot to eat."

Dylan patted his hand. "I'm sure she'll just be happy you're going to be okay."

The bell over the door rang.

"Henry, you here?"

Dylan looked up to see Cleetus standing in the middle of the shop.

"Hey Doc Roberts. What you doing behind the counter?"

"Thank God you're here, Cleetus. Henry's fainted and I need help getting him up."

For a big man, Cleetus was quite fast, before Dylan knew it, he'd whipped around the counter, scooped the older man up and sat him in one of the chairs near the front window for customers to use. Dylan went into the back of the shop and found the refrigerator. Inside were bottles of water and some small containers of orange juice. She searched the drawers and found some packets of sugar, along with a blood sugar checking kit.

God bless Meg for being prepared.

"What happened?" Cleetus was asking when she came back.

"I just got a little dizzy is all," Henry said, trying to stand.

The big deputy laid his hand on the frail man's shoulder and shook his head. "You need to sit right there and let the doc check you out. I'd hate to tell Meg you acted foolishly."

"Now, there's no need to get Meg all riled up, Cleetus," Henry protested, but settled back in the chair.

Cleetus met Dylan's eyes and winked. "Anything else I can do, Doc?"

"Could you go over to the café and get Henry a sandwich?" she asked then turned to Henry. "What would you like?"

"Roast beef would be fine." He tried to reach into his hip pocket.

"Don't get your money out, Henry," Cleetus said already heading for the door. "I got this."

"Cleetus?" Dylan said, squatting beside Henry's chair.

The big man stopped with the door open. "Yeah, Doc?"

"Let's keep this between just the three of us for now," she said, wanting to keep the gossip mill to a minimum. "I'll tell Meg as soon as Henry is better. Okay?"

"Gotcha," he said and headed out the door.

"You really don't have to fuss, doctor," Henry said as she pricked his finger and gathered a drop of blood onto the test strip.

"It's not fussing, Henry," she gave him a reassuring smile and held a little two-by-two gauze pad onto his finger to stem the blood flow. Then she handed him the cup of orange juice she'd mixed a little sugar in and sat in the chair opposite him. "I'm always curious about facts and scientific things. Used to drive my sisters crazy with my questions. So, I'm just wondering how low your sugar got."

The monitor beeped and she read the result as he drank the juice. Sixty-four. Low but not dangerously low. She needed to stay with Henry until his level was normal, but knew Meg needed to be told. Normally, she'd call Bobby, but her sister really didn't need the added stress right now, so she dialed the only other person she trusted to discretely find Henry's wife and not panic her.

"Hey, Doc."

"Callahan, I need a favor."

"Sure. What is it?"

"Could you go to the market and get a message to Meg Dubois for me?"

"Sure. What's the message?" he asked, and she could tell he was already headed out the door of the newspaper.

"First, it's not an emergency and Henry is okay. His blood sugar bottomed out, but he's drinking some orange juice and going to have a roast beef sandwich. I do think if she can, she should come back to the shop. I am staying with him until I'm sure his sugar is stable."

"Got it. I'll bring her right away."

"Don't panic her, Sean. Henry should be okay by the time you get here."

"No panic. See you soon."

After hanging up, she checked the time. Five minutes since she checked Henry's blood sugar. Five more and she'd recheck it. "How are you feeling now, Henry?"

"Much better, thank you." He looked at her and his eyes appeared more focused than they had before the juice, which was only half gone.

"Why don't you finish the juice and then we'll recheck your sugar in a few minutes?"

While he complied with her suggestion, she studied the bouquet of flowers he'd arranged for her sister. "You really are quite the floral artist, Henry. Have you done this all your life?"

He chuckled. "No, I followed my father into the banking business. When I retired from that fifteen years ago, Meg said I needed to find something to do. She said after fifty years of marriage I was suddenly always under her feet. I saw the advertisement in the paper that the shop was for sale."

"How did she feel about it?" she asked as she wiped his finger with and alcohol swipe, then punctured it with the needle and drew a drop of blood onto the new monitor strop.

"I thought she'd laugh and tell me I was crazy. But she didn't." He stopped his tale to look at the reading on the monitor. "Ninety-two. I thought it was back to normal. I feel much better."

"Your color is improved, too." She patted his arm just as Cleetus returned with a to-go bag from the café. "And here's Cleetus with your food."

"Roast beef and Swiss on sourdough. Lorna also sent some fruit salad and one unsweetened tea with lemon," Cleetus said handing the bag over.

Henry pulled the food out of the bag and set it on the table. After he'd taken a few bites, he paused. "Where are my manners? Would you like some, Dylan?"

"No, thank you. I had lunch earlier. You need to eat the protein to keep your blood sugar up. The juice pushed it up, but we don't want it crashing on the rebound. Why don't you finish your story about Meg's reaction to the flower shop?"

He took another bite, chewed and swallowed before continuing. "Like I said, she surprised me. When we drove into town to tour the shop, she fell in love with how quaint it was. Not just the shop, but all of Westen. Of course, it didn't look like it does now, a bit run down back then, like a lady wearing old clothes. Many of the shops here now have changed hands, but the remodeling has kept the small town feel, even in the signs. Meg liked that she could hand deliver flowers by walking or riding her bicycle. She saw potential in the town and in me," he said with a little shy smile.

Just then the bell over the door chimed and the whirlwind that was Meg Dubois flew into the shop, Sean on her heels.

"You forgot to eat lunch, didn't you?" she said, coming over and hugging her husband. Releasing him, she stepped back and frowned at him with narrowed, disapproving eyes. "You promised me you'd eat on time."

"I meant to, Megs. But there was a steady stream of customers and...I just forgot. But the doctor here took good care of me." He gave a sheepish nod Dylan's direction, then lifted his sandwich. "And Cleetus got me something to eat. I feel much better now."

"Yes, but what if Dr. Roberts wasn't here? You could've fallen, hit your head, and I wouldn't have known and..." she paused to wipe at a tear and catch her breath. Then she seemed to stand a little taller as if she'd made an important decision. "That just settles it. We're going to hire another helper, besides Caroline. If we're going to have a regular booth at the market, we'll need someone here with you so I can make deliveries and help Caroline run the market shop." Turning, she focused her attention on Sean. "Can I get an advertisement in tomorrow's paper?"

He nodded. "Sure. Give Marta a call and she can get the details. We could post something online, today if that will help?"

Meg gave him a firm nod, then turned to Dylan. "Thank you for being here and taking care of Henry."

"I'm glad I was. He was making me an arrangement for my sister when he started having symptoms. But his blood sugar was back to low normal range before he started eating. Perhaps he should go see Dr. Preston after he eats, just to be sure everything is okay?"

"I'll give Harriett a call," the older woman said with a nod. She turned to look at the counter. "Is that the arrangement for your sister?" she asked with a nod at the fiery vase with the warm colored flowers.

Dylan stood and they walked over to the sales counter. "Yes. I love it and Henry explained to me what all the flowers mean. He nailed Chloe perfectly with his suggestions."

"He does that. I think it's what makes his arrangements so special. I'm glad he used this vase. I wasn't sure we'd ever be able to find the right customer. But now I see how it would be your sister."

"I didn't choose the vase," Henry said coming over to join them. "The doctor did."

"Well, I'm still happy you both used it," Meg said stepping around the counter and grabbing a box large enough to hold the vase. After setting it inside, she grabbed some green florist's tape and began securing the vase so it wouldn't wobble when being carried. "When the little girl who made it brought it in, I wasn't sure about it. Now I can let her know the vase sold and give her the money."

"Is she a local artist?" Dylan said, fishing her credit card out of her wallet and handing it over to Meg.

"She's the granddaughter of Harvey Kennedy. His farm is about ten miles east of town," Meg processed the transaction and handed the card back, along with the receipt. "She showed up about a year ago out of the blue and has been living with Harvey ever since."

Dylan glanced at the receipt. "Meg, you only charged me for the vase."

The older lady laid her hand on Dylan's. "Doctor. I'm not about to charge you for the flowers. If you hadn't been here, and I came to find Henry dead..." She stopped to swallow and once more wipe tears from her eyes. Henry wrapped his arm around her shoulders and hugged her tight.

It was Dylan's turn to swallow. Here were two people who had been married for decades and you could see how they still supported and loved each other. She never got to see that with her parents, but she liked to think they'd be the same way.

"How about I carry that for you, Doc?" Sean said with a smile, coming to everyone's rescue in the awkward moment. She could've kissed him.

CHAPTER 18

The day had been one of the busiest this year. Even more than right before holidays. Despite the stress and chaos that happened with walk-ins on top of scheduled clients, Twylla still felt uneasy. When she'd been out front earlier, she would've sworn the man walking away from her had been Ricky Saunderson.

It had been nearly two decades since she'd seen him, but the back of the man and the purposeful stride was exactly the same as Ricky's, although a little older. Had she really seen him? Or had it just been the memories of her baby that produced the mirage?

If it was Ricky how had he found her? More importantly, why was he here?

Myles.

The only reason Ricky would be in Westen was because Myles somehow knew where she was after all these years. How? She'd always been so careful.

From the moment she climbed onto that bus in New York she reverted to Twylla Howard once more, the shy girl from a small midwestern town. She'd gone almost to the border of

Canada and stayed a week in a roadside motel before catching another bus to Buffalo, then a third bus took her to Cleveland. That's where she finally had the courage to sell one of the diamonds she'd brought with her. One diamond was all she dared sell at that time because even though Cleveland was a large enough city for a reputable diamond broker who would buy her diamond at true worth, not a pawn shop owner, but the brokerage world was small enough that if several high-quality diamonds hit the market at once, word could get back to New York where Myles had to be watching for such a sale.

And he would be watching. It was his worse traits, obsession and ego.

For all the months she'd been in his control, he'd thought himself superior to her and everyone around him. That no one would dare stand up to him and no one would risk their lives to steal from him. However, his ego blinded him to those around him. Especially her. He'd torn down her defenses with his derogatory comments, shattered her faith in herself with sarcasm and hateful words, and believed he'd destroyed her independence with his fists. His self-assurance that she wasn't any kind of a threat to him had him relaxing his guard around her.

More than one of her beatings took place in their bedroom. The first time she lay in a heap on the floor between the bed and his closet, he'd gone inside to change his bloodied clothes and she'd gotten a glimpse of the three-foot tall safe inside. It intrigued her. With each subsequent beating, she focused her attention on the metal box and not the pain.

Why did he have a safe? What was in it? What was the combination to get inside?

Then one night after he had a meeting with a client she knew he supplied drugs to, she watched him go into the safe. It was another little detail he'd overlooked. If he didn't close the closet door completely the full length mirror on the inside could be seen from just the right angle of the bathroom mirror. That's when she watched him place a small black bag into the safe. A jewelry pouch.

"You really need to watch how you talk to me, Meri-girl. (God, how she hated that nickname now.) *When you're sassy, you force me to discipline you," Myles said moving deeper into his closet.*

She lay on the floor, the metallic taste of blood gagging her and trying to see out of her left eye, unable to open the right one. The pain so intense, she just wanted to die. What had she done to deserve this? Simply said she didn't like olives? It was the truth, the briny, almost bitter taste of them turned her stomach. The words barely out of her mouth when the back of his hand whipped across her face.

This beating was different. This one she'd planned. Intentionally provoked him. Knowing it would set him off, she thought she'd be ready for that first attack. He still caught her off guard. Dazed and seeing stars, she'd been unable to defend herself as he grabbed her by the hair and dragged her into the bedroom, the one area of the house off limits to his bodyguards and crew members. He delivered the next blow to her jaw, and she crumpled onto the floor, remembering to curl into a ball and protect the small life growing inside her.

Kicks followed, which she used to crawl away, just a little closer to the closet. Intentionally.

Another punch to the face right in her eye, and a twisting of her arm making at least one tendon in her shoulder tear so he could haul her around and scream into her face.

"Bitch, don't ever spit out food I give you. I don't care if it's dog shit. I give it to you, you eat it! You hear me?"

She managed a nod.

"Good." *He dropped her like a heap of trash on the floor and stepped over her.*

"Now I have to change again before I go out. I should beat you again just for causing me the aggravation." *He shrugged off his shirt and tossed it at her. "Have that sent out to be cleaned and they'd better be able to get your damn blood off it." He paused and looked at the gold Rolex on his wrist. "Great. I'm going to have to send this watch to the jeweler's for cleaning now."*

Curled back into a ball, she gathered the shirt close and tried to keep tears from her eyes as he knelt in front of the safe's door. She needed to focus on what he was doing. The spot where she landed was just close enough to see the dial as he turned it—right to six, left to twenty-eight, right again to seventy-two.

She should've guessed. His birthday.

Her mission complete, she closed her eyes and gave into the pain. When she finally heard the roar of his sports car leave the drive, she knew it was time to make her escape.

If it had been her first beating, she doubted she'd have the ability to move even one muscle. Myles thought he was breaking her down with his punishment. Instead, he'd conditioned her to not only tolerate the torture, but endure it. Slowly, she rose to her feet, stooping for a moment to catch her breath and keep the dizziness at bay. Once her vision cleared and she could straighten, she made her way inside his closet, careful not to touch any of his clothes, or the shoes he had scattered about. Another thing she knew about Myles was he never did anything unintentionally. If he left his closet a chaotic mess, it was so he would know if someone came into it and disturbed anything.

She knelt before the safe door and using the shirt he'd flung at her to keep from putting her fingerprints anywhere on the safe she turned the dial in the exact sequence she'd witnessed him doing earlier. When she heard the final tumbler click into place, she inhaled and exhaled slowly.

Her heart racing, she strained to hear any noise in the house. With Myles off to whatever meeting or event on his schedule, the security would be lax, the minions had either followed him in another car, or retired to their rooms in the smaller house on the compound. The guards at the gate would be looking for anyone trying come through the gate. No one, not even Ricky who always accompanied his boss, would be looking in on her. The only fear she had at the moment was Myles' returning.

Quiet. That's all she heard.

Grasping the handle of the safe with the shirt, she pushed down hard. Without any sort of alarm going off, the door easily opened when she pulled. In all her attempts to secretly watch Myles when he was in his safe, she'd never really gotten a look at the contents besides the jewelry pouch she'd watched him deposit inside. Stacks of bundled hundred dollar bills filled the bottom shelf. There had to be over a hundred thousand dollars. On the top shelf were file folders.

She took out the top one. A local congressional candidate's name was on the outside. She flipped it open, and quickly closed it. The man was naked with another man and two women doing things she'd never wanted to see. Quickly she put it back, not wanting to see what the other files might contain. Knowing Myles, he used their contents to blackmail people.

In the corner of the top shelf, she saw the black velvet bag. She pulled it out into her lap. It didn't feel heavy like some sort of gold chain or a broach. Opening it, she poured the contents into her hands.

Diamonds. Some big, some small. All reflecting the closet light like little sparks. There must've been a hundred of them.

The final key to her escape plan was in place. After closing the door to the safe and pocketing the pouch of diamonds in the pocket of her jeans, she hurried to her room and gathered up her backpack she'd filled with the meager belongings she still had from before moving in with Myles. He'd wanted her to get rid of everything, but she'd told him the clothes were mementos of her past. He'd allowed her to keep them as long as she never wore them in his presence. Like he was some sort of king and non-designer clothes were offensive to his grand personage.

She'd just slipped the pouch of diamonds and his wadded up, bloodied shirt into the bag when her door opened.

"Ricky!" she gasped, clutching the bag to her as if it were a shield to protect her from whatever was hurled her way.

"Oh, my God!" Ricky said. The tall, lanky man who'd won her heart, hurried over to put his arms around her. "I'm going to kill him. I swear it."

"No. You can't. I won't have you going to prison because of me." She stepped back, slightly wobbly. "But I do need your help."

Myles had gone to the girl he was courting as a replacement for her to spend the weekend and dismissed his crew for privacy, keeping only one bodyguard nearby. Ricky had returned to check on her. With his help, they concocted the plan to distract Myles in another direction, then Ricky smuggled her out of the compound in the trunk of one of the cars. Lucky for her, no security cameras taped the coming and going of the compound. They'd arrived at the bus station in time for her to bid Ricky farewell and disappear.

For the first few years she'd watched for him to show up in Westen. Even though she'd never told him about her hometown, her wounded heart and spirit desperately wanted him to make the effort to find her. After time passed and she was busy starting up the Dye Right, her need for him diminished as she gained her self-confidence again. Somewhere along the way she realized that the idea of Ricky as her knight in shining armor saving her from the monster that was Myles faded away, transforming into the knowledge that she'd been the one to save herself. In the depths of her fear and physically traumatized, she found the strength to get out of the situation.

She'd also taken precautions to keep Myles off her trail. Reverting to her birth name and never telling anyone in town about her brief career on Broadway as Meredith Charbeaux, even avoiding singing in the choir or anywhere else, afraid someone might recognize her voice. She'd evaded all photos, even when Sean Callahan had done a large piece in the newspaper and online about the Dye Right. She'd asked him to never put her picture in the paper. He'd surprised her by always honoring that request. Over time, she'd formed her own family of friends and employees, even feeling like a grandmother to Sylvie's little girl Sunshine.

After all these years, if Ricky really had shown up in town it didn't matter why. She didn't need him in her life anymore. And she'd be more than happy to tell him that.

CHAPTER 19

"I'm sorry I dragged you away from your staff meeting," Dylan said as they finished their dinner. "I didn't want to send Bobby to get Meg, she needs to rest off her feet. And I was afraid Meg would get really concerned if I asked Gage to go."

They'd stopped at the newspaper office long enough for Sean to give instructions to Marta about Meg's ad, find out that the paper would be going to press on time and get in his Mustang once more. He'd even stopped at the local grocers and ran inside to grab steaks, asparagus and potatoes for dinner tonight, which she had to admit was delicious. Who knew he was quite the gourmet chef?

While he'd been shopping, she'd taken the time to call the clinic and give Emma—who thankfully answered the phone and not Harriett—the details of what had occurred at the flower shop and Henry's first and second blood sugar readings. Emma said Meg had already followed through with making an appointment to come in and Clint ordered a blood workup on him, including an A1C to check how his sugars had been doing the past few months.

"Don't worry about it," Sean said. "The meeting was short and productive. I was more than happy to go and Meg is pretty unflappable, well, except for when it concerns Henry. And you were right."

"I was? About what?"

"Sending your six-foot-four-inch always intense brother-in-law into the fair would've had Meg afraid Henry had been robbed."

Dylan laughed, leaning back to stroke Wöden's back as he lay by her chair, sated from the grilled steak Sean had given him. "He's not that bad."

Sean gathered their empty plates and put them in the sink, then stood very straight, hands on his hips and gave her a one-brow-lifted gaze that Gage had perfected years ago. "I'm the law around here. Don't give me any trouble."

She laughed at his impersonation. "Okay. He *is* pretty intense, but it's just because he loves this town and all the people in it, even you." She finished her wine and carried both their glasses to the sink.

"Whoa! Let's not go crazy," Sean said as he rinsed the dishes and loaded them into the dishwasher. "Gage tolerates me as an improvement over the guy before me."

"The guy who used the town as a base for his illegal drug lab? The guy who tried to blow up the town? The guy who nearly killed him? Yeah, I can see how he'd think anyone was an improvement, even you," she teased, leaning one hip against the counter to watch him work. Something she'd discovered the past few nights. Sean didn't expect her to do clean up and he was very efficient at it. "I've learned one thing about Gage since he's been married to Bobby. He doesn't put up with bullcrap out of anyone. He's a straight shooter. If he likes you, he likes you. If he doesn't. You will know it. So take the win, Callahan."

"You're the only person I know who can make my last name

sound sassy and sexy," he said, smiling as he wiped his hands dry with a towel.

Surprising him, she wrapped her arms around his neck. "That's because I think you're very sexy."

"Oh, you do?" he said with a grin, another thing she found sexy about him.

"Yes, I very much do." Moving in closer, she pressed her lips to his in a slow, seductive kiss. His arms wrapped around her to hold her tightly against his body. Heat surged through her as she parted her lips, tasting the sweetness from the wine and the decidedly masculine flavor of him.

He fisted his hands into the back of her top, tilting his head and increasing the pressure on her lips, taking over the kiss. Her pulse raced and she moaned at the desire flushing through her. More. She definitely wanted more of this man, more of his kisses. Gripping his shoulder with one arm, she ran the fingers of her other hand up into his hair, letting him know what she wanted.

Suddenly, he eased back, lessening the kiss until he finally lifted his mouth and pressed his forehead against hers, his eyes closed. "Damn, Doc. I can't keep doing this."

"Can't keep doing what?" she asked, feeling confused and hurt at the same time, anger slowly igniting inside.

His eyes snapped open. She read both desire and tenderness in their green depths. "Stopping myself from carrying you into the bedroom, stripping you naked and making love to you like I so, so want to do."

Wow! Talk about a way to douse the anger and put cooling salve to her hurt. It made her want to fist pump her victory as a woman successfully seducing her man. Slowly she smiled. "I don't know why you keep stopping. Sounds like a very good plan to me."

"I'm trying to be honorable here and you're making it very difficult."

"I am?"

"Yes, because you're so tempting. You're beautiful inside and out. Smart. Caring. And sometimes just vulnerable enough to make me want to fight off all the dragons threatening you. If I give in. If we go further than just some very enjoyable kisses, I'm going to want more."

"And the problem with that is what?"

He lifted his head and stroked one hand down her cheek. "The problem is, sweetheart, you are at a crossroads in your life. I'm not. I know exactly where I'm meant to be. Right here in Westen."

She tilted her head trying to determine where he was headed with this conversation. "I know that. What does that have to do with us having sex?"

"Because I don't just want casual sex with you. I want something more. Something sustainable. Permanent." He inhaled and slowly exhaled. "I always have."

"You have?"

"Yes. From the first moment we met. But I always knew you had things to accomplish. While my world was just starting here, in Westen. It's where my heart beats truest. I love being part of this town, watching it grow, yet keep the smalltown friendliness that is its core. I'd love to share this life with you. But." He paused long enough to hold her gaze as if willing her to understand what he was saying. "But, you have to want to stay here because you believe this is where you're meant to be. Not because people have pressured you to do so. Not because of our physical relationship. If you gave up your lucrative medical career for that, eventually you'd come to resent me. And that's the last thing I want." Again, he paused, this time his eyes wary, searching. "Does any of this make sense?"

"It does," she said automatically, her mind still processing all he'd said and her emotions rolling up and down with those same words. "You're right. My life is too up in the air to step full-force into a relationship, even if I really, really want to."

His soft slight smile eased some of her anxiety that she might be selfishly hurting him. "I hope I made it clear, that I do, too."

"You did." She ran her hands over his shoulders and down to rest on his arms that still encircled her. "I guess I still have a lot of thinking to do. I think I should head to bed early tonight. I want to have things all clean and ready for Chloe and the baby when Wes brings them home."

"Still want me to stay?"

"Would you hate me if I said yes? If I'm alone, I'll just listen to every cricket, frog and owl sound and not sleep a wink."

He chuckled and pulled her into a hug. "I'll be happy to protect you from all animal sounds for another night. Besides the sofa is pretty damn comfortable, but don't tell Wes I said that."

A low moan sounded near the front door. They both turned to see Wöden sitting patiently in front of it, tail wagging patiently.

"I'll let him out, then lock up while you get ready for bed," Sean said, stepping away.

She wished he'd kiss her good night, but knew how unfair it would be to him. Despite his presence in the cabin, she doubted she'd get much sleep anyways. Without a word, she headed into the guest bedroom, her mind full of what ifs and questions.

As she washed her face, brushed her teeth and pulled on the over-sized sleeping shirt, she considered her personal situation.

For years she'd been so consumed with her studies and training that she'd only had time for the cursory date, always keeping the man at arm's length both physically and emotionally. Intellectually, she knew it wasn't fair to them, her patients or even herself to step into a relationship at that point in her life.

And how she felt about Callahan was different from any of the men she'd occasionally dated, more intimate. It had started slow. Companionship, camaraderie. Someone to relax with over beer, burgers and pool. Someone she wasn't competing with for a position in a residency program. Someone who made her laugh and always seemed genuinely happy to see her. If she was honest with herself, coming to Westen wasn't just about seeing her sisters. More and more it had been to spend time with Sean.

Now that she'd completed her education and training, she found herself wanting something more personal. But did she want something permanent like he'd said he was looking for? He'd been honest. He wasn't planning on leaving Westen.

She really was in a dilemma. To pursue this attraction she had for Sean, she'd have to give up her dream of being a trauma surgeon in the city where she'd help all kinds of people. Would it be worth it? Would she regret the decision? What if it didn't work out?

If she continued down the path she'd been on since that horrible day, she knew her skills could save many lives, but at what cost to her? Nothing but hours elbows-deep in blood and guts, fighting for the lives of gang-bangers who shot each other over drugs or turf? The occasional visit with her sisters and their families over holidays? A meal with Sean here and there? All work. A life of loneliness? Is that what she really wanted?

Yes, she had co-workers and colleagues, but had there ever been anyone she wanted to spend time with in a non-professional way? Someone to share her fears and workday stories with? Yes. There had been Bulldog. Of course, at first he'd wanted to get into her personal life because she'd been a protection detail assignment. Once that danger was past, he'd persisted in finding ways to hang out with her. Yet, when he'd needed her, she couldn't do a damn thing for him.

Would walking away from what Callahan was offering really be the better choice?

After all these days in Westen, she really wasn't any closer to making a decision. Her feelings for Sean only mucked up the water worse than ever. What she needed was a great big neon sign from God, saying DO THIS!

Rolling over in the bed, she slammed her hand into the extra pillow, then pulled it in tight. Somehow, she didn't think God was planning on doing that.

CHAPTER 20

A light knock sounded on her back door.

Startled, Twylla glanced at the clock. Ten-fifteen. No one in Westen came visiting this late at night unless it was a problem. And then it was to your front door.

Already on edge from all the memories that had been flooding her over the last few days, her heartrate increased. She headed to her kitchen, stopping at the pantry to pull out the baseball bat she kept stored there. The gun she had in her bedside table was for a sudden attack while she slept, something she'd often experienced with a drunk Myles. For unexpected visitors here? She could swing the bat like a major leaguer disarming without risking actually killing someone.

Thankfully, the kitchen lights were still off. She peeked out the window to see a tall, slim silhouette on the porch. Definitely not Myles.

Gripping the bat with both hands, she inhaled and exhaled slowly, willing her heart to slow and her mind to clear. She was in control. Then she approached the backdoor.

"Who's there?"

"Meri, it's Ricky."

She relaxed, but only slightly. Continuing her grip on the bat with one hand, she flipped the deadbolt, opened the backdoor and stepped back. "Come in."

He opened the screen door, stepped into her kitchen and quickly closed both doors behind him.

She flipped on the overhead pot lights. "Why are you here?"

"You're still so beautiful," he said, his eyes seeming to skim over her face and his tentative smile almost melting her heart.

"Thank you, but that's not what I asked."

He took a step towards her.

She lifted the bat and retreated two steps. "Don't come any closer."

His smile faded and his hands came up, palms out. "Whoa, Meri. I'm not going to hurt you."

"It's Twylla. But you already know that don't you? Answer my question, why are you here?"

"Myles is on his way."

All the oxygen on earth seemed to just evaporate and the world closed in around her. She stumbled backward, clutching the bat with one hand and catching her balance on the edge of her kitchen table. "H-how?" she managed to gasp out.

"A picture on the internet."

"A picture?" she asked, trying to wrap her head around the words. She'd always avoided any pictures. No social media after it became popular. Even advertising for her salon was all about her shop, the stylists and clients. Never her.

"Why don't you sit down?" Ricky said, coming closer and pulling out a chair for her.

She slid into it, still holding onto the bat loosely with her left hand. "I don't understand. I'm never in any pictures and certainly not on the internet."

Ricky took a chair across the table from her. "It was at a baseball game."

She'd seen the pictures Sean Callahan had posted from that game. She hadn't been in them. He'd kept his promise and cropped her out of them. She shook her head. "No. I saw those pictures on the newspaper site. I wasn't in any of them."

"It wasn't in the local paper." He pulled out his phone and typed something in. "A realtor agency was using the little league team to do PR work on social media. You're in the far corner of the picture. And only those of us who know you well would be able to tell it was you."

He passed the phone over to her. It was just as he said.

"Nora," she muttered, shaking her head. One woman's ego and need for attention had destroyed all her years of hiding.

"Myles found it before I could get it deleted. It's the way you were standing," he said, enlarging the image and pointing to her right arm curved so her hand rested on her heart.

"You're always saying the pledge," she said, repeating Myles' well-worn complaint about her.

"Apparently, that's what caught his attention." He laid his hand over hers. "I'm sorry I didn't get to it before him. For years I scoured every newspaper that came into the compound to be sure there was nothing of you in them. I paid off private investigators to not look too closely into what happened to you. I guess I got complacent, thinking he'd stopped talking about you because he'd give up the search."

"But he hadn't."

Ricky shook his head. "No. He'd just decided to do it himself. With the internet and his tablet, he spent his spare time scouring social media pages for anything that might link to you."

"And Nora just served me up."

"I'm sorry, Meri...uhm Twylla. After eighteen years, three wives, and five kids, I thought Myles had finally given up his obsession over you."

"He won't give up until one of us is dead," she said, repeating what she'd known since the day she pulled that little black velvet bag out of his safe.

"Then we have to get you out of town. Tonight."

"No."

Incredulity written all over his face, he stared at her. "What do you mean no? You just said yourself he won't stop until you're dead."

"I said, he won't stop until one of us is dead," she clarified, pulling her hand from beneath his. "I'm not running again. This is my home and I'm not going anywhere."

"I don't think I made myself clear. Myles knows where you are. Either I bring you back to him, or he's going to send someone here to kill you, sweetheart."

"Don't call me that."

"Sweetheart? Your life is in danger, and you want to argue over a word?"

"You gave up the right to call me any kind of endearment when you didn't get on that bus with me. When you sent me off by myself in fear for my life. When you didn't show up in my life a week, a month a year, or even a decade later."

"You know why I couldn't come. Even though I love you, I had to stay behind to keep your trail cold. Hiding you solo was much easier than giving him a pair of targets to hunt."

She studied him, this man she once thought she loved but who was now a stranger, in the dim light from the single bulb she kept on over the stove at night. "You really believe that, don't you?"

"That I had to stay behind to keep you safe?" he asked. "Of course I did."

"No. I don't believe you did. But that's not what I was talking about."

He drew his brows down in confusion. "What?"

"You really believed you loved me, but could let me leave,

injured to fend for myself. I thought so too, but I was wrong. You were wrong." Fear now gone, she let the anger she'd held for how Myles and he had treated her back then. "I was nothing more to you and Myles than a plaything. Some toy you both wanted to own and abuse."

"Myles was the one who used you like a punching bag. I never hurt you," he said, his voice raising in anger.

"You're right Myles did beat me like I was a worthless piece of crap. But you're also wrong. What you did hurt me far worse than Myles' fists or feet ever could." Setting the bat against the chair next to her, she slowly stood to stare down at him, her arms crossed in front of her. "You gave me hope for a better life with someone who said they loved me. I believed I was more important to you than Myles."

He held out his hands to her. "You were. You are. I had to send you away to save you."

"You know, for the first few weeks on my own, I actually believed that. I was busy traveling through upper New York state, staying in barely habitable motels, scared Myles would find me or some local creep would attack me. But being alone like that, I had more than enough time to think. To really examine my choices and the people I'd let into my life. And you know something? I learned that in all my life, only two people had ever really loved me. My mother and myself."

"But—"

She held up her hand to stop him from saying another word. "So, I picked myself up out of the bed where I'd been sick with the flu for a week and climbed yet another bus, this time heading back here. To my home. To my mother. And you know what I found then?"

He shook his head.

"I found out that in the year I was with Myles turning myself into a doormat for him, my mother had died."

"I'm so sorry...Twylla," he said, and she could read the sympathy in his face.

She didn't want to soften towards him. Right now, her anger felt like armor. Armor she was going to need to get past him and defend herself from Myles when he reared his head.

"Don't! I don't need you feeling sorry for me. I was very sick when I got home. It was the kindness of people here that got me through it. These people supported me when I had nothing and championed me getting my salon running. They helped it become a success. They are my family and I'm not leaving again no matter what you say and no matter what Myles threatens me with. So, you can leave now," she said, going to the backdoor and opening it.

"Twylla, you're not being reasonable," he said as he stood. "Myles has stewed for nearly twenty years. His need for revenge on you for leaving him isn't something you can talk him out of. He said if he didn't hear from me by tonight, he would send one of his other men. One of the ones he'd send to end a problem."

"One of his hitmen," she said, still holding the door and willing herself not to panic.

"Yes," Ricky said, moving closer. "You have to get out of town, at least for a little while."

She shook her head. "No. It's about time this ended. I won't live the rest of my life hiding from him. When you talk to him tonight, you tell him I said that."

"You're really going to stay." It wasn't a question. He finally understood. "You'll die."

"Maybe. Maybe not. But whatever happens, it's going to be on my own terms, not his."

Shaking his head, Ricky walked past her onto the back porch. He turned to close the screen door.

"You should leave town, Ricky. It's time you lived your own life out from under Myles' thumb. You might just find some peace," she said before closing the door and turning the deadbolt once more.

Standing in the dark long after he'd exited her yard, she listened for his footsteps in the alley to fade away. Despite what he thought, she wasn't planning to play the martyr and just wait for Myles or one of his other henchmen to show up and murder her. Closing her eyes and clearing her mind, she prayed for guidance on how to handle this problem. Finally, she knew what to do and went for her phone.

Unsurprising, the number she dialed was answered on the first ring, even this late at night.

"Harriett?"

CHAPTER 21

"So, what brings you by the clinic this fine afternoon?" Clint Preston asked from behind the antique oak desk in his office. "I thought you'd be doting on your sister and new nephew."

Dylan smiled, leaning back in the chair across from him. Sean left after breakfast to get prepped for his morning meeting with Congressman Rawlins at his home, so she'd spent the morning cleaning up and preparing for her sister and nephew's arrival. The conversation still on her mind while doing that, she'd called and checked to see if Clint had a little time in his schedule to talk with her. So, here she sat in the office of the Victorian-era house his uncle had turned into a medical clinic.

It was a warm room, full of family pictures and pictures of Westen's citizens with Clint's uncle Doc Ray, the town's former general practitioner. A huge picture window behind Clint looked out onto a green space resembling something similar to an English garden, complete with stone walkways and benches spaced underneath tall maple and oak shade trees. A place where someone recovering from an illness or injury could spend time outdoors.

Built-in floor to ceiling bookshelves covered the other two walls with books. Medical journals, classic and contemporary novels, non-fiction and biographies. And on one shelf, toddler height, were stacks of children's books, some of which she remembered being read to her by her parents and sisters in her own childhood.

"Wes brought Chloe and Benjamin home about two hours ago" she said. "By the time she got inside, fed the baby and ate lunch Chloe was worn out and ready for a nap. Apparently one of her nurses warned her this would happen and then told her for the next few days at least she should sleep whenever Benjamin does."

Clint nodded. "Good advice. People, not just new mothers, don't realize how exhausting just getting home from the hospital can be. And glad to hear she's listening to the OB nurses. Their experience with new mothers and babies is instrumental for new parents to get through the first few weeks. Trust me, even though Emma had already been a mother to the twins eight years earlier, she and I relied on the nurses' help when we first had Belle and then Wyatt, too."

"My control-freak sister, Chloe is certainly out of her element, that's for sure. Since she, Benjamin and Wes were all down for a little while, I decided to come chat with you about something that's kind of personal. Doctor to doctor, if you don't mind."

Clint leaned back in his chair, studying her with the serious doctor-wondering-what-your-symptoms-are-and-how-bad-is-this-going-to-be look. "Sure. What's on your mind?"

"It's not a medical question and I'm quite healthy, so you can relax," she said with a smile as he did just that. "What I want to know is what made you give up your ER practice for a general practice here in Westen?"

"Ah," he said. "When Uncle Ray asked me to fill in for him, I was fighting a bad case of burnout. So, I thought coming to Westen would give me some time to get my head back in the game. I'd only planned to be here for a few months while he and Aunt Caroline were on their around the world cruise."

"What made you decide to stay? And please don't say love."

He chuckled, crossed his arms over his desk and leaned in over them. "But it was love. I fell in love with Emma, her boys, her mother. But it wasn't just that love that gave my life more meaning. And I suspect Uncle Ray knew that's what I was looking for when he asked me to step in. Working in a big city ER, I saw lots of action, lots of interesting cases. Life and death on a daily basis. But also heartbreak cases. Some because there was no hope of saving them. Others were heartbreaking because no matter what we did, their living situation was hopeless and no matter how many times we sent them home patched up, at some point they weren't going to make it."

She nodded. "I've seen lots of those as a resident."

"Trauma surgery has to have its own challenges."

"Some nights it's like being on the front lines of a war zone. Quick decisions both in the triage and in the OR can save or cost a life."

"But they're starting to just be bodies you work on?" he asked, hitting the question she'd been feeling for a while.

It wasn't the last case of her trauma fellowship that had her wondering about her professional choice. That case had been a two car collision and although the injuries on her patient had been serious, nothing she hadn't done before. And thankfully, her patient and everyone in the other vehicle all survived.

"What has me questioning things is the month of gang shootings I worked on. Night after night, chasing bullets inside the body of kids who should be going to basketball games or senior proms, trying to repair organs and blood vessels while blood is pouring out onto the floor faster than the anesthesia staff could pump it in." She paused and licked her lips, then propped her elbow onto the arm of the chair and rested her suddenly weary cheek against her fist. "More and more I'm finding myself disconnected from the people I went into this profession to save."

He nodded as if he knew exactly what she was saying. "I'm not going to lie to you and tell you that I walked into the clinic that first day and poof I suddenly knew I belonged here. Hell, the first thing I had to accept was that I wasn't in charge here. Harriett was."

Dylan laughed sardonically. "Oh, she gave me a tour of the farms and lined up loads of patients whose lives were impacted with no trauma surgeon in the area."

"She doesn't mince words," Clint said, nodding sympathetically. "But once I got used to her, I started to see patients with all kinds of problems like broken wrists—those were Emma's boys."

"Your stepsons both had broken wrists?"

Clint nodded. "At the same time."

"How did that happen?"

"They jumped out of a tree. Seems they heard Lorna, Harriett and Emma's mother talking about how she needed to meet me. The boys decided to do something about it," he said with a wry smile.

"How tall was the tree?" Dylan asked.

"I went out after getting their arms fixed. The lowest branch was about fifteen feet." He shook his head. "The more dangerous aspect of their escapade was the mammoth-sized bull that lived in the field where that tree grows."

"Oh, my God! They could've died."

"That's what Emma said."

"I bet." She shook her head sort of admiring the twins for taking the initiative, even if their actions were dangerous.

"Poor guys ended up in trouble for a while. So, they were my first patients that had me reconnecting with why I wanted to be a doctor. As I took care of more of Westen's residents I slowly realized that maybe there was enough emergency cases to keep my adrenaline pumped, but enough human connection to make me want to go to work every day."

"And now you have a family here."

"I have a big family, which includes your sister Bobby, since she married Emma's cousin. And I have a community family I'd do whatever I could to keep healthy and safe." He fixed his steady gaze on her. "For me, coming to Westen let me connect with my patients on a more personal level. It also allowed me to know I was making a difference in their lives. Which is what I was missing. I guess the question for you is, what are you missing? And can you find it in Westen?"

She sighed. "I can see how much Westen has grown since the first time I came to see Bobby. So, there's no doubt that there's a need for more doctors in the area." She paused and gave him an apologetic smile. "Not that you're not doing a great job."

He laughed. "Trust me, I don't mind the competition. Between the extra hours and patients in my practice these days, and working with the hospital board, meeting with architects and construction contractors, I'm lucky to have Sundays off to be with the family. If Emma didn't work here with me, I don't know that we'd ever have time together some weeks. And besides, if you decide to start a medical practice here you really wouldn't be competition. You'd be focused on pre-op, surgical and post-op care of patients. Ones I'd be happy to refer your direction."

"That is one of my other questions. I've toured the new hospital and love the OR suite. Performing routine surgical procedures would be fantastic and with the growing community, I'm sure I'd have enough work for building my surgical practice. But you know I just finished my year-long fellowship in trauma surgery. I have to wonder if those skills and all that training would be wasted here in Westen."

"I can see your concern. You're leaving a big city with all the variety of trauma that occurs there—stabbings, shootings, vehicular accidents—to come live in what most people consider a sleepy little rural town."

She nodded and glad he understood her dilemma.

"But since I've been in Westen, we've had several shootings, a major tunnel collapse on your brother-in-law that could've been worse than it was."

"I'll say. A broken arm is probably the least injury he could have sustained in that situation."

"I've stitched together more than one farmer with injuries from farm equipment. And being near the highways we see our fair share of accidents. And in the winter, at least one pile-up due to sleet, freezing rain, snow or a combination of all three every year."

A knock sounded on the door. Before Clint could say come in, it popped open and there stood Harriett. "Lunch break's over. Your one-o'clock's here, Doc. And Emma's taking over."

"She is?" Clint asked. "This is usually her day out of the office. Where are you going?"

"None of your business," Harriett said and turned. In a blink she disappeared back down the hall.

"I guess that's my cue to be on my way. I'm sorry you had to miss lunch to meet with me," Dylan said, standing and heading to the door, Clint on her heels.

"I didn't miss it. I ate before you got here. Harriett made sure I had a little extra time after my last patient, but just enough time for a sandwich, mind you," he said with a grin.

"Thank you for answering my questions. You've given me something to think about." She paused in the doorway and leaned back to whisper. "If I stay, promise me one thing."

"What's that?"

"That Harriett stays *your* office nurse. I don't want to inherit her."

He laughed. "I don't think I could get rid of her, if I tried."

"I heard that," the nurse called from down the hall.

CHAPTER 22

"It took me a few years to figure it out, but I'm not as stupid as you seem to think," Myles said pacing in front of the chair he'd tied Ricky to in the hotel room. "At first, my anger clouded my vision. I didn't see you stabbing me in the back. Then after the second private investigator reported he hadn't found any clue to her trail then promptly left town, I figured it out. Someone was working very hard to keep me from finding the bitch."

Unable to verbally refute Myles' words over the cloth gag he'd tied over his mouth, Ricky tasted his own blood from his busted lip and broken teeth soaked into the cloth. He'd spent the night outside, watching Twylla's place after she threw him out. When he arrived back at his motel room this morning, he'd collapsed on the bed, only to awaken to the pounding on the door. The moment he opened it, Myles had sucker-punched him. Before he could fight back, two of his henchmen had him bound and gagged in the chair, ears ringing and one eye swollen shut from the repeated fists to his face. Myles wasn't interested in anything he said in his defense. He wanted something to hit. Better him than Twylla.

Besides, there was no denying his accusations. He'd done exactly what he'd accused him of doing.

Another fist connected with his jaw. Something cracked.

"So, I kept you close. I waited. I watched you. But it became clear to me that you didn't know where she was either. That's when I started searching for her on my own." Finally, he stopped pacing and sat on the end of the bed and held out his hand. One of the others laid the white hotel towel in it. Slowly, he wiped his blood onto it, turning it rusty red and brown.

"You know, I didn't need to send you off looking for her. I'm just as capable of searching the origins of that picture as you were. I wanted you to know I'd figured out you were the one who helped her escape. I just wanted to know if you knew where she'd hidden them."

Them? Had he heard him correctly? There was more than one?

He'd known she was pregnant. She'd told him one night before she escaped, when he'd accompanied her to an art exhibit. Myles hated being around anyone in the arts but wanted to invest in pieces to hide some of his assets, so Meri always went in his place with Ricky escorting her.

But she hadn't been very far along when she left. Had there been twins? And had she gone through with her plans to have them? And where were they?

Another fist connected with his cheek, sending his head sideways and more pain searing his brain. Stars circled stars as he blinked and tried to clear his vision. This time it was the larger of Myles' two minions rubbing his fist with glee.

Myles leaned in to block his vision of anything else. "Do I have your attention now?"

Ricky swallowed blood and spittle but stared straight into his torturer's face. He'd be damned if he'd let this mountain of excrement see his fear.

"Good. I'm going to ask you again. Do you know where she hid them?"

Slowly he shook his head.

"Okay. Do you deny helping her get away with them?"

Again, he shook his head. It was the truth.

"Did she give you one in payment?"

Payment? He thought she gave him a child? Myles knew he didn't have a kid. What the hell was he talking about? His cocaine had finally fried his brain. He shook his head.

"Does she know I'm here?"

He'd only warned her Myles was on the way, so technically she didn't know he was here already, so he shook his head once more.

"Good." Myles stood and paced in front of him again. When he stopped, Ricky watched him screw the silencer muzzle to his weapon. "I was going to keep you alive long enough for her to see me kill you for your betrayal, but frankly, I don't need your baggage weighing me down. I've waited long enough to get back what belongs to me and make that bitch pay."

This was it. This was how he betrayed Meri...Twylla. He was going to die in a hotel room in this podunk town and she would never know how much he loved her.

The zipping sound filled his ears a second before pain exploded in his chest.

~

"What's going on, Callahan?" Bobby asked as Sean stepped into the sheriff's office.

"Just finished meeting with Tobias over at his house and thought I'd do a walking tour of the downtown area on my way back to the office. Tons of people in town," he said, pulling one of the guest chairs over near her desk and sitting.

"Tell me about it. Gage is out making rounds in the squad car right now and I'm sitting in here being useless with my feet up." She wiggled her feet on the chair she had them propped on. "How was the interview with Tobias?"

"Informative," he said, sinking back in the chair and resting one foot on the opposite knee. "He gave me a complete list of all the bills he either helped sponsor or voted on that he thought helped the people of Westen."

"Oh, that will be fun to write about," she said with just enough sarcasm to make him chuckle. "That's Tobias, always politicking."

"If I just wrote the article as a list, then it would be boring for sure, but he also had some news I think the people of Westen would be interested in hearing. Apparently, the state is investing in trade schools to train people who don't want to go to or can't afford the expense of college."

"That's a good idea," Bobby said, nodding her head. "Not everyone is meant for an academic life. Take Joe Gillis over at the Knobs & Knockers. Sure, he inherited the hardware store, but his father had him apprentice with a local carpenter, plumber and electrician right out of high school. He said he wanted Joe to not just sell tools and equipment but be able to instruct people on how to use them."

Sean nodded. "He's passing that training on to the young man he hired from the Westen House, Geoff, with the side business in remodeling and flipping houses. I did an entire series on Joe for a fall exposé. With all the new people in town, I thought we should do pieces on citizens that were here before the explosion changed things."

"Hang on a second," Bobby said, lowering her feet and wiggling out of her office chair. "My bladder is the size of a lemon these days. I want to hear more about Tobias' plans if you can wait a moment."

Sean chuckled as she slowly walked to the rear of the office. He didn't know how women went through all the changes in their bodies to have kids. But given the leap in the town's birth rate, they must be willing to put up with every ache and pain. He knew he couldn't do it.

Staring out the window he watched pedestrians walking up and down the sidewalk. He didn't kid himself. He was hoping to see one very unique and tall silhouette among the crowd. It was one of the reasons he'd taken a chance to stop by the sheriff's office in hopes that Dylan would come in to visit her sister. On his way back from Tobias' place, he'd driven by the medical clinic and saw her BMW parked outside. He didn't think there was anything physically wrong with her, but she also hadn't said she had plans to go to the clinic, either.

When he'd left the cabin this morning, there'd been a bit of strain between them. He'd wanted to kiss her goodbye, but after their talk last night he didn't want to confuse the situation even more. So, they'd had a quiet breakfast then he'd packed up his backpack, knowing he wouldn't be needed to spend another night with her in the cabin and headed out, so many things left unsaid between them.

The opening of the bathroom door drew his attention away from the street once more. Bobby walked over to the office break area and pulled out a bottle of water from the mini-fridge. "Would you like one?" she asked, pausing with the door open.

He shook his head. "No. I'm good."

She closed the door and returned to her seat, wiggling back then elevating her feet once more. "It's a never-ending cycle. I have to drink to stay hydrated, but then I have to pee." She laughed. "And that was way more information than you wanted to hear. So, tell me more about Tobias' latest plans for Westen. I have to admit that when I first met him, I didn't think much of him. He was sort of a caricature of small-town politicians I'd seen in bad b-film movies as a teen. Who knew Gage almost getting killed in that explosion would kick his civic duty gene into activation mode?"

"He has stepped up to the plate," Sean agreed. "When I first got to town and heard about the whole incident and the money the state was frantically pumping into the area as sort of hush money for the DEA's inadvertent involvement with the near tragedy, I was skeptical about what Tobias and the council would do with it. I watched him with a cynical eye. It surprised me when instead of pocketing the funds or using them on frivolous things, he led the movement to develop a plan for improving the town and the surrounding area both aesthetically and financially."

"So, what's the newest project?" she asked, then took a large drink from the water bottle.

"Apparently, Tobias has been meeting with heads of the state trade unions about coordinating their apprenticeship programs under one roof and locating it in the new business corridor where the microchips manufacturing building is going to be located. He wants to also offer elective business courses for the apprentices if they want to eventually run their own plumbing or electrical companies."

"What a great idea."

"He also met with business and a man interested in expanding his bolt, nut and screw manufacturing company approached him for information about the town's manufacturing corridor to possibly build here. So, lots more job opportunities coming to town."

The office phone rang, and she reached to answer it. "Westen Sheriff's office, Deputy Justice. Hey, Mayor what's going on? Yes, Gage is planning on being at the hospital opening an hour before the ceremony tomorrow to set security."

With one ear listening to Bobby's conversation, Sean took

the moment to scan the street outside once more. Still no sign of Dylan or her car. Damn it, he really wanted to talk with her, to see for himself that she was doing okay with what she could think was tantamount to a rejection of her. Which wasn't what he intended.

Then something caught his eye.

He stood and wandered over to the window.

Cleetus, dressed in regular clothes and not his deputy uniform, exited the Peaches 'N Cream Café with a large bag of to-go food in his hands. That wasn't unusual for the deputy, but he wasn't headed towards the sheriff's office. Instead, he walked in the direction of the Dye Right. Directly back to where he'd seen the big man sitting outside the shop on his way into town.

"Everything okay, Sean?" Bobby asked.

"Yeah," he said, suddenly curious about what Cleetus was up to. Because although he might be dressed casually, the deputy still had his weapon holstered on his belt. The last thing he wanted to do was worry the very pregnant Bobby, because his journalist gene was tapping the merengue down his spine. He turned and smiled, then walked to the office door. "I think I'll be on my way. If you see Dylan, can you tell her I was asking about her?"

Before Bobby could question him about that last comment, he exited and headed for the Dye Right. If he didn't know better, he'd swear Cleetus was working semi-undercover in a protection detail. He'd seen enough of them in New York to recognize one. Usually with high-profile targets.

But at the Dye Right?

CHAPTER 23

The bell rang as the Dye Right's door opened.

"May I help you, sir?" Molly, who was manning the receptionist area for the afternoon asked.

At the word sir, Twylla stood up from her desk and moved to the office door to listen to the conversation. Used to be they'd steer any male customers down the street to the barbershop where they could get a cut and shave. Lately, with all the new families and young working executives moving into the area, they'd had men who wanted more of a styling coming into the salon.

"I'm in need of a haircut," a very deep and very familiar voice said. A voice she hadn't heard in eighteen years, but one she'd never forget.

Twylla sucked in her breath and pressed her back against her office wall. He was here. After her talk with Ricky last night, she knew Myles was on his way. She'd hoped she'd have a little more time. Time to prepare herself for this confrontation.

Cleetus had been keeping quiet guard out front all morning in hopes that his presence would deter Myles from attacking her during business offers. But Myles had to have been watching the shop and when the deputy had gone to make a food run for the girls, he made his move. There was no one to help.

It was up to her to keep the others safe.

Across the hallway, she saw Darcy, Sylvie and Gretchen doing their clients hair, along with Mara, managing the broom and dustbin full of hair clippings. Two middle-aged ladies and one lady near seventy were seated at the stations. She needed to get them out of the shop, out of the line of fire when Myles' temper blew. And it would definitely do that the moment he saw her.

She glanced out her door at the reception area. No one could see her.

Going back to her desk, she grabbed her cell phone and punched in a number.

"Yep."

"Harriett, it's happening."

"Stick to the plan. I'll be ready."

Then it went dead.

With a quick steadying breath, she darted across the hall. Stopping at Gretchen's chair first, motioning Sylvie, Darcy and Mara to join her.

"What's up?" Darcy asked.

"Listen to me and keep your voices down," she said, hoping the music playing overhead would muffle any conversation they had.

The four younger women nodded. "I think we're being robbed," she said, better to lie and get their immediate cooperation, than trying to explain things. "So, I want you to get your clients out the back of the salon, and I'll keep them occupied."

"But Molly's up there," Darcy said looking wide-eyed towards the front of the shop.

"I'll take care of Molly," she said, hoping it was true, then moved her staff back to their clients.

"I'm only halfway finished highlighting Nicole's hair," Gretchen said.

She fixed her I'm-the-boss-and-in-charge look at her newest stylist. "This could be life or death. You have to go *now*. If there's any damage to her hair, I'll reimburse her for it and the repair. Just go. All of you."

The urgency and firmness in her voice must have registered. As if a light went off over all their heads, they quickly hurried to their chairs, gave a quiet explanation to the clients and maneuvered them all out the backway where Mara held the door open.

Twylla inhaled and exhaled. Now all she had to worry about was how to get Molly safely away. It was her responsibility to protect her employees, her girls. She'd always known one day Myles would show up in her life demanding his diamonds back and he'd take his revenge out on her. But she'd be damned if an innocent life would be lost to him.

"Meri, I know you're here," Myles called out.

She slipped her phone into the pocket of her sweater and grabbed her car keys off her desk and slipped them in too. She already had a plan in place for if he came to her house. Now she just had to implement it here. Head held high, she walked to the front of her shop. She wouldn't give this monster the satisfaction of seeing her fear. Not anymore.

There he stood in his fancy, expensive suit, holding a gun. The grey hair around his temples would've given him a distinguished air if he hadn't gained nearly a hundred pounds and years of drugs and alcohol hadn't turned his skin sallow and wrinkled. Beside him were two younger men flanking a pale and shaking Molly.

"You okay, Molly?" she asked, rather than acknowledging her own personal nightmare.

Molly, wide-eyed with fear simply nodded.

She returned the nod and faced her nemesis. "Hello, Myles. I've been expecting you."

"I'm sure you were. Got a heads up from your old lover, Ricky, didn't you?" he said with a sneer in his voice.

"Ricky was never my lover. Just my friend."

"Your friend? Like this little girl is your friend?" he said, jerking Molly up against him. Her eyes looked like a frightened puppy and tears welled up in them.

"Let her go, Myles. You don't want to hurt her," she said, drawing his attention back to her. She steeled herself for what's about to come next. "It's me you're mad at. Me, who stole from you."

That's all it took to get the rage in his eyes focused on her. "You're right." He flung Molly to one of his men and with two steps had his hands gripping both her arms, lifting her to stand on her tip-toes. A favorite intimidation act of his. "Where are they?"

~

Just as Cleetus stepped off the sidewalk to cross over to the other side of main street several women including his wife Sylvie came running out of the side parking lot. Sylvie waved for him to come join her.

"What's going on?" he asked, nearly dropping the to-go boxes with their lunches as she threw herself into his arms.

"Oh, Cleetus, someone's robbing the Dye Right!"

"Robbing it?" he asked, setting the boxes on the top of one of the new benches the town council had installed up and down Main to encourage people to spend more time in the business end of the town.

"That's what Twylla said," Sylvie said, stepping back and looking a little calmer.

"Where is she?" he asked.

"She and Molly are still inside," Darcy said as she and the three women who looked like they'd fled the shop mid hair styling—one complete with layers of tin foil and goop covering her head—gathered in close. Mrs. Bailey, the oldest of the clients, shook a little and was paler than usual.

"Okay, let's get you sitting down, Mrs. Bailey. Okay?" he said, taking the elderly woman's elbow and maneuvering her to the bench by the food. "You going to be okay?"

"Yes. It's all just a bit scary. And my bag with my medicine is still inside."

"You're safe out here and I'll get your bag as soon as I can," he said to reassure her then he turned back to his wife. "How many robbers were inside?"

"I don't know," she said, shaking her head.

"At least two," Darcy said. "Twylla said she'd keep *them* occupied while we escaped."

"What's going on, Cleetus?" Callahan asked hurrying up to the group.

Cleetus was glad to see him, this many scared women made him more anxious than what was happening across the street. "There's intruders in the Dye Right. I need you to stay with the ladies here, so I can go see what's going on."

"No!" Sylvie said, grabbing at his arm. "It's too dangerous."

Cleetus laid his hand against her soft cheek and stared into her green eyes. "Sylvie. It's my job. You're safe. I need to make sure Miz Twylla and Molly are, too."

For a long moment he stared into her eyes, wanting her to know how much he loved her, but that it was his responsibility to try and help her boss and friend. It's why he became a deputy sheriff. To help people, no matter the cost.

Finally, she blinked and hugged him hard. "You be careful."

He turned to go when Callahan grabbed him by his arm.

"I should go with you, Cleetus."

"No. I don't need another civilian in this mess. You stay here and call for help. I don't have a radio with me."

Callahan nodded, then pulling out his phone, he stepped between the women and the street. Blocking them like a human shield.

Cleetus, pulled his weapon out of the holster on his belt and darted across the street, staying to the side of the large windows. With a steadying breath, he slowly inched his way closer to peek inside without giving his presence away.

When Gage called him at home early this morning, he said Miss Twylla might have some trouble today and he was to be outside as a visible guard to keep that trouble away. He didn't have any strangers making him suspicious all morning, so when Sylvie suggested he go get their lunch real quick, he didn't see a problem with it. Dang it. Gage was gonna be mad at him. If he had just stayed at his post none of this would've happened.

He inched a little closer. Finally able to see inside. Three men, one holding on to Molly, while the other two that flanked him stood in the center of the window with their backs to him. Suddenly, Miss Twylla came into the front of the shop. Although he couldn't hear what she was saying, she seemed to know the man holding Molly's arm.

With a glance back across the street, he zeroed in on Sylvie standing beside Callahan who was talking on his phone. Man, how he loved that little woman, the mother of his little girl who was going to look just like her. He had every reason to be super careful. Then he looked back in the shop trying to determine how best to get inside just in time to see the older, bulkier man toss Molly towards one of his men like a rag doll and grab Twylla by the arms.

One of those women was going to get hurt.

Time to make his move.

CHAPTER 24

After her talk with Clint at the Westen clinic, Dylan decided to stop in and check on her sister Bobby at the sheriff's office since it was on the next block down from the Peaches 'N Cream café. As she was leaving Emma handed her a note from Harriett instructing her to stop by the café for some food to take home to Chloe and Wes. Emma had informed her that it was a tradition in the town to provide meals for the new mothers for the first two weeks and Lorna was always the first meal. She liked this idea since Chloe's idea of a balanced meal was a grilled cheese sandwich, tomato soup and two bags of potato chips.

She pulled into an empty parking space out front of the sheriff's office and climbed out of the driver's side, glancing down the street to see Sean walking in the direction of the Dye Right. Strange. She thought he'd be in the newspaper office writing up his interview with Congressman Rawlins.

"Hey, Bobby," she said as she entered the door. "You in here?"

A hand waved from behind one of the computer screens. "Right here," Bobby said, slowly rising from her knees in front of her desk.

"Oh my gosh, are you okay?" Dylan asked rushing around the desk to grab her sister's elbow and assist her to standing once more.

Bobby let out a sigh, then grinned, if a bit wearily. "Yes. I dropped my cell phone and it went under the desk. I just had to go get it."

"You shouldn't be doing that," Dylan said, holding onto her arm until Bobby was back in her office chair.

"Yeah, right. If Gage called me on it and I didn't answer immediately, he'd be storming in here as if I was under assault by armed terrorists."

"True. You shouldn't complain though. You're lucky to have someone that worships the ground you walk on like he does," Dylan took one of the other office chairs.

"I know I am. And usually, he realizes I'm quite capable of taking care of myself, our son, the house and working here. It's just when I'm pregnant, he goes into overprotection mode. It can be exasperating." She reached for a bottle of water and took a long drink. "Speaking of men who worship the ground someone walks on, Callahan was just in here. He told me to tell you he'd been asking about you."

She didn't deny her sister's assessment of Sean's feelings for her. After last night's conversation and confession from him, she knew exactly how he felt. "I thought I saw him walking down the street as I was coming in. Did he say where he was headed?"

"No, just said he had to go. I assumed it was back to the office since he'd had an interview with Tobias this morning. Why?"

Dylan shrugged. "He wasn't headed across the street to his office. He was walking down the block towards the Dye Right."

"Well, that's odd. Who knows with a journalist." She leaned back and managed to get both her feet up on the chair opposite her. "Did Wes get Chloe and the baby home safe and sound?"

"Yes. They got in before noon and all three looked exhausted. Chloe said thank you for the gift basket of fruit, cheese and snacks Gage dropped off. When I left, they were all going to take a nap."

"Even Wes?" Bobby asked a little surprised.

Dylan laughed. "Our big bad brother-in-law looked like he needed it the most."

"So what have you been up to?"

"I had a long talk with Clint over at the clinic."

"About what?" she asked, then her face grew very concerned, and she laid one hand on her arm. "Are you okay? There isn't anything wrong, is there?"

Always the concerned big sister. Dylan smiled and squeezed her hand. "Yes, mom. I'm fine. It was more a professional chat between colleagues."

"Oh, good. I don't need another thing to worry about right now." Bobby squeezed her hand back, then laid it with her other one lightly resting on her pregnant belly. "Can I ask what it was about or is that like a HIPAA violation?"

"No, it was nothing like that. I simply wanted to know how he made the adjustment from big city medicine to smalltown medicine and if he thought it had been worth it."

"And what did he say?"

Before she could decide how much to confide in her sister the office phone rang.

"Hold on," Bobby said, sliding her feet out of the chair and turning to answer it. "Westen Sheriff's office, Deputy Justice speaking—"

∽

"I'll tell you what you want to know," Twylla said, trying not to gag at Myles' cigarette laced breath as he spoke inches from her face. She'd always hated that smell as much as the pain from his fists. "But you have to let Molly walk out the door first."

"You don't get to tell me what to do," Myles said, then did what he always did.

The meaty flesh of his hand stung as it connected with her face in an open hand slap. Her head snapped to the side and stars filled her vision, but she refused to moan from the pain.

"You can beat me until I'm dead, I won't tell you where they are unless you let her go." She wasn't going to provoke him to harming Molly, which he'd do just to spite her. Time for a bit of appeasement. "I promise to take you right to them if you do."

Suddenly, the door behind them opened and there stood Cleetus with his gun drawn.

"Sheriff's department. Freeze!"

Dammit! No! She didn't want anyone innocent to get hurt because of her. Certainly not Sylvie's husband. She tried to pull away from Myles.

A gunshot rang out, followed by another.

~

"Bobby, it's Sean Callahan. Cleetus asked me to call. The Dye Right's being robbed."

Bobby blinked, not believing what she'd just heard, but standing up anyways. "What?"

"Someone's robbing the Dye Right," he repeated. "Cleetus wants you to call Gage to come right now."

"Someone's robbing the Dye Right?" she repeated even as

she met her sister's eyes and reached for the radio to contact Gage in his cruiser.

"Yes."

"Where's Cleetus?" she asked.

"He's just outside."

A pause.

"Oh shit, he's going inside."

A large crack of sound came across the phone. Followed by another.

CHAPTER 25

Molly screamed at the same time Twylla gasped and froze staring at the two men who landed on the floor.

"Cleetus!" she yelled, trying to pull away from Myles.

The man holding Molly released her to go check on his counterpart.

"Is he dead?" Myles asked.

The man shook his head. "Nope, but not looking good."

"Leave him then, we're out of here," Myles said, pulling Twylla towards the front door.

"Out back," she said, wanting to keep him away from what was going to quickly be a mass of onlookers on the sidewalk.

Myles nodded, pivoted and headed the other direction, his hold on her still like a vice grip.

"What about her?" his last henchman asked, going after Molly.

"Leave her. I got what I came for," Myles said over his shoulder as he dragged Twylla through the shop.

Footsteps pounded behind them. She turned her head at the

door to see Myles' man running to catch up. Molly leaned down near Cleetus.

"My car's right here," she said, pulling her keys out of her sweater pocket. She needed to get Myles out of the shop and out of town before anyone else got hurt.

He grabbed them from her and hit the unlock button, tossing the key to his man over the hood. "You drive." He opened the back passenger door and shoved her inside. "Get over," he ordered, pulling a gun out of the shoulder holster he always wore under his suit jacket.

The gunshot across the street was followed by a second one.

Sean clutched the phone as he watched Cleetus disappear below the bottom of the Dye Right's front window inside the shop.

"Cleetus!" Sylvie screamed and darted forward.

Sean caught her and pulled her back.

"Let me go!" she said, trying to break free.

"Sylvie. We don't know what's going on in there. Let me go."

"But, he's my husband," she pleaded, tears pouring down her cheeks.

"And he'd want you to be safe. Wasn't that what he said?"

She nodded. He motioned for Darcy to come stand with her. "Call 9-1-1 for the paramedics," he said, tossing them his phone.

Then with a quick glance up the street, he darted across just out of view of anyone inside the shop. Once there, he plastered himself against the brick wall and caught his breath.

What the hell was he doing? He wasn't a lawman. He wasn't a hero. They had guns. He had? Nothing. Obviously, this was stupid but that was Cleetus, Molly and Twylla in there. And there was no one else to help.

Like Bruce Willis said in one of those *Die Hard* movies, *"When someone needs to do something, I'm that guy."*

Yep. He was that guy right now. And the longer he was out here might be reducing Cleetus' chances of surviving.

Dammit.

Keeping low, he moved to the door and opened it, looking onto a scene he'd experienced in Iraq, never in the states. One man lay sprawled on his back, blood pooling beneath him like thick red goo. Cleetus was slumped against the receptionist's counter, blood flowing from his right shoulder and his face pale. Molly knelt beside him, tears rolling down her frightened face.

Beyond them something moved. He caught the backside of a man disappearing through a door.

"They got Miss...Twylla," Cleetus said, attempting to point to the back of the store with his other hand, blood dripping off his fingertips.

Sean grabbed a towel off one of the shelves near the receptionist's desk and hurried back to put pressure on his friend's wound. Cleetus poked him in the side. He looked down to see his service weapon, butt first. "Got...to stop them. He's...gonna hurt her."

"Your shoulder," Sean said, pressing the towel in place.

Cleetus nudged him again with the gun. "I'll be...okay."

Sean stared into the big man's eyes, they were pain-filled, but clear. He took the weapon and Cleetus pressed his own hand on the towel.

Dammit, he'd become *that guy*, again.

And without another thought he ran to the back of the salon.

∼

"Callahan!" Bobby yelled into the phone, looking more frightened than Dylan had ever seen. Bobby didn't scare easily. Her own heartbeat jumped into fast mode as she leaned over and hit the speaker button on the old-fashioned land line.

"Cleetus!" Sylvie screamed in the background.

The sisters stared at each other in fear as they listened to the conversation on the other end of the connection.

"Oh my, God," Bobby said, interpreting what they were hearing. "I think Cleetus has been shot. And Callahan's going in the salon."

Dylan was at the office door in a heartbeat.

"Dylan!" Bobby yelled and she paused halfway out the door.

"I have to go, Bobby. It's what I'm trained to do."

Her older sister nodded. "Be careful. I'm calling Gage and the EMTs."

Without another word, she sprinted out the door and across the street, dodging onlookers who were suddenly stopping to wonder what those loud bangs and screaming were about. Because of her long legs, she'd been encouraged to run long-distance track in high school and college. Right now she wished she'd been a sprinter. She couldn't get to Sean and Cleetus fast enough.

She reached the shop and flung open the door. There lay Cleetus slumped up against the desk holding a blood soaked towel to his upper right chest, a frightened young woman—Molly, if her memory was correct—huddled beside him. On the floor beyond was a stranger, who didn't appear to be any threat, given the level of blood around him.

"Cleetus," she said kneeling down and laying her hand on his over the towel, "how you doing?"

"Got a bit...of a problem...Doc," he said, but his voice was steady, eyes focused.

Sliding her fingers over his wrist until she found a pulse, she counted as she watched the second hand of the old-fashioned clock on the wall for six seconds. Nine beats. Nine times ten. Pulse rate of ninety. Not too bad.

"Where's Callahan?" she asked as she pulled his hand away from the towel so she could see the wound. Looked like a shot to his shoulder. Luckily far enough away from the neck to miss his carotid artery and jugular vein. Until she got some x-rays and a sono, she wouldn't know exactly what had been hit in that area. Due to his size any number of big vessels could be there, not to mention the clavicle or scapula in the back could've been hit. She'd know better when she got in there to repair things. She pressed the towel back over the wound.

"He ran out back after the men who took Twylla," Molly answered her.

"What?" She whipped her head around to stare at the rear of the salon as if her sheer will could make him appear.

Suddenly, another gunshot rang out. Followed by two more.

Dear God! Not Sean. She couldn't lose someone else she loved.

"Go, Dylan. I've got this," a voice whispered behind her.

She turned to see Sylvie crouching beside her, laying one hand on her husband's face.

"Keep pressure on this wound until help gets here. Bobby called them," she said and hurried to the back of the building. The door to the side parking lot stood open. As she peeked around it a black SUV peeled out and headed the opposite direction of town.

Where was Sean?

She stepped out into the parking lot scanning the area. Then she saw legs clad in jeans and hiking boots, Sean's boots, sticking out from beside the large trash dumpster.

"Sean!" She hurried to his side. He was holding his hands over his right thigh. Blood soaked his pants and covered his fingers. A gun lay on the ground near him.

"Hey, Doc," he said.

"What the hell were you trying to do?" she asked, already squatting beside him, and pulling his hands back to look at his wound. The sounds of sirens filled the air.

"Trying to stop them from taking Twylla," he said and hissed as she poked her fingers into the hole in his pant leg, ripping it up and away from the hole in his leg.

"And you were going to play super-hero and save her?"

"Seemed like a good idea at the time," he said with a bit of self-deprecating humor in his voice.

"Glad you realize how stupid that was," she said as she continued to work the opening until she could see his thigh from knee to three inches above his wound. Blood continued to pour out of the hole, but since it was on the lateral part of the thigh, she figured he hadn't hit a major artery or vein. Those were all located medially on the inside on the leg. She ran her fingers around the back. There wasn't an exit wound. *Dammit. The bullet was still in there.*

"You know that's sexy," Sean said.

She blinked and looked into his eyes to see if he had some sort of concussion. "What are you talking about?"

"The way you're looking all doctorly at me." He leaned closer to stare back at her. "I find it sexy how your mind works, Doc. And no, I didn't hit my head. I ducked in here when the guy manhandling Twylla fired his first shot. I fired mine high so not to hit the car with her in it. That's when he shot again and got my leg."

He shifted position and moaned. That's when she saw the blood on his left side, where his lower ribcage was.

Crap.

Quickly, she started pulling his shirt up to get a look. "You got shot in the chest, too?"

He blinked and looked down surprised to see all the blood. "I guess, I did. I thought it just hurt because I hit the side of the dumpster." He took a deep breath and hissed. "Damn that hurts."

Okay, he probably broke a rib at the very least. Possible punctured lung, given his pain on breathing, but not necessarily. The bullet might've just followed the curvature of the ribs on its path through his body. She slid her hand around back. An exit wound. Thank God. At least that bullet wasn't in there causing more damage. They'd know more after x-rays.

"Hey, Dylan, want some help?" a female voice asked.

Dylan and Sean both peeked around to find Aisha, one of the county's EMTs and Deputy Löwe coming through the door.

"Sure do," she said wiggling to the side to make room for Aisha. "I thought Cleetus might be in worse shape, but I just found a second bullet wound here."

Aisha nodded as she pulled out a tourniquet and some sterile compresses. "My partner Carlos is working on Cleetus right now."

"The other man?" Dylan took another compress and pressed it to the chest wound while Aisha got the tourniquet onto Sean's thigh several inches above the bullet hole. Then she handed a blood pressure cuff to Dylan, along with a wrap to secure the occlusive dressings to cover his chest wounds.

Next, Aisha got out an IV line and a bag of solution. "LR okay with you?"

"Works for me," Dylan said as she worked on Sean's chest. Ringers Lactate—commonly referred to as LR by medical personnel—was similar to normal saline, but didn't cause decreased blood flow to the kidneys, so she liked using it on her patients. She read the numbers on the BP as Aisha started the IV. "We're one-eighteen over fifty-six. Pulse is one-oh-two."

"Other guy's dead," Daniel said coming closer. "Did you see which direction the men went with Twylla?"

"East," Sean and Dylan said simultaneously.

Daniel nodded, then stepped a little bit away to talk into his phone. "Yep, Gage. You were right. She's got them headed your way."

Dylan drew her brows down and looked at Sean who shrugged his head in just as much confusion as her.

Twylla knew this was going to happen? What was going on?

"Yes," Daniel said. "I'll follow to be sure they don't backtrack towards town. Keep your eyes open. We already have two wounded…Cleetus and Callahan…Doc Roberts and the EMTs are with them. They're stable," he said with a look to Dylan, who nodded. They were for now. "I double checked there wasn't anyone else…Leaving now."

He hung up and came closer. "I've gotta go. Twylla's still out there."

"I want the story…when this is all done," Sean said, grimacing as Dylan and Aisha maneuvered him to get the wrap around his chest to hold the compresses tightly in place, front and back.

The deputy nodded, then sprinted out of the lot towards the front of the store.

"We're ready to roll up here," Carlos said, sticking his head out the door. "You?"

"Gonna need the gurney, but he's good for transport, too."

"Where are you going to take them?" Dylan asked, moving out of the way as Carlos brought out the stretcher. Now that they were both working on Sean, she needed to get out of their way and let them do their thing. They were highly trained for field trauma. She wasn't.

"To the new hospital," Bobby said, standing in the doorway now.

"It isn't open yet," Dylan said, her eyes not leaving Sean as the EMTs worked on him. Opening his shirt completely, they placed EKG leads on his chest and hooked him up to the monitor.

"It's been staffed for two months preparing for just this thing. I already called and they're waiting on you to get there," Bobby said coming closer.

"I'm not on staff there, Sis," she said, holding onto the stretcher to steady it as Aisha and Carlos lifted Sean onto it. Once he was in position, they used the gurney straps to stabilize his legs, especially the wounded one, in case the femur had gotten hit by the bullet.

"You're here. The trained personnel are here. The hospital is here. Do you really want to waste precious time trying to get them to Columbus?" Bobby asked in that way that always made her feel silly for even asking the question.

Suddenly, Sean gripped her hand and squeezed.

"You...got...this," he said, sounding weak and in more trouble that she'd thought. He loosened his hold as they carted him out of the lot towards the front of the building and the waiting ambulance. She stared after them, her heart heavy that he'd been so hurt.

"You're wasting time, Dylan," Bobby said coming up behind her. "Go."

CHAPTER 26

"At the next street, turn left," Twylla said to the henchman behind the wheel.

"I can't believe you were stupid enough to bury the diamonds out in the woods where any yahoo could dig them up," Myles said, grabbing her by the hair and pulling her closer. He shoved the muzzle of his gun up under her chin, something he always liked to do to prove how in charge he was. "They'd better be where you buried them or I'm going to kill you."

Not that she believed he planned to let her live when he got what he wanted anyways. "They're exactly where I buried them. I promise you they're safe."

"You better hope they are," he growled, then flung her back against the door. She barely had a chance to keep her head from hitting the window when his fist hit her face again. The urge to cower up against the door filled her, but she fought it. No longer was she the young, naïve woman who had been dependent on this man for everything. For almost two decades she'd on her own. Not only had she survived, she'd thrived.

Slowly, she straightened, keeping her left hand gripping the door handle and stared out the front windshield at the road up ahead. If this was going to work, she needed to pay attention to what was coming. "If you knock me out, I can't tell you where I buried your diamonds."

A growl came from beside her, but no fist followed it.

The driver made the turn and ended up on the highway and they passed over the Old Wilson Bridge.

"How far now?" Myles asked.

"About two miles. There are two turns in the road up ahead. After the second one, there's a hill. You have to make a sharp right turn into the woods."

Quiet descended inside the car, which made Twylla more nervous than if Myles were screaming at her.

"What I can't figure out," he finally said and she relaxed, but only a little. It was never good to relax around a rattlesnake. "How did you get into the safe to steal the diamonds?"

"You got too complacent with your torture sessions." She turned to meet his gaze, hoping to keep his attention on her and off of the road ahead. She didn't want him to see what was coming.

"What the hell does that mean?" he asked with a sardonic sneer.

"You thought you'd knocked me unconscious and left me laying on the bedroom floor, just close enough to see inside. You forgot to be sure I was out," she said, seeing the first turn coming up.

"I always made sure to block the view of the lock." He seemed incredulous that she'd tricked him.

"It took a few times, I'll grant you that, but I was willing to take the beatings to see what you were putting in there. My patience paid off when I saw you put in the jewelry pouch. That really was your biggest mistake," she said, knowing questioning his perfect ego would trigger his anger again.

"What are you talking about? I don't make mistakes."

She slowly smiled at him as they neared the second turn. "Yes, you do. The first mistake was making me curious as to what was in the pouch. I just had to find out the combination and look inside. Using your own birthday was the second mistake. A rookie mistake. I bet all your passcodes are the same."

Predictable as always, he backhanded her hard. Her head hit the window this time. She used the reaction to grab a tight hold onto her seatbelt as they hit the almost ninety-degree turn that locals knew to slow down on at the same time sirens filled the air.

She narrowed her eyes at him. "Your third mistake was thinking you could trust me this time."

He lifted the gun at her.

A loud bang sounded as the front tire suddenly blew out. The car swerved.

"What the hell?" Myles bellowed, as beltless, he was flung sideways into the opposite door.

"I think a tire just blew," his henchman said, trying to right the car which was curving off the road.

Another loud bang as the rear tire on the same side blew. The speed of the car's momentum carried it up onto the side. Twylla held on tight. The sound of his gun deafening Twylla. Pain seared her side.

Suddenly, they were flipping like in a stunt movie. Twylla held on despite the pain as her body was thrust against the side of the car, her head hitting the window again and again. Myles' heavy body landed on top of her and the gun inside the car went off again.

The driver slumped forward on the wheel. The engine gunned.

The car flipped again. This time, the car door opposite her flung open.

Centrifugal force thrust Myles outside.

The car rolled over his body and continued down the hill until slamming to a stop against the large oak trees on the edge of the forest.

Twylla gave into the darkness.

~

"Damn, Harriett, how many shots did you fire?" Gage yelled, as he bolted from his car hidden in the side road just around the bend in the road, headed to where the SUV was wedged in between two trees the front end accordioned in on itself.

Harriett appeared out of the forest several hundred yards back up the road from where the car flipped, slinging her rifle bag over her head and shoulder. She jogged almost as fast as him. "Only two. Front and back tires."

Behind them the town's second EMT squad pulled up. Deke and his third paramedic, Caleb Hoskins hopped out and ran to the scene.

"Was the plan to kill them all?" Deke asked.

"The plan was to neutralize the threat to Twylla," Harriett said, already kneeling beside the driver's door. She reached in to feel for the driver's pulse. "He's dead."

"Not surprised, given the head-on into the tree they took."

She leaned in for a closer look. "That's not what killed him."

Gage looked over her shoulder. "Looks like a shot to the back of the head. I thought you said you only shot out the two tires."

Harriett gave him that don't-you-dare-doubt-me look. "Two shots only. Both to the tires. Like we planned."

"She's strapped in good. Appears to be breathing," Caleb said drawing their attention to the back of the vehicle where he'd climbed in from the passenger side to check on Twylla.

"Facial contusions and a busted lip. More like I'd expect in domestic abuse than the collision."

"You're probably one-hundred-percent on that call." Harriett moved to the back driver's side. "Twylla?" she said into the busted window.

A moan answered.

"Let's get her out of there," Gage said. A sheriff's squad car pulled up to the scene. Daniel climbed out. "Check on that body over there," Gage said to him, pointing to the heavy-set older man who'd been thrown from the SUV.

Gage and Deke pulled on the semi-mangled door until it popped open. Harriet quickly reached in to stabilize Twylla so she wouldn't get hurt any worse. Caleb wedged himself in beside her, using a flashlight to assess her from head to toe.

"Twylla, it's Harriett. Open your eyes," she said in that voice no one ever ignored. She'd used it on him for years.

Slowly, Twylla's eyelids fluttered open, and she peered through little slits at Harriett. "It hurts."

"I warned you, just didn't expect the car to flip that much," she said, running her hands over the other woman's body, then brought her hand out covered in blood. "Crap. We've got an entry wound to the upper left quadrant of her abdomen."

"He had...a gun," Twylla whispered.

Gage pulled out his phone and dialed the new hospital's ER number.

"Westen Mercy ER, how may I help you?"

"This is Sheriff Justice," he said to the female voice on the other end. "We've got a third gunshot victim. I don't know all the details, but let the docs know we're coming."

"Do you have an ETA?"

"Not yet. She was in a motor vehicle, and we have to extract her from that first."

"Ok. We'll be ready."

He hung up. "What do you need me to do?" he asked.

"If you and Deke can get the gurney while I start an IV," Caleb said, already getting his supplies from the bag he'd brought with him. "Don't forget the monitor."

Gage and Deke jogged over to the squad.

"You think the guy in front was shot by the one thrown from the car?" Deke asked as he set the portable monitor box onto the gurney.

"Had to be. Harriett said she made her shots," he said as he lifted his end of the gurney out. Daniel joined them. "The other guy?"

"Not breathing, no pulse," his deputy replied.

Gage nodded as they hurried with the equipment over to the car, where Caleb and Harriett were working as a team to stabilize their patient. "Probably best for Twylla. Once we get her on the way to the hospital, we'll start processing the scene. Can you block off traffic at both ends?"

It wasn't a highly used road. For that reason and the hairpin turns, Harriett, the mastermind of the plan, had chosen it. When she and Twylla came to him late last night with the problem, he'd wanted to arrest the man the moment he showed his face in town. Harriett pointed out that the Myles guy hadn't committed a crime that they could prove in court. It was Twylla who suggested catching him trying to kidnap her.

They thought they'd have time, since the perpetrator hadn't shown his face in town, but when he got the call from Bobby about the salon being robbed, they'd moved their plan forward. From his time undercover he knew that any strategy to take down the bad guys—well planned and organized or last minute and off the cuff—had the potential for things to go wrong.

Luckily, Twylla was still alive. For now.

CHAPTER 27

The ER was already a buzz of activity when Dylan hurried in. Staff in various shades of blue scrubs moved around as if in some sort of medical ballet loading IV solutions onto electronic pumps, setting out packs of sterile equipment that might be needed on metal tables and positioning both the med cart and defibrillators within reach.

Despite this being a new facility and her not really knowing anyone, she suddenly felt right at home. This was her element. Part of who she was.

The charge nurse, Josh, she'd met days before, separated from the group and approached her along with another younger man wearing a doctor's lab coat over his scrubs.

"Didn't think we'd be seeing you in this capacity so quickly, Dr. Roberts," he said, motioning to his companion. "This is Dr. Tony Moreno, one of the senior surgical residents rotating to our hospital from Ohio State."

She shook hands with both of them.

"What can you tell us is coming in?" Josh asked, motioning his staff to join them.

"Two gunshot victims," she began, filling them in on the

specific details of both Sean and Cleetus' wounds and status as of the moment she'd watched them get in the emergency squad. "We're going to need x-rays and sono to find the bullets and what damage was done inside."

A tall thin young man with thick auburn curls straight out of the seventies raised his hand. "I got that. Liam, radiology."

She gave him a nod. "Lab work, including type and cross-match on both, in case we need it."

"We have O negative on standby in the blood cooler for quick transfusion if needed," a thirtyish woman of middle eastern descent said. "Mya, lab."

Sirens grew loud outside as the squad arrived. The team broke into groups, some going to the patient bays, while others went outside to help receive their patients.

"Want to come with me, doctor?" one of the older women from the group asked. Her name tag said Beth, RN. "I can get you scrubs and some place to change."

"I need a medium top, but I guess large pants for the length, if you have them," she said as they hurried to a door at the end of the hall.

"We have women's extra tall. Two of the nurses here are six feet, although they won't admit it." Beth opened the staff lounge door and pointed to another one. "That's the women's locker room. Scrubs are on the shelf behind the door. There's a restroom in there and two empty lockers near the window. We didn't assign those to the staff, so doctors would have one to use."

"Thank you," Dylan said, hurrying to the far door.

"We're glad to have you here, Dr. Roberts," the nurse said, then disappeared.

With a quick search of the shelves, Dylan found the right sized scrubs. As she changed, she ran through all she knew about Cleetus and Sean's injuries. Had she missed anything?

Were there wounds she'd missed out in the field? First responder assessments weren't her specialty.

Hurrying back to the patient care sector of the ER she listed in her head all the labs and tests she'd ordered, making sure she hadn't forgotten those. Normally, she wouldn't be questioning herself. Her training was too thorough. This was different.

This was two people she knew and cared for.

This was Sylvie's big, loveable husband Cleetus.

This was Sean.

Even though she'd focused in on his injuries from the very first second, her heart ached knowing he'd been hurt. She didn't want to see him suffer. Concerned something might have happened to him on the trip here, she quickened her pace, almost running by the time she hit the doors into the unit.

The place resembled the outside of an ant hill she saw once on a trip to Texas. Everyone was moving in all different directions. She scanned the two patient care bays. Cleetus was easy to see on her left, sitting on his stretcher with the head elevated about forty-five degrees. Sweeping her gaze to the right, she found Sean sitting in the same position, but more people working on him.

Needing to see for herself that his condition hadn't deteriorated during the transport to the hospital, she hurried to his bedside.

"Hey, Doc," he said, holding his left hand out to her.

Someone had cleaned most of the blood off it and the IV Aisha had started out in the parking lot was secure in his arm. She took his hand and squeezed it. "How you doing?"

"Not too bad. Aisha gave me some meds on the way here." His slightly slurred speech confirmed his words.

She looked at the nurse, Beth, standing on the other side of the bed. "Toradol thirty milligrams IV. Standard protocol. We have the x-ray results for you."

"That was quick."

"Liam did his first. We released the tourniquet after he was finished and the bleeding is just a low trickle now. He's over doing Cleetus' now." Beth hit the button on the computer right next to where Dylan stood and up popped the film of Sean's thigh.

"Good." She leaned forward to see where the bullet had stopped in Sean's thigh.

"What's the verdict, Doc?" he asked, his hand still squeezing hers.

"Well, the reason there isn't an exit wound is the bullet hit your femur, fracturing it," she said, pointing to the two parts of the long bone of the thigh. "That impact shattered the bullet into lots of little pieces," she pointed to what looked like bits of shiny gravel in the x-ray. "So, you're going to need surgery for that."

"That sucks," he muttered.

"It could've been way worse," she said, but only half-scolding him for taking such a chance. She didn't believe in picking on someone who was injured. She'd wait until he was one-hundred percent to have that conversation. She looked at Beth. "How about the chest wound?"

The nurse hit a button and the film switched to Sean's left rib cage.

"It's a through and through, like you said," Doctor Moreno said, coming to stand on the opposite side of the stretcher. "I took a quick look once the film was done. Looks like the bullet's path curved along the ribs. I didn't see any sign a rib was nicked."

"That's a good thing, right?" Sean asked.

"It means no ribs were broken, but there was internal tissue damage, so there will be bruising and pain from that," the resident answered.

"So, no surgery?" Sean asked.

Dylan shook her head. "You're not that lucky. No chest surgery. We'll just stitch up your bullet holes front and back. The thigh? That's going to require hardware to get your thigh back together and we'll have to extract all the bullet fragments."

"Sound like fun," he muttered, releasing her hand and relaxing back into the stretcher pad, closing his eyes. "How's Cleetus doing?"

"I'll check. I wanted to see how you were first."

That brought a small lift to the corner of his lips. "I like being your priority."

"I'll be back as soon as I find out what condition Cleetus is in."

He didn't reply. Even though the monitors confirmed he was stable, she let her gaze focus on his chest a moment to watch the steady rise and fall of it to reassure her the modern electronics were correctly evaluating his status. Silly, she knew. But this wasn't just another patient. This was Sean. Her Sean.

Turning on her heel to force herself away from his bedside, she marched directly over to the other occupied patient bay to check on Cleetus. As she stepped into the cubicle, another sudden flurry of activity among the nursing staff caught her attention.

"What's going on?" she asked as Josh hurried by with another IV pole fitted with an infusion pump.

He paused. "Just got a call, another patient is coming in. Car accident, possible gunshot."

Dylan sucked in her breath. *Twylla.* It had to be. Or what if it wasn't? What if it was one of the men who'd taken her. One who'd shot both Cleetus and Sean?

"Male or female?"

"Sheriff Justice called it in. Said it was a she."

Definitely Twylla.

"Do you have any details?"

The charge nurse shook his head as he walked away, saying over his shoulder, "That's all we got when he called."

She prayed her friend was okay but knew there was nothing more she could do for her until the ambulance arrived. Best to see what shape Cleetus was in. Stepping into the patient bay, she stood at the foot of the stretcher to assess the situation. The beeping monitors showed all his vital signs were steady and within normal limits. Remembering one of the first things a surgeon taught her fresh out of medical school—*Look at the patient. What color is their skin? Are they in pain? Are they alert? Is their breathing labored or easy? You're treating a human being, not the monitors*—she shifted her attention to the big man filling up the stretcher.

"Hey, Doc Roberts," he said, his vision clear, his skin color only slightly paler than usual, and no labor to his breathing. Beside him stood Sylvie, holding his hand and stroking her other hand over his short cropped brown hair in a soothing fashion.

"How you doing, Cleetus?"

"Not the first time I've been hurt on duty," he said, referencing the injury he'd sustained the day of the Meth lab explosion.

"They gave him something for the pain," Sylvie said.

Dylan nodded. "Makes it easier to care for him, if he isn't in too much pain. Did they get the x-rays done?"

"It's right here, doctor." A tall African American nurse, her name tag said Michelle, turned on the computer screen, similar to the one she'd viewed in Sean's room. No bone splinters were visible, but the bullet had torn through his pectoris major muscle, missed the clavicle, bounced off the scapula and wedged into the fascia—thick connective web-like tissue—that stretched across it. She leaned in closer and studied the scapula. And there it was, the hairline fracture. He'd need surgery to stabilize that and sew up those muscles and tissue so the shoulder would work right again, but all the large muscles on Cleetus' frame had kept this bullet from doing more damage.

"His bleeding has slowed significantly. I've changed the dressing once since he arrived. The first was soaked through." The nurse opened the ace bandage to let Dylan observe the new dressing herself. A small circle of blood had soaked through the pressure dressing, about the size of a quarter.

"Keep an eye on it and let me know if the bleeding picks back up. I'll repair any bleeder when we go in to get the bullet."

"He'll need surgery then?" Sylvie asked, worry etched on her face.

Dylan went over and put her arm around the diminutive woman's shoulders for a reassuring hug. This was her friend, not just the wife of a patient. "Yes, we don't want to leave the bullet in there, and some of the muscles and tendons will need repairing, too. We want him back in good working order to carry that baby of yours around."

Sylvie gave her a watery smile then patted her husband's good shoulder. "Sure do."

Just then the overhead speaker sounded that the other patient was arriving. "I have to go. But we'll get you into surgery as soon as possible, Cleetus."

As she and the nurse stepped out, she closed the curtain to prevent Sylvie from seeing who was on the stretcher. She didn't need to see her boss and friend injured on top of worrying about her husband. "Please keep that closed for a while. Until we know what's happening with this new case."

Michelle nodded. "I'll keep her distracted."

Dylan gave her a brief nod in thanks, then hurried to the ambulance bay door, praying that if this was Twylla coming in, her condition wouldn't be too grave.

Standing at the scrub sink in the Operating Room hallway, Dylan worked the antiseptic soap in between each of her fingers of one hand with the sterile nylon sponge brush, being sure to work around her nails at the tip and all the way down to the palm, her mind focused on a plan of action once she got into Twylla's abdomen.

The ER staff had stepped into its usual chaotic dance as they wheeled the stretcher in from the ambulance bay.

"The patient is a forty-two year old female from a motor vehicle accident with a gunshot wound to the right upper quadrant of the abdomen," the paramedic said, walking with the team and handing the IV he'd started on Twylla to one of the nurses, who immediately fed the line into the IV pump. "BP is ninety-four over fifty-eight, pulse one-ten, O-two sat ninety-seven, respirations twenty-two, but unlabored at this time. She's been conscious despite multiple contusions to the face—cheek, nose and lip."

"He hit me...before the car...flipped," Twylla managed to say, staring right into Dylan's eyes. She'd grabbed her friend's hand as they brought her off the squad and she wasn't letting go.

"Did you hit your head with the accident?" she asked, and Twylla gave a slight shake of her head. Dylan squeezed her hand. "We'll look at those injuries later, I need to see where he shot you."

Releasing her hand, she moved to the other side of the stretcher where one of the nurses was cutting away at the bandage the EMT had placed over a pressure dressing.

"We found the penetrating wound from the bullet, but no exit wound," the middle-aged paramedic said. "I'd guess she lost about a pint of blood at least."

"She's O negative," a familiar terse voice said from the patient cubicle door.

Dylan glanced that way to see Harriett standing there, dressed in what looked like military fatigue camo. The older woman might be the best nurse this town had ever seen, but they were in her territory now and she was calling the shots.

"Good to know, since we have that readily available." Standard procedure in trauma units. O negative blood was considered universal donor type blood and could be given to most people with little problems. "But we'll type and cross-match her per protocol, just the same."

"Figured you would."

As the nurse finished removing the bandage, Dylan got a good look at the gun-shot wound. The blood flowed out with the pressure dressing removed, but it wasn't pumping as if from the hepatic artery, which was a good thing.

"Let's get the fast sono in and see what we're looking at," she said and a young woman quickly moved her machine into place to begin the non-invasive procedure. Within a minute the sono showed about one-hundred milliliters of fluid around the liver and right kidney. She could also see the bullet behind the large right lobe of the liver.

"BP is ninety over forty-eight," one of the other nurses called out. "Pulse is one-twelve."

The sono tech removed her machine and nurse Josh and the resident surgeon, Dr. Moreno placed a new pressure dressing over the site.

"Okay, she's deteriorating. We need to get her to the OR and stop this bleeding," Dylan said, making decisions like she had so many times before. "Let's get some vasopressors on board and start some blood."

"I'll call the OR and let them know you're on your way," Josh said, grabbing his phone. "Although they had the OR teams prepped for a case and anesthesia is already up there."

Dylan gave him a nod, then took her friend's hand again. "Twylla, we're going to take you to surgery right now. I'm going to have to go in and get that bullet and close up some holes it made. Okay?"

"What about...Cleetus? Callahan?" she asked, sounding weaker than she had moments before.

"They're both stable for now. You get to go to the front of the line. Sort of going first class," she said as the team started moving the stretcher. She walked along side, not letting go of Twylla's hand until they arrived in the OR suite.

Now here, she stood as nervous as the first day she scrubbed in on a case as an intern. It wasn't because the liver was so vascular an organ and its structure so unique with the added biliary structure intertwined with those vessels. Due to the size of the liver, it was the most commonly injured organ in a trauma situation, so she'd done many surgeries to repair lacerations, stabbings and gunshot injuries.

No, this was different because she not only knew the patient but cared about her. It was up to her to save her friend.

She worked the soap up her arm to the elbow as she watched the scene inside the operating room through the observation window. The anesthetist sat at the head of the bed monitoring Twylla whom she'd just intubated and put to sleep for the surgery. The main IV pumped fluids to keep her hydrated and gave them access for delivering medications. The second IV dripped in whole blood to not only replace the oxygen carrying red cells, but also clotting factors found in the plasma that would help repair the injuries to her body.

As she dipped one arm, hand raised so water would drip from her fingertips to her elbows to rinse off the soap, Dylan just hoped all their efforts would be enough to save Twylla.

"God gave you the smarts and the skills Doc," Bulldog said to her before a very traumatic case early on. *"Just put your trust in Him and go do your thing."*

She closed her eyes holding her arms up over the sink. "Please God, guide me, use me. Save my friend."

Snapping her eyes open, she hurried to the OR door, leaning her back against it to swing it open. "How's she doing?" she asked the anesthetist as she accepted the sterile towel from the scrub nurse to dry her hands.

The other woman read her the monitor readings. "BP's ninety-eight over fifty-two. Pulse is still a little tachy at one-twelve. O-two sat's ninety-six."

"Good." She said as the circulator and scrub nurses helped her into her sterile gown and gloves, then she stepped up to the operating table and gave a nod to the resident on the opposite side.

"Scalpel," she said, holding out her hand for the blade handle.

~

With a glance at the clock on the OR wall, Dylan marked the time. Thirty minutes in. They were making good progress. A Transplant Hepatologist who'd helped tutor her during her fellowship held with the belief that *"the less time you spent mucking around in the liver, the better"*. He insisted you get in and get out in less than sixty minutes.

So far, they'd retrieved the mangled bullet that had done the damage and repaired the main fissure it had carved in the anterior superior segment of the right upper lobe.

"Let's take a quick look at the kidney and see if we missed anything back there. If not, we can start packing her for closure."

The kidney lay behind the liver and they'd already suctioned out the pocket of bloody fluid in the space between them visualized on the sono in the ER. Dylan wanted to be sure no damage from the bullet had happened to the kidney that needed repair before they started packing the liver back together.

A quick, but thorough inspection of the kidney and area around it showed everything looked in working order and no active bleeding appeared.

'We're good to go here," she said, gently laying the liver back in its place.

A remarkable organ, the liver could regenerate itself if given time. The newest protocols in hepatic surgery were to pack sterile cloth sponges around the different segments of the liver lobes to put pressure on any minor bleeding spots and seal the whole thing in a sterile plastic pouch.

"Sponge one going in," she said as she placed the first surgical cloth over the actual spot she'd sutured closed. The circulating nurse, who kept minutes of everything happening with the patient in the OR, recorded each sponge as it was inserted. In a day or two, depending on Twylla's condition, Dylan would open her back up and retrieve all the sponges.

"Lap sponge two," she said wrapping this one around the right upper lobe and all its segments.

As she held out her hand for the next sponge, the swinging door to the room opened. She looked up to see Clint standing there, activity in the OR hallway behind him indicating another case was starting across the hall. The intense concern in his eyes above his surgical mask hit her hard.

"What's happened?" she asked, already knowing it was something to do with Sean. Her knees wobbled, but she braced herself against the steel OR table.

"Callahan's vitals dropped," he said. "One of the bullet fragments moved and nicked a small artery."

"Dear God," she said, her eyes filling with tears. "I need to be in there, but I can't leave here."

"It's okay. We've got it covered," Clint said. "Dr. Gibson, our new ortho surgeon was with him. They're going in now."

She gave him a nod and he stepped back out of the OR. Blinking to clear her vision, she stared at the wooden doors as if she could suddenly see through them at what was happening beyond.

Sean.

Bleeding.

In trouble.

"Sponge, doctor?" the scrub nurse beside her asked, bringing her back to Twylla and the need to finish her surgery.

With a nod, she held out her hand. "This is number?"

"Three," Dr. Moreno across from her said.

"Right. Sponge three going in."

Somehow, almost from rote memory, she finished putting in the remaining four packs and wrapping the liver and packs in the clear sterile plastic drape. As a precaution, she placed two drains to help remove fluid that might accumulate.

"Suture." She held out her hand for the handle of the needle driver, which didn't come. She looked over at the scrub nurse who had the instrument loaded with the suture needle in her hand, but a sheen of tears in her eyes.

"I can close if you want to go across the hall," Dr. Moreno said, drawing her attention to him. "Continuous sutures, not too tight, easy to remove when you go back in for the packing. Antibiotics prophylactically against any post-op infection."

Her heart suddenly racing, Dylan nodded and stepped away from the table. At the door she stripped out of the sterile gown and gloves and hit the swinging door with her hip to keep her hands fairly clean. Across the hall, she changed masks, then stopped at the observation window and searched the room until her gaze focused on Sean's pale face at the head of the table.

She closed her eyes and prayed. Prayed that he'd fight to survive. Prayed that he wouldn't be taken from her before she could tell him how much she loved him and how there wasn't any doubt in her heart where she belonged.

A hand landed on the middle of her back. Startled, her eyes snapped open and she turned to see Harriett standing beside her.

"You need to get in there."

"I don't think I can."

"Of course, you can. He needs you. You've trained your whole life for this. No one cares about him more than you. And if you don't, you'll question yourself forever if everything was done right."

Harriett was right.

She stepped around the diminutive nurse and squeezed some of the alcohol based fast scrub onto her hands, rubbing it on thoroughly. Her hip hit the swinging door to the operating room just as blood shot up in the air.

CHAPTER 28

"Hey, Beautiful," a raspy voice said from beside her.

Dylan woke instantly from where she sat beside the bed with her head laying on the corner of Sean's mattress. Straightening up, she stared into his clear and alert green eyes. Despite the rhythm of the monitors beeping beside them, she slid her hand over his wrist and felt his pulse steady beneath her fingertips. Assured he was okay, she let out the breath she'd held and smiled at him tenderly. "Hey there, yourself."

"Everything okay?" he asked.

She nodded. "Seems to be. Although you gave me quite the scare there." Tears welled in her eyes, and she quickly dashed at them with her free hand.

"Water, please?" he asked.

"Sure." Thankful for something to allow her to gather herself together, she hurried from the patient cubicle in the surgical ICU in search of...she paused, trying to figure out where she could get a glass of water for him.

"Can I help you Dr. Roberts?" a middle-aged woman asked from the center desk.

"Uhm, yes. I need some water for Sean, uhm, Mr. Callahan," she said, a little out of her own sorts and still shaking off the sleep she'd barely had. "And what time is it?"

"It's o-four-twenty," the nurse said, coming around the desk and pointing at the clock on the wall behind Dylan. "Let me show you where we keep the water and snacks for patients and visitors. You didn't get to have a tour before all three of your patients were admitted to us. I'm Amy, Mr. Junkins' nurse for tonight."

"I remember," she said, following the nurse to a small room down the hall, barely registering their brief conversation when she'd arrived in the ICU and gotten reports on both Cleetus and Twylla. Twice during the night she'd made rounds on them to assure herself they were still stable, but her mind had been on Sean.

The moment she'd walked into the OR and saw the arterial blood shooting out of him, her world had focused on nothing else. The microscopic moment of panic had been quickly shoved into a corner of her brain as she shifted into automatic, her training and skills taking over. The bullet fragments had shifted a second time, another nicking a small artery in Sean's thigh. She'd stepped in to help clamp that while the ortho surgeon continued working on the other vessel that had caused Sean's blood pressure to drop dangerously low in the ER.

Once that was under control and the nurse anesthetist assured them he was stable, she and the other surgeon worked in tandem to mechanically rejoin his femur bone parts with two plates and several screws, which would hold the leg straight while the body healed it with new bone cells. Then they'd taken the time to clean the leg from not only bullet fragments, but small shards of bone from where the femur had shattered along the jagged diagonal break.

All in all, it took longer to do that than Twylla's entire liver surgery.

From then on, the rest of the night blurred between checking on her patients with hourly rounds and watching the monitors in Sean's room. She had a new respect for the families of her patients. Keeping vigil at the beside of someone you loved was exhausting.

"Is there anything else I can get you, Doctor?" Amy asked, holding a large patient pitcher of ice water with an adjustable straw sticking out of the lid. "There's fresh coffee in the break room."

Dylan realized she'd been staring off into space. "Oh, no," she said, taking the offered cup. "I'm more of a Diet Coke drinker than coffee."

"Well, you're in luck, we have that stocked in here for patients." The nurse opened the fridge and Dylan saw not only her drink of choice, but other pops, juices and cups of jello lined up nice and neat. "Probably won't look this good in a few weeks, once we're busier. Although I was surprised when I got the call to come to work last night."

"We all were." Dylan grabbed her drink, then walked out into the hall. "I'll come see Cleetus in a bit."

"He's doing well," Amy said as she led the way back to the nurses' station. "I finally got Sylvie to go home around midnight."

"You're friends with Sylvie?" she asked, realizing that many of the staff here might be friends with Twylla, Cleetus, Sean, and even her own family.

"She does my and my sister's hair over at the Dye Right. We love her so much. It was hard to see her so worried about her husband. I reminded her she had a little girl that needed her mother to be healthy, so she finally went home for a while."

"Isn't it hard to take care of people you know?"

Amy shook her head. "I think it's better. If Sylvie and I weren't friends, I wouldn't have known about Sunshine and used her love for the little girl to get her to take care of herself. It's one of the perks of deciding to work here in Westen and not all the way in Columbus where I used to work."

"What kind of perk?"

"The kind that lets me be sure those I love are given the best care possible."

Dylan considered those words as she slipped back into Sean's room. He'd drifted off to sleep again, so she settled into the chair beside him and cracked the tab on her pop and took a long drink.

"Ask for water, she gets herself something instead," he muttered with his eyes closed.

"I figure I need to be awake to take care of you," she said, setting the can on the bedside table. Lifting the water, she brought the straw to his lips. "Go slow."

Leaning forward, his eyes held hers as his lips wrapped around the straw and he sipped. Then he released his hold and leaned his head back against the pillows, licking his lips. "Manna from heaven."

"I thought manna was bread," she teased.

"Bread, water. I don't care. It tastes heavenly."

"More?"

He shook his head. "Maybe in a bit. Tell me what happened."

She gave him the edited, less gory details of why he'd been rushed up to the OR and what they'd done to not only save his life but repair his injuries. His hand settled on hers as she talked. She flipped hers over until they were palm to palm, their fingers intertwined. When she finished, he slowly lifted her hand to his lips and placed a kiss on the back of it.

"Thank you. It must've been hard to do that."

"Harriett said something to me that made sense."

"Harriett? She was in the operating room, too?"

She shrugged. "She was there when I came out. Somehow, I don't think anyone tells Harriett what she can or cannot do."

"What did she say?"

"That I wouldn't be satisfied no matter the outcome if I wasn't in there to be sure everything that could be done for you *was* done. And she was right." She blinked a few times, then stared into his eyes. "I think I've made my decision. This is where I'm meant to be."

Sadness crossed his features. "Don't."

She blinked. "Don't what?"

"Don't tell me you're staying because I need you. I love you, Doc, but I don't want your sympathy."

Stunned, she kept herself from pulling her hand away from his and tilted her head to one side, fixing him with her best I'm-the-doctor-and-don't-mess-with-me stare before speaking, slowly and succinctly. "Just be glad you're in this bed with more stitches in you than a worn out rag doll or I'd probably sock you for that comment." She leaned in close so he could see her very clearly. "I'm trying to tell you something if you think you can rest your ego long enough to hear what I have to say."

That got his attention. He nodded, but kept his mouth shut.

"Good. First, I'm going to chalk that statement up to the fact you have pain medication dripping into your IV, Callahan, and not your being a stupid jackass. Second, long before you decided to play superhero and get yourself shot, then need emergency surgery to keep you alive, I knew I loved you. That was never part of my issue. The problem, in fact, wasn't about you at all. It was about me. Would I fit in here in Westen? Would I be needed? Would my skills be utilized? Also, could I work on people I knew and not just total strangers?"

She paused for a breath. He wisely kept watching her without saying anything.

"Somewhere along the way, whether it was this week visiting everyone or all the times I've come to Westen, I fell in love with the whole town. When I was able to help the paramedics in the field work on you and Cleetus, I started to see the possibility. Then in the ER, my training came into play, but seemed more needed, because it was for people I cared about. Cleetus, Twylla and you. Especially you, if I'm being honest.

"Then I walked into the operating room and went to work on Twylla doing massively technical surgery quicker than if we'd tried to transport her to another city. And then you took a turn for the worse, and thankfully you were right here where I could get to you. I hate to think what would've happened if that artery had gotten nicked while you were in transport—" She paused and a shudder ran through her.

He released her hand and laid it on her head, pulling her over to rest on his chest. "I love you, too, Doc."

For a few minutes she stayed right there, letting her tears slowly flow as the tension of the day and night eased. Then she leaned up and kissed him.

"I'm staying in Westen. This is where I belong." She kissed him again. "Loving you?"

"Yes," he said, slowly smiling.

"That's just a bonus."

EPILOGUE

*T*hanksgiving was tomorrow. Earlier in the year, Dylan had received the news about Bulldog's death. It devastated her and she didn't know if she'd ever find her place in the world. Now, she had many things to be thankful for.

A week after the shootings, Bobby had gone into labor and safely delivered her daughter, Blythe. So now she had two nephews and a niece to spoil on her days off. Almost from the minute she told Sean she'd made the decision to stay in Westen, her medical practice had taken off. Thankfully, there hadn't been anymore shootings in the area, but the number of traumas from vehicular and farm accidents amazed her. She'd also had to evaluate a number of football and soccer players—high school, middle school and even pee-wee—in the ER. But the best changes her life had taken were the ones spent with the citizens of Westen, her family and especially Sean.

Once he was transferred out of the ICU to a regular patient care room, he'd gone back to work remotely from his hospital bed and then his home, covering the armed attack at the salon and Twylla's kidnapping. His ortho surgeon, Doctor Darius Gibson, insisted he stayed physically off work for the full six weeks, so it wasn't unusual for her to walk into his apartment over the newspaper to find all the staff meeting with him. Marta had taken over almost all the duties for the paper except for the editing, which Sean insisted was his job. Both Dax and Laurel had done numerous articles on all that had happened that day —even the sheriff deputies finding a mutilated male body in one of the motel rooms on the outskirt of town—although no one had been able to get Twylla to talk about why this man Myles had kidnapped her.

Which was why she and Sean, along with many of the older town members, were seated in the social room of the Baptist church. Twylla had invited them all to be here so she could explain what was behind the incident that caused so much turmoil that day.

"Since tomorrow is Thanksgiving," Twylla said from the corner of the sofa, with Harriett seated beside her, "I have a lot to be thankful for this year and most of it is because of you all. Lord knows things could've turned out much differently if you all hadn't been here to help me."

"We love you, Twylla," Sylvie said from another sofa where she sat happily nestled against a fully recovered Cleetus with Sunshine in her arms.

She smiled at her friend. "Believe me, I've come to realize how much I'm loved by all of you and how much you've come to mean to me. But I fear I put you all in danger by keeping my secrets. Had I told them years ago, we might've prevented so many from being injured and nearly killed that day."

"Exactly who was this Myles Compton to you?" Gage asked, sitting beside Bobby and their daughter, while Luke played with blocks on the floor in front of him. Obviously, her brother-in-law had done his research on the man who'd caused all this havoc in his town.

Dylan knew a little bit about him through Sean, who'd

written about his business dealings once or twice while living in New York. Shady was the best description.

"Myles was my lover years ago," Twylla said. "He came to one of the off Broadway shows I was in. He courted me and swept me off my feet. Unfortunately, I was too naïve to see the predator he was. Before I knew it, I'd become his punching bag for any perceived slight, or just a change in mood."

"Oh, no," Darcy, who was sitting with Molly, said, covering her mouth.

"It took me a while, but eventually I managed, with the help of...a friend to escape," she said after the hesitation. "That's when I came back to Westen."

"Why didn't he just come here to get you then?" Chloe asked.

"Because he never knew my real name. To him I was Meredith Lane, my stage name I adopted the moment I left Westen."

"That's why my dad could never find you when your mother asked him to all those years ago," Gage said.

Twylla nodded. "It was childish and arrogant of me to change my name that way. I know it hurt my mother. But in the long run, it kept me safe for eighteen years when I came home."

"Was the friend the man we found in the hotel room? Richard Saunderson?" he asked.

Again, Twylla nodded. "Ricky was Myles' number one employee, I guess you'd call him. At one point I thought I'd fallen in love with him, and he'd be my knight in shining armor. In the end, I realized he'd never really stand up to his boss and it was up to me to devise my own way out of the situation, especially when I realized I was pregnant."

Many of the others in the room exchanged slightly shocked looks. Dylan wasn't surprised. She'd pretty much surmised Twylla had been with child when she arrived in the clinic and lost him after hearing her singing in the small graveyard. Looking across the room, her eyes met Harriett's and the other woman gave an almost imperceptible nod. It amazed her how long that woman could keep a secret. What other secrets did she have stored away?

"What happened to the baby?" Sylvie asked.

Twylla gave her a wisp of a smile. "I'll get to that. But there's more to the story."

"Was that why he wanted to find you after all these years? Because of the baby?" Molly asked.

"No. I never told him I was pregnant. I didn't trust how he'd respond, and the baby was safer if he never knew."

"Then why did he come after you? Was he obsessive and still angry because you left? After all these years?" Wes asked.

"No. He came because I took something of his when I left." She opened her hand and held it so everyone could see the lone, very large diamond in her palm.

"Wow."

"A diamond?" Bobby asked. "He came to kill you over a diamond?"

Twylla closed her hand again and rested it in her lap. "No, he came for all of them."

"How many diamonds did you take?" Sean asked, his newspaper curiosity finally getting the best of him as he sat forward to listen to the story.

She told them the story of how she discovered the safe, how she'd watched Myles put the jewelry pouch inside, then how she'd taken them and her harrowing trip through upper state New York and over to Cleveland. "When I got to the hotel room there, I finally opened the pouch. I was shocked. There were close to one hundred diamonds inside. In desperate need of money by then, I took one to a diamond broker in Cleveland. He bought it for a substantial price. Enough for me to come home and sustain myself until I knew what I wanted to do. I've only sold two more over the years. One to buy the Dye Right and one to expand it four years ago.

"I knew if I flooded the market in Cleveland with high-quality diamonds Myles would figure out where I was and come to kill me. When he found me from the picture of the little league team—"

"Wait. How did he find you from that picture?" Sean interrupted. "I edited you completely out of it before we published it in the paper or online."

"It was Nora," Sylvie said, with a bit of a snit in her voice.

"Ah," Sean said, relaxing back beside Dylan. She rested the hand bearing the diamond engagement ring he'd given her the week before on his thigh. She knew he'd gone to great efforts over the years to protect Twylla's privacy.

"When Twylla called me and explained the pickle she was in, we devised a plan to get the monster out of town, assuming he'd come after her when she was in her apartment alone."

"Wait," Sean said, "you wanted him to take her?"

Harriett nodded. "Plan was to have Twylla tell him she'd take him to where she buried the diamonds, then have him drive out on the highway to the hairpin turns. I'd take out the tires and we'd capture him away from all the people in town for the festival and hospital opening. Thought it might be the best way to keep people from getting hurt."

"Didn't work too great," he muttered.

"Things don't always go how you plan," Harriett said, then pressed her lips tighter than the Sphinx.

"It was a very good plan," Twylla said, coming to her friend's defense. "I should have known that Myles' arrogance would have him walking into my shop. And I knew he always carried a gun, but I didn't expect him to shoot his own driver. So, I am very sorry you were frightened, girls," she said to her stylists.

"And I'm very sorry both you, Cleetus and you, Sean, were injured because of my past."

Both men smiled and nodded. They might not say it, but Dylan knew both of them would take a bullet again to save someone in their town.

"So where are the diamonds?" Mayor Maggie asked.

"Come with me," Twylla said, walking out the side door to where the cemetery was. Outside, she grabbed the shovel by the door and led them all to the small white fenced area, stopping at the small grave marked Philip. "Gage, if you wouldn't mind?" she said, handing him the shovel.

He used the shovel to loosen the edge of the headstone and gently set it aside. Then he dug a hole about a foot deep, hitting a metal box. He pulled it out, then dusted off the dirt before handing it to Twylla.

Dylan and Sean exchanged looks. Had she buried the diamonds with her child in a locked box?

"I can tell what you all are thinking. No there isn't any tiny skeleton in here. You see, I did have my baby. He was a very early and had to go to the Children's Hospital in Columbus. I was very sick and when I was well enough, I made the decision to protect him the only way I knew how."

"You gave him up for adoption," Dylan said, understanding the enormity of the sacrifice Twylla had made for her child.

"I did. So, in case Myles ever somehow learned I was pregnant, I would use this gravestone to make him believe Philip had died." She took a key from the chain around her neck and opened the locked box. She pulled out the black velvet bag and opened it, pouring them into her hand. They sparkled in the autumn sunlight.

"What are you going to do with them?" Dylan asked.

"I think I'll sell them and use the money for something good. Perhaps scholarships for the graduating seniors each year for whatever career path they choose, college or technical training, but first I want to share it with my family. All of you." She plucked one out and handed it to Dylan, then to each of the other women and men standing there.

Dylan had to smile as they headed back inside.

"Your second diamond in two weeks," Sean whispered in her ear. "Is that what has you so happy?"

"No. Although it was very generous of her. It's what she said about family."

He stopped and pulled her into his arms. "That we're her family?"

She nodded. "It's what I think of Westen now. It's where all of my family lives. And I belong here. Close to my family."

NEWSLETTER SIGN-UP

**Thank you for reading
CLOSE TO FAMILY**
Want to know more about my books and new releases?
Please consider joining my **newsletter** mailing list.
I promise not to SPAM you.
Your email will NOT be sold to other sites
and is only to be used for the purpose of sending
out my newsletter.

ALSO BY SUZANNE FERRELL

WESTEN SERIES

Close To Home, book 1

Close To The Edge, book 2

Close To The Fire, book 3

Close To Danger, book 4

Close To The Heart, book 5

Christmas Comes To Westen (book bundle):

Close To Santa's Heart

Close To The Mistletoe

Close To Christmas

EDGARS FAMILY NOVELS

Kidnapped

Hunted

Seized

Vanished

Unmasked

Exposed

Drained

NEPTUNE'S FIVE

(EDGARS FAMILY PREQUEL SERIES—WWII)

Shanghaied

Tracked

HISTORICALS

Cantrell's Bride

Turner's Vision

ABOUT THE AUTHOR

USA Today bestselling author, **Suzanne Ferrell** discovered romance novels in her aunt's hidden stash one summer as a teenager. From that moment on she knew two things: she loved romance stories and someday she'd be writing her own. Her love for romances has only grown over the years. It took her a number of years and a secondary career as a nurse to finally start writing her own stories.

The author of 20 novels and an Amazon best-seller for both her series, the Edgars Family Novels and the Westen series, Suzanne's books have been finalists in the National Reader's Choice Awards--SEIZED (2013) and VANISHED (2014). Suzanne was also a double finalist in the **Romance Writers of America's** 2006 Golden Heart with her manuscripts, KIDNAPPED (Long Contemporary Category) and HUNTED (Romantic Suspense).

Currently working on more books for her Edgars Family

series (KIDNAPPED, HUNTED, SEIZED, VANISHED, EXPOSED and Capitol Danger) and the Westen Series (Close To Home, Close To The Edge, Close To The Fire, Close To Christmas, Close To The Mistletoe, Close To Santa's Heart and Close To Danger), Suzanne hopes to bring readers more passionate and suspenseful books to fill your reading moments.

Suzanne's sexy stories, whether they are her on the edge of your seat romantic suspense or the heartwarming small town stories, will keep you thinking about her characters long after their Happy Ever After is achieved.

You can Find Suz at:

Website: http://suzanneferrell.com/

Made in United States
Troutdale, OR
12/04/2023

15291360R00166